Beg, Borrow or Steal

Susie Tate

Created with Vellum

Contents

For all my medical school friends.
I couldn't have done it without you.

Chapter 1

Sleepy Girl

Jamie's gaze swept through the young, eager faces of the medical students in front of him, and he grinned. He loved teaching the newbies. Straight from their first two pre-clinical years, with no practical experience yet and barely out of their teens, they were generally keen as mustard to be in the thick of it. His smile faded as he caught sight of a girl near the back; like the other students, she was facing him and sitting upright in expectation, her pen poised over her notes; the only difference was that her eyes... seemed to be closed.

He frowned and cocked his head to the side. After a few more seconds had passed he realized that she wasn't just looking down at her paper or taking a long blink; she was asleep. Jamie wound his way through the students' chairs to get to her, and the excitement on their faces faded to confusion as they followed his progress to the back of the room. Once he reached Sleepy Girl he squatted down so his face was level with hers, and held up his hand to the student next to her, who was about to nudge her awake.

He studied her for a moment: long, dark lashes casting

shadows over her high cheekbones, an enormous amount of dark hair piled on top of her head and secured with what looked like a rubber band and various hair grips (almost as though some sort of battle had been waged against it to keep it in check), no make-up whatsoever (unusual, in his experience, in that age group), loose-fitting jumper over what looked to be a slim frame, dark smudges under her eyes, heart-shaped face surrounded by tendrils of the dark hair that had won their battle and escaped from their confines.

She looked too young to be out of school – and the most naturally pretty girl he had ever seen. He cleared his throat and her eyelids fluttered for a moment, but then settled back down.

"These are not the droids you're looking for," she muttered bizarrely under her breath as she shifted to a more comfortable position in her seat, her head gradually falling towards her friend's shoulder. The friend had a fair few actual dreadlocks in her hair, threaded with brightly coloured material. Jamie made a mental note to have one of the ward sisters give their "appropriate appearance for clinical medicine" lecture – in all honesty both these girls looked like they needed it, but more would be achieved if they were both awake at the time of delivery. Jamie's hand reached forward to touch the sleeping girl's arm, but he thought better of it at the last moment and pulled away to rub the back of his neck.

"If it's not too much trouble," he said, his deep voice sounding directly in front of her, causing her to start in her sleep, "I might not be a hard-arse," Jamie lied, "but I do at least require my students to be conscious."

She blinked twice, and he sucked in a breath when her gorgeous bright blue eyes snapped to his. This girl wasn't just pretty; she was almost breathtakingly beautiful. He felt like he had been punched in the stomach. Her mouth dropped open for a moment before her perfect small white teeth bit into her bottom lip.

"What the varp?" she whispered, sitting up a little straighter in her chair and glancing around the room at the other students, before her gaze came back to his. "Um... sorry, what was that?"

Her voice was soft and still a little gravelly from sleep, making him think about how she would sound in the morning... He shook his head to clear it, reminding himself that he was *not* a pervert that lusted after the medical students, and rose back to standing so that he was no longer at her eye level. She was *so* attractive he actually felt a little shaken by it. Jamie made it a rule *never* to even flirt with the med students. He was thirty-three and a consultant. The age gap alone would make it inappropriate, but the fact that he was in charge of the medical student training for anaesthetics at St George's Hospital made it downright wrong. And Jamie never, ever did anything to risk his career; work and his reputation meant everything to him.

He turned away and stalked back to the front of the room, now even more annoyed with this girl, not only for falling asleep in the middle of his teaching (he was charismatic, funny – a bloody great teacher, goddamn it), but also for making him inappropriately horny while at least twenty sets of eyes focused on his every move.

"Right, well," he snapped, dragging Sim-Man (the life-sized plastic "patient" they used for simulated clinical scenario training) up the bed and dumping him with a loud thud down at the end. (Probably ill-advised, seeing as Sim-Man cost at least £70,000, but Jamie was beyond clear thinking at this point.) "If we are all now fully conscious, I'd quite like to move this along. Who's keen to try their hand at the first one?"

Silence.

Jamie wasn't surprised. Simulation training was intimidating and potentially embarrassing; but it was by far the best way to learn. Better a solid fuck-up with a plastic dummy than a live patient. The days of see one, do one, teach one were on the way out in this generation.

He sighed – then caught sight of Sleepy Girl stretching in her chair. At this stage he would have hoped that the students would have grown out of the selfish-brat mindset enough not to party all night and come in hung-over and tired.

Suddenly a hand in the front row shot up and Jamie dropped his gaze to the stocky guy who had volunteered, giving him an encouraging smile. "Okay ..." Jamie glanced at the chap's ID, "Toby. Well volunteered. Come up here, mate." Toby stood next to Jamie, then crossed his arms over his chest, exuding confident-little-shit vibes in abundance.

"I just need one more ..." Jamie trailed off, and then a slow grin spread across his face as his gaze came to rest on Sleepy Girl. "You," he barked suddenly, causing most of the room to start in their chairs. He took in the horrified look on Sleepy Girl's face with satisfaction as she realized he was pointing straight at her. "Yup, you; semi-conscious burning-the-candle-at-both-ends girl. Up you come. Time to learn medicine now."

At the back of his mind Jamie knew he was being a bit of a knob, but somehow he didn't seem to be able to claw back his normal controlled attitude. Sleepy Girl stood up slowly and made her way to the front of the room with obvious reluctance. She wasn't that short, but next to Toby, and swallowed by that awful jumper, she looked tiny.

"Okay, guys," Jamie said, laying his hand on Sim-Man's shoulder and dragging his gaze away from Sleepy Girl. "This fella here is going to be our patient. He's not like the Resus Annies you're used to: he can breathe, he can talk, he can demonstrate clinical signs, and we use him to train you lot; because if you're going to make mistakes it's better that they're with this chap than on the real thing." He moved to the computer monitor by Sim-Man's head and started programming in the first scenario. An image of Sleepy girl's serene unconscious face flashed through his mind, making him clench his jaw in frustration. Unfortunately he let his anger choose the scenario for him. *Let her try and sleep through this one*, he thought to himself with an evil smile.

"Right. Toby. And ..." Jamie looked for Sleepy Girl's ID.

"I'm Libby," she said, tucking some of her hair behind her ears and shifting nervously on her flat shoes. Toby a.k.a. Cocky Little Shit was still cool as a cucumber.

"Okay, Libby and Toby. I'm the ward nurse and I've fast-bleeped you to the acute medical unit. It's two in the morning. You come into the cubicle and this is your patient."

Jamie pressed the button on the monitor and Sim-Man started convulsing on the bed, causing even Cocky Little Shit to jump with surprise. Libby blinked, before looking at Jamie with a panicked expression. An uncomfortable ten seconds passed whilst Jamie suppressed the urge to roll his eyes.

"It's shaking," Toby said, frowning down at Sim-Man. Jamie pressed another few buttons and foam started coming from Sim-Man's plastic mouth. "What the fu–"

"Age? Medical history?" Libby's now-alert voice cut Toby off. She had come to stand next to Sim-Man's head, opposite Jamie, and had started to check the airway.

"Forty, diabetic, alcoholic," Jamie rattled off, watching as she efficiently tilted Sim-Man's head back and lifted his chin.

"Um ..." Libby hesitated for a moment and colour swept high across her cheekbones as she bit her lip. Jamie's breath left him in a sudden whoosh as he took her in; she was insanely beautiful. Control was important to Jamie and he was annoyed to feel it slipping as he looked at her. Coming out of her trance, she felt in Sim-Man's neck for his carotid pulse. "We need to do a BM and I need some rectal diazepam." She turned to a frozen Toby. "Can you help me roll him?"

Toby snapped out of his inertia and stepped forward to help roll Sim-Man so that Libby could give the rectal diazepam.

"Okay that was a good start, you two," Jamie said after they had both been working on Sim-Man for a few more minutes: he had stopped fitting and had a Gudel airway in place. "Libby, nice effort for your first time. Toby, don't worry, a lot of people freeze up in the first scenario with Sim-Man; you'll get used to him." Toby's face was flushed and his mouth was set in a hard line, but he gave a short nod. "Can one of you tell me what you forgot though? What do you want to be happening now?"

"We should have intubated him," Toby said quickly, eager to make up for the last ten minutes.

"Give him a chance, slugger," Jamie replied with a small smile. "And remember you're only an F1 in this scenario, you wouldn't be going around tubing people."

"Call for help," Libby cut in. "We didn't call for help."

"Yes!" Jamie smiled across at Libby and then watched in fascination as her gorgeous face broke into a wide grin. In contrast to her perfect features, her smile was just slightly off balance, with one side of her mouth hitching up a touch more than the other. Strangely, that added even more to her appeal. "You guys need a senior review and possibly an anaesthetist – like *me* – as everyone knows we're the best at handling acutely unwell patients."

What? Why was he boasting about his specialty like some sort of insecure wanker? He cleared his throat to continue. "In this scenario I wouldn't even have blamed you for putting out a crash call."

Jamie tore his eyes away from Libby's wonky smile when he heard a muffled snort from the other end of the bed. He turned to see Toby stalking back to his seat, red-faced and with his jaw clenched so tight that a muscle was ticking in his cheek. He heard a small sigh from Libby as she returned to hers. Jamie was still watching Toby's face as she walked past him, and frowned when he caught a surprisingly fierce expression – one of actual rage and loathing – flash across the boy's features.

"Libby-Lou." Libby heard Kira hiss and felt her shoulder being shaken. She pulled away slightly and burrowed her face further into her arms on the table. "Come on, Libs. I have cancer-laden processed food of Satan, plus evil corporate-giant caffeinated drinks."

Libby's eyes flickered as the delicious smell of bacon wafted up to her nose. Before she could manage to open them fully however, her eyelids were both forcibly pulled back Clockwork Orange-style, so she was made to look at Kira's frustrated little freckle-covered face. Those green eyes stared back at her with concern. "Come on, loser. I had to set aside nearly all my principles to buy you this stuff. You know I'm a vegan this month and I'm boycotting all big corporate products." Libby managed to push up to her elbows and laid her head on Kira's shoulder, on top of her dark red, partially dreadlocked hair.

"Ugh," Libby grunted, stretching out feebly towards the bacon bap just out of her reach. Kira rolled her eyes and gave the bap a shove in Libby's direction.

"Are you totally non-verbal today or what?" Kira asked. Libby was attempting to open the bottle of Fat Coke, prompting Kira to sigh, snag it from her and twist off the top before passing it back.

Libby nodded and took a life-restoring swig of the good stuff. She'd feel better in about ten minutes after the sugar and caffeine kicked in, and then she'd have about an hour before crashing.

"I love you, Ki-Ki," she said as her teeth sunk into the soft bread and bacon with just the right amount of ketchup. "I wish we were lesbians and we could live together in a lesbian commune for the rest of our lives."

"Libs, we all wish we were lesbians. But I'd like to point out that that wasn't what you were saying earlier after your little sesh with Triple G."

"Bugger off," Libby muttered, her mouth still full.

"I'd like to show him a scenario or two," Kira said through a smirk. "I'd scenario that boy's arse off."

"He's hardly a boy, Ki-Ki," Libby put in, frowning down at her bacon. "He's... I don't know... thirty or something. And he's in charge of training. You shouldn't be inappropri–"

"Oh come on, goody-two-shoes. Don't tell me you haven't thought about it? Those smoldering eyes, that strong jaw, ripped body. If he'd have got me up there I'd have been bent over Sim-Man crying 'Oh teacher please help me save the patient. Let's save him *real* good.'"

Libby choked on her Coke, trying to stifle her laughter. "Shut up, Kira," she said through gritted teeth. "The whole bloody canteen can hear you."

Kira rolled her eyes. "Lighten up, loser. I'm trying to inject some life into your zombie-self with my hilarious banter." She turned to Libby and raised her eyebrows. "I suppose it's a lost cause asking if you'd come out tonight?"

Libby grimaced at even the thought of a night out in her sleep-deprived state and shook her head so vigorously that the elastic straining to contain her hair popped free, leaving the heavy mass to settle down her back, across her shoulders and around her face. She growled as she looked under the table for the elastic, wishing, not for the first time, that she could just cut the whole sodding ridiculous lot off; but for Libby, as with a lot of other things in her life, that was not going to happen.

"Where did it... ?" she trailed off as she noticed that Kira now had her hand over her mouth in horror. "What?" Libby asked, tucking her hair behind her ears. Kira widened her eyes at Libby to almost comical proportions; then she jerked her head to the side, towards the next-but-one table. Libby looked across and saw her hair band resting on the top of a plate of pasta. The fork that was suspended over it, held by a large, male hand, slowly lowered. When she finally dragged her gaze up to see whose food she had contaminated, she froze. Familiar hazel eyes stared back at her and she took in a sharp breath of surprise. It was him: Dr Grantham, the anaesthetist from this morning, who had already been labelled Triple G: "Gorgeous Grantham the Gasman". She stood up from her chair, feeling her face heat and wishing fervently that the floor would swallow her up. Kira snorted a suppressed laugh.

"Uh... hi, Trip... I mean, Dr Grantham," she said once she had reached his table. "I'm so sorry but ..." She trailed off as he hooked her hair band with his fork and held it up. She snatched it off and screwed it up into a tight fist despite the pasta sauce covering its underside. "Sorry," she whispered.

"It's fine," he clipped in that cut-glass accent of his. Libby had done a fairly good job of neutralizing her own accent over the last two years but she knew it still held a slight, unmistakable Cockney vibe. For a moment she couldn't move. Maybe it was the sleep deprivation, but she became hypnotized by the sight of a small muscle ticking on his tanned and stubble-covered jaw.

"I'm sorry but do I know you?"

Libby turned her head sharply and took in the attractive Mediterranean-looking man sitting opposite Triple G who had asked the question and was looking up at her with curious eyes and a wide, bright, dazzlingly white smile. Libby stiffened.

"No." She forced a smile. "No, we've not met."

"But I could swear I ..." The man trailed off, his dark eyes narrowing.

"Um... thanks," Libby said, frantically gathering up her hair and trying to stuff it back into the band. "I'd better get–"

"Oh... that's it!" Mediterranean Man said suddenly as she was turning away, and a cold feeling of dread swept over her. "I know where I've seen you!" He was excited now, his finger raised and pointing at her. Her hands dropped down from her hair-wrangling and she turned to him. She gave a tiny shake of her head and her wide eyes pleaded with him to stop. The grin on the guy's face slowly dimmed and he blinked once.

"Sorry," he said quietly. "My mistake, okay?"

Her eyes closed briefly in relief before she gave a quick nod and rushed back to her table. Once she had sat back down she found that she had lost all appetite for the now rather sad-looking bacon sandwich, and pushed her tray away. She glanced to the side as she continued to bundle her hair up into the elastic, stuffing hairpins in as she went for good measure. Triple G was frowning across at Mediterranean Guy, asking him something. Luckily for Libby, the man just shook his head and avoided eye contact. Whether he didn't want to admit where he had seen her before, or whether he had taken pity on her, she wasn't sure.

Some men could be decent.

Most were scum.

She should know.

Chapter 2

Everyone's fighting their own unique war

"For the love of God, please make it stop," Jamie pleaded through gritted teeth as the first chords of the next Justin Bieber song sounded obnoxiously throughout the enclosed space.

"You know as well as I do, me old mucker, that the surgeon gets to choose the songs," Pav said from his position at the end of the bed, between the patient's legs. His dark head was bent to concentrate on his task, but Jamie could just about make out the smirk he wasn't trying to hide. "This isn't a democracy you know. I need this kind of existential beauty to soothe my soul and help me focus my genius."

"You are forcing me, and the entire theatre staff to suffer for your own satisfaction. You hate this stuff as much as the rest of us, you sick bastard."

"Aren't you a true Bielieber then, Grantham?" Mick the ODP's low voice rumbled from the other side of the patient. ODPs, or Operating Department Practitioners, were the anaesthetist's right-hand men and women. Without Mick on side, Jamie would be royally screwed.

"No, Mick," Jamie said slowly. "No, I am not." Mick shrugged his massive shoulders, exposing some more of his elaborately tattooed forearms. He was bald and about as wide as he was tall.

"Not averse to a bit of the Biebs. Little fucker can sing, after all." Mick delivered this in such a deadpan voice that the theatre staff who didn't know he was a purely heavy metal man probably thought he meant it. The other half were sniggering. They all enjoyed Jamie's torture sessions during these urology lists.

Ever since Jamie had let slip to his best friend that Justin Bieber gave him the creeps and his music made him feel physically ill, it had been playing on loop every Friday morning for months. *Months.* Pav was a persistent and diabolical wind-up merchant; if something amused him he would keep it going well past the tolerance of any other reasonable human being.

"It's not like you really need to concentrate anyway," Jamie complained. "It's just a TURP. You're not removing the bladder or anything; just making sure that this guy isn't going to be pissing every five minutes."

"I'm not sure that if you were the one with a metal bar up your cock, getting your prostate hollowed out, you would agree."

Jamie rolled his eyes. "Saving the world one dick at a time."

"Damn right I am. I'll have you know–"

The double doors to the theatre crashed open and all eyes swung to the dishevelled figure that stepped through. Her scrubs were inside out and massive on her, her theatre shoes were different colours and sizes, and her hair was a huge mess on top of her head, secured with multiple elastic bands and clips. She was trying to shove a torn theatre cap over the mass as she moved through the doors. Jamie smoothed down the front of his perfectly fitted scrubs and frowned.

"Dr Grantham," she said as her wide bright blue eyes met his, "I'm so sorry I'm late." She was out of breath, her cheeks were flushed pink, and despite the crazy disarray of her appearance she looked absolutely stunning. Pav had stopped squinting down his "metal rod" to take her in, and was openly smirking. Jamie shot him a warning look before turning to deal with the latecomer.

"One of the most important things in anaesthetics is preoperative assessment," he said, frowning down at her and trying unsuccessfully to block out how bright her eyes were after her rush to get here, or how full her bottom lip was as she bit it. "You've not only missed assessing the patients on the ward but also the anaesthetic itself."

Libby released her lip and took a deep breath in. For a moment her eyes clouded with the strangest look of bone-deep weariness and defeat that he almost wished he could let her off the hook. But by the time she spoke, that look had been replaced with hard determination.

"It won't happen again," she told him. "I just had–"

"Let's forget about it," he cut her off. He'd heard too many lame excuses from medical students burning the candle at both ends over the last few months since he'd agreed to be Educational Director. To Jamie it was black and white: you turned up, you put the effort in and you got the job done, end of story.

"You may as well come up this end, newbie," Pav put in, having gone back to operating. "The Gasman has already done big syringe, little syringe. All he does now is listen to the inane beeps and watch porn on his iPhone."

"Pav, will you please, for once, shut up," Jamie snapped. "And turn this goddamn music *off*. I feel like I want to rip my brain out through my nose."

"Boys, that's enough," the theatre sister snapped, thankfully shutting off the Bieber. "No swearing. *Ladies* are present."

Pav snorted a laugh (they'd already heard this particular *lady* using the c-word when referring to a theatre manager before the list started), which, under the sister's glare, he managed to turn into a cough. Jamie waited until he'd caught Pav's eye and gave him a long stare before turning back to Libby.

"Okay... Libby is it?"

He knew her name. He'd been thinking about her name, her hair, her eyes, her skin, even her baggy bloody jumper way too much over the last few days. But he wasn't about to reveal that to her or anyone else for that matter. She nodded, her breathing still fast, and Jamie had to put all his concentration into not looking down at her chest as it rose and fell rapidly.

"Right, Libby. Sit up on here." He gestured towards a stool next to the monitors at the patient's head end. "We'll go through some of the equipment and what the 'inane beeping' actually indicates (without it the patient would be dead). So, contrary to what Testes Twiddler over there thinks, our job is a little more involved than watching porn on my iPhone."

Libby gave a nervous laugh and sat up on the stool. Jamie had had too many med students pass out in theatre to risk having one who was obviously a party animal standing for an hour.

"Is that the CO_2 tracing?" she asked, pointing at the screen. Jamie gave a short nod and ignored Pav's long-suffering sigh as he started explaining the physics behind the tracings and equipment.

"Jamie," Mick interrupted him mid-flow a few minutes later. Jamie looked over at the big bastard in frustration and was shocked to see what might pass for an actual smile on his craggy face.

"Yes?" he asked, raising his eyebrows in expectation.

"Give it up, mate."

"Mick, what are you – ?"

"She's outters, zonko, dead to the world: you've put the poor girl to sleep."

Pav, who was unfortunately finishing up with the prostatic resection, let out a loud bark of laughter as Jamie slowly turned to face a sound-asleep Libby. She was still perched on the stool, her back surprisingly straight and her pen in her hand poised over her notepad; but her eyes were shut, her long lashes forming shadows over her cheekbones, and her breathing had evened out.

"I knew you were a boring fucker but this is the first time I've seen a female fall unconscious whilst you were mid-sentence," Pav managed to get out through his hilarity. Jamie shot him an irritated look before focusing back on Libby, whose hand had now gone lax, causing her pen to drop to the floor. As she started leaning dangerously to the side Jamie caught her arm to stop her from falling, and she scowled.

"Hands off the merchandise," she mumbled as she attempted to slap his hand away. "No touching."

At this Pav started another round of sniggers, closely followed by the rest of the theatre team as they prepared the patient for recovery and cleared the equipment away. Libby continued to fall off her stool, no more awake than before, despite being able to form sentences. Jamie caught her before she could hit the ground and, on instinct, lifted her small body up against his chest, and then watched as her eyes fluttered open to focus on his face. She blinked once, then her body went stiff before she gave a small yelp and struggled out of his arms.

The entire experience, including the feel of her against him, the smell of her light perfume mixed with her shampoo, and the incredible beauty of her eyes close up, somehow short-circuited Jamie's brain. His arms actually tightened to try to keep her suspended close to him, as his body seemed to have decided that this woman was right where she needed to be. It took a few long seconds for reason to kick in and override his almost overwhelming attraction to her. At that point he let her go abruptly and, much to his horror, she fell in a heap at his feet.

"Shit," he muttered, extending his hand, which she ignored as she staggered upright. "Are you okay?" The theatre had now fallen deathly silent. Pav's registrar was writing up the notes as Pav watched open-mouthed, his eyes widening as if to question Jamie's sanity.

"Fine," Libby snapped, looking unsteady and disconcertingly fragile now that she was standing on her own. "Sorry, I've always been a bit clumsy but I–"

Jamie, being a *little* bit of a control freak, and not relishing embarrassing himself in front of the entire theatre, not to mention his fury at her ability to fall asleep mid-teaching session (okay, so he knew the physics behind the anaesthetic machine was unlikely to butter everyone's bagel but he wasn't that dull, was he?) was suddenly furious. Nobody had actually *lost consciousness from boredom* whilst he was speaking before. In all honesty, he was used to a very different reaction when it came to the opposite sex, and it certainly didn't involve them falling asleep. He gritted his teeth.

"You were *asleep*," he told Libby, holding onto his temper by a thread.

"Oh no, I couldn't have been. I'm sure that –"

"You were asleep, and this is the *second* time it's happened," he snapped. The sharpness of his tone must have cut through even Pav's amusement because the atmosphere in theatre was thick with tension. Libby lowered her head and rubbed her temples, before clasping her hands together in front of her chest and looking up at him with wide, pleading eyes.

"I can explain," she whispered. "You wouldn't believe what a–"

"It may have escaped your notice, Ms Penny, but there is still a patient on the table. Maybe we could finish this up before we get into the gory details of your life?"

The patient was transferred to another trolley in near silence. After he had been taken to recovery, and with all of the theatre staff still milling around on clear-up, Jamie turned to Libby.

"Ms Penny," he said sharply, and Libby appeared to brace. "I know you probably think you have a valid excuse for today, but I've heard every excuse under the sun for below-par performance from medical students, and I'm afraid that they all equate to the equivalent of 'the dog ate my homework'. You are in your third year now. You're not dealing with lectures and paper; this was a *real* patient having a *real* operation. I'm keeping him alive during it *and* taking the time to teach you. There is no excuse for coming in half awake; there is no excuse for not listening. It's April, you will have already had one clinical attachment before you started on Anaesthesia and Elective Surgery. All the induction is finished now; it's time to knuckle down to some real work. You will not pass this rotation if you carry on like this and you certainly will not become a doctor if you keep up this attitude."

"But, I–"

"Just go. Sleep. And for God's sake buck up your ideas tomorrow."

Libby's mouth closed and her shoulders slumped. She glanced around at the theatre team before nodding, tucking her hair behind her ears and muttering, "I'm sorry," in a barely audible whisper as she backed out of the double doors.

There was a long pause as they all watched the doors swing

shut. Jamie looked over at Mick, who was frowning at him, with his big, tattooed arms crossed over his chest.

"What?" Jamie spat, stalking back over to his chart as the surgeons backed away from the table.

Mick just raised an eyebrow, as if that said it all for him, and then started to clear away the ventilation equipment.

He turned to Pav, who was also uncharacteristically somber.

"I can't let them get away with that shit," Jamie explained.

Pav put the rigid cystoscope back up on the theatre trolley and narrowed his eyes at Jamie. "There's a time and place, Jamie. That was a bit of a public dressing down. She's only just starting out. You could have let her explain.

"Oh, come on," Jamie scoffed. "You know as well as I do why she's tired: young, beautiful student? Falling asleep in clinics? Think what we were like for Christ's sake."

"Don't judge her by your standards, Jamie."

"You know what I mean."

"*You* know nothing about that girl's life. When did you become such a hard-arse? Everyone's fighting their own unique war, man. Wait until you know hers before you judge."

Chapter 3

"How high?"

"That request is inappropriate."

Libby waited for Dr Morrison to continue, but that was apparently all the bitch of a radiologist had to say.

"Um... okay," Libby said slowly, feeling another chunk of her hair work its way out of the elastic bands and holding back a sigh. Dr Morrison's hair was fastened at the nape of her elegant neck in a sleek chignon, her make-up was flawless, her clothes immaculate; she was Libby's complete opposite in appearance.

Libby was wearing one of her two work outfits – the sleeves of the oversize jumper were frayed, her trousers were a nasty polyester, and her flat chunky leather shoes had an unfortunate hole in the sole. Looking at Dr Morrison, Libby had to concede that clothes would need to work their way up her priority list somewhat. She felt like a homeless person next to this woman's perfection. The problem was, Libby's priority list was long and filled with things that just wouldn't wait – sacrifices had to be made, and so far it had been okay for her appearance to take a back seat. But now that she was no longer able to hide in the back of lecture theatres, that would have to change.

"Would you mind... I mean, could you possibly give me a reason to tell them?" Libby asked, pasting on a fake smile.

Dr Morrison's eyes flashed very briefly to hers before looking back at her computer screen; it was the first time she had even glanced in Libby's direction. She then continued to flick through the x-ray films on the monitor, but with her brows now drawn together and her mouth tight.

"Are you a foundation doctor?" she asked.

"Uh... no, actually I'm a medical student."

Dr Morrison's jaw clenched further at this information, but she didn't glance up again. Libby felt herself start to sweat, and she did what she always did when she was nervous: she fiddled. There were three paperweights on the desk in front of her. She picked one up to turn it over in her hands, but quickly returned it when she saw Dr Morrison look over out of the corner of her eye. After she put it back at random, Dr Morrison immediately adjusted it so it was again in perfect alignment with the other two, her movements jerky, either with stress or annoyance: Libby was guessing it was the latter.

"Sorry," she whispered, her face flooding with colour.

"Tell them to consider a CT. An ultrasound is just a waste of time," Dr Morrison said, not bothering to look up at her again.

"Chin up, love," Dr Philips, the much more jolly, white-haired radiologist who shared the office with Dr Morrison, said. Libby had heard that he was a good decade over retirement age – but he looked about a hundred and two. "Don't worry, we've all been there, haven't we, Millie?"

Dr Morrison's shoulders tensed but she didn't say anything in response, and Libby took that as her cue to leave.

"She said that it wouldn't be appropriate. Her advice was to request an urgent CT," Libby told Peter, the ICU registrar, when she got back to the unit.

"Ugh," he spat, pushing away from the central desk in disgust. "For fuck's sake. Did you tell her the bloody history?"

"Well... yes. I told her everything you said, and the results of the echo, and I–"

"*One thing* I ask you to do, and you bugger it up," he said, standing up to loom over her.

In her other world, her other existence, men like this idiot would be dealt with as soon as they threatened her in any way. It was ironic, really, that she felt more vulnerable in this environment than where she was arguably more exposed. But there were no huge bouncers here waiting in the wings to give this guy a well-deserved punch in the face, no women with inch-long nails ready to claw his eyes out should he dare to touch her. She took a small step back and watched irritation flash across his face.

It was only her first week of her ICU and anaesthetics attachment, and she had run into trouble of the male variety already. This particular unpleasant specimen of misogyny had spent the first day of her placement standing too close to her and talking to her breasts; then, after handover, he'd asked her out for a drink. Libby gave him a totally unambiguous *no*. She'd made the mistake too many times before with men like him by being polite, unwittingly making them think they stood a chance. In the long run it was better to be blunt.

Libby knew she was beautiful. Men and boys had been watching her since she turned thirteen and went through puberty in the space of a few weeks. As a teenager the attention it garnered her was exciting... until it wasn't. Now she viewed her beauty with a kind of pragmatic detachment. If she needed to use it, she would. Of course, there were advantages, but in this environment, and without a willingness to use her looks to get ahead, they became a distinct drawback. This prick of a registrar being a case in point.

"Well, at least *try* to make yourself useful," Peter sneered. "Go and cannulate Mr Westbeach."

Mr Westbeach was an intravenous drug user. There was no way Libby would be able to find a vein on his arms, or even feet. She knew for a fact that two junior doctors had already tried and failed.

"I don't think–"

"Bloody hell," Peter spat, his face turning red with anger as he took a step towards her and into her personal space. "When did you students get so full of yourselves? In my day if my registrar asked me to jump, I would ask, 'How high?' Your problem is–"

"Pete," a sharp male voice cut off Peter's tirade and Libby turned to see Dr Grantham striding towards them, his brows drawn down into a frown and his eyes sparking with fury. When he reached them he crossed his arms over his broad chest and looked down at Peter, who went from seeming physically imposing to looking like a bit of a weiner. "What is your problem?"

"My problem is that this medical student can't handle simple tasks and thinks she's too good for the ward work," Peter said, and Libby clenched her small hands into tight fists to stop herself from doing something she would regret. Dr Grantham's gaze shot between her and Peter for a moment and he frowned. Libby's heart sank. She knew that with her less-than-stellar performance where Dr Grantham was concerned so far, he would be unlikely to take her side.

"What 'simple tasks' exactly are we talking about here?" Dr Grantham asked.

"He sent me down to request an ultrasound for Mrs Tyler. Dr Morrison told me the request was inappropriate." Libby kept her voice as neutral as possible, simply conveying the facts.

Dr Grantham's eyebrows lifted and he turned back to a rather more uncomfortable-looking Peter, who shot Libby a poisonous look before meeting Dr Grantham's gaze head-on.

"Pete, medical students do not go and request investigations from consultants, especially not a consultant like Dr Morrison, who is so cold you could freeze ice on her arse. And, that *is* inappropriate. You should know by now that we go straight for CT to investigate possible abdominal sepsis. Now, what ward work is she refusing?"

Peter, who was now the one with his fists clenched and virtually trembling with rage, muttered something under his breath. Libby could just about make out the word cannula.

"Which patient?" Dr Grantham asked in a tightly controlled voice.

"Bed nine," Peter said with great reluctance, his attention now focused on the floor. Dr Grantham sighed and rubbed the back of his neck as his eyes went briefly to the ceiling before settling back on Peter.

"Mr Westbeach is waiting for a central line, Pete. Seeing as nobody, not even the consultants, can get IV access. Just bugger off and cover the emergency list, will you?" he gritted out. Peter went to dart around him at top speed but was halted by Dr Grantham's hand on his arm. "I don't want to see you pulling this shit again, you hear me?" His voice was quiet, almost a whisper, but somehow that made it more menacing.

"Fine," Peter hissed, shaking off Dr Grantham's hand to stalk out of the unit.

Once they were alone, Dr Grantham looked down at Libby and he sighed.

"I'm a fair man," he told her, and Libby blinked.

"Okay ..." she said slowly, unclenching her fists and taking a deep breath to brace herself for whatever he might say next.

"I'm sorry about Pete; he can be an arrogant sod, but I've never known him to reach quite that level of arsehole before." He narrowed his eyes at her as if assessing how she had managed to bring out his registrar's worst behaviour. Despite the slightly contemptuous look marring the apology somewhat, Libby gave him a wide smile. She was an expert at hiding behind banal facial expressions, and they worked particularly well for her with men.

His gaze dropped to her mouth and his frown deepened – not a typical reaction in her experience.

"No problem. And... and I know I should have been on time the other day, it's just that..." She trailed off and her mouth snapped shut. For some reason, she was reluctant to give him any more information about her life. If he had been interested he would have let her explain at the time. The very last thing she wanted was for him to think she was trying to wheedle out of her mistakes with some sort of sob story. "Well... I won't let it happen again."

He was still watching her mouth. Then, to her complete shock, he reached up as if to touch her face but withdrew sharply at the last minute. Her eyes widened and she took a jerky step back, this time coming up against the side of the central island and wincing in pain as her hip struck the hard surface. After snatching his hand away, he tried to shove both of them into his pockets – only he was wearing scrubs, so they simply slid down the sides of his legs at speed. Libby would have laughed, had she not been so terrified of his reaction.

After a moment of stunned confusion, he looked down at himself and then back up at Libby, before his face broke into a small smile as the tips of his ears turned red. For a moment Libby forgot how to breathe. So far, Dr Grantham's expressions had been less than happy around her, and with good reason. Even with the irritation she seemed to provoke clouding his features, he was still gorgeous; but with a genuine, self-deprecating smile on his lips and his eyes sparkling with humour, he was insanely attractive. A surge of what was likely oestrogen caused heat to flood her face and she had to look away to pretend to fiddle with the tie on her scrubs.

"Sorry," she heard him say and lifted her gaze to his again. "It's just, you've got some pen... um... here." He made to reach for her face again but Libby, truly believing that another oestrogen surge would render her unable to stay on her feet, flinched away. He pulled back, his ears burning even redder, and instead swiped his fingers over his own cheek.

"Oh... Varp," Libby mumbled, furiously scrubbing at her face to get the pen off, and then surreptitiously pulling down the long-sleeved top she had on under her scrubs to hide the notes she had scribbled earlier on her forearms. To be honest, Libby wasn't really the type of woman to normally be bothered about a bit of pen on her face, messy hair, holes in her shoes – she barely had time to glance in the mirror before she left for clinics, and she *never* wore make-up outside of her other work. Even then her boss at the club had to give one of the other girls extra tips to trowel on Libby's war paint for her after her dismal attempts had been rejected early on.

So no, Libby's appearance, which in her experience often led to uncomfortable confrontations and situations (case in point Mr Entitled Arsehole anaesthetic registrar), meant very little to her. But for some reason, in front of this beautiful man, she was suddenly wishing she maybe looked *slightly* less disheveled.

She bit her lip and Dr Grantham stared at her, his eyes becoming a bit unfocused before he coughed and took another step back.

Chapter 4

For badger's sake

Jamie felt his palms start to sweat. Here he was, her supposed knight in shining scrubs, rescuing her from that fucking lech Pete, when all he could think about was how soft her lips would be under his, how easily he could lift her small frame up onto the island and... Bloody hell, he needed to get some sort of handle on his perverted mind. He felt like a randy teenager again and he had to force himself to remember that she practically *was* one. Hell, with her fresh-faced innocence, messy hair piled on top of her head with various pens sticking out at weird angles, and those little scribbled notes he'd caught on her forearms before she yanked her top down, she looked about *sixteen*.

He searched the ICU to find a suitable substitute for Pete who she could shadow; but the only other options were the SHO (who Jamie was pretty sure had actually drooled at handover whilst staring at Libby) and Tony (one of the other consultants, famous for making an art form of seducing junior doctors and would be more than likely to turn his charm to stunning medical students, given the way he'd been eyeing

Libby since she'd stepped onto the unit). Why, today of all days, was the ICU full of predatory males? Where were the female consultants and trainees when you needed them? Jamie sighed.

"I think you should come with me for the rest of the day," he told her, making sure not to drop his gaze down to her mouth again but finding that her blue eyes surrounded by thick, dark lashes were just as disconcerting. "Okay," he said briskly, breaking eye contact and turning on his heel. "Let's start the ward round."

Moving through ICU with Libby in tow was a new form of torture for Jamie. He'd worked with attractive women before, but somehow this felt different. It wasn't just that she was beautiful; it was other stuff, small stuff: the way she shoved tendrils of dark hair, when they escaped from the mass on her head onto to her cheeks, behind her ears; the focus she employed when watching a procedure or listening to anything he or the nurses had to say (unlike other medical students, Libby did seem to appreciate that the nurses had just as much to teach her as he did); the way her cheeks flushed when she answered a question correctly (which, considering her propensity to fall asleep sitting up, was surprisingly often).

Despite all this, Jamie managed to be studiously professional... that was until he heard her sing to herself under her breath whilst doing a practical procedure. He'd listened in during the second cannula, when she thought he was still reading the notes. "*Putting on the tourniquet, tap along the vein, open up the packaging, swab the area ...*" and so on. When she'd finished, having sung throughout the entire thing about what she was doing, to the worst rap in recorded history, she turned and gave a little start to see him standing right behind her, smiling a totally inappropriate smile.

She rolled her eyes (which unfortunately was goddamn adorable as well). "I'm not used to doing this stuff, okay? I read that it helps cement memories if you sing what you're doing as you're going along."

Jamie nodded, his grin still very much present as he said, "Yep. Totally normal."

She gave a little cute huff of annoyance but her lips tilted up in amusement.

"Tell me though– does it *have* to be Ant and Dec? Or do other dodgy nineties classics look in? Some Chesney Hawkes maybe?" he asked, and then sucked in a breath at her answering smile. That smile was dangerous; it should have been quarantined immediately for the safety of mankind. He took a step back, his own smile fading rapidly as he shook his head to clear it.

It wasn't just her beauty that was throwing him though; it was her intelligence, her quirkiness, her complete disregard for her appearance... But okay, the fact that she was unbelievably, mind-blowingly hot didn't help either.

The next day Libby was allocated to his list again and, unlike before, she was early. By the time he arrived, she had already reviewed all the patients' notes and was ready to go round with him to assess them. She listened in theatre, did her cute little rap whilst she cannulated each patient (by this stage Jamie was pretty much addicted to hearing it and moved closer as soon as he saw her approach the equipment). She even managed to soften the big man: Mick had cracked a smile with her that morning (Jamie could count on one hand the number of times he'd seen that bastard smile) and he'd taken to plucking pens out of her hair to write on the charts, apparently pleased with the convenience of such a ready supply.

She was good with the patients – she told a particularly nervous one that Jamie could put her to sleep with just the power of his voice, so adding in a little propofol would knock them right out. This earned a bark of laughter from Mick so rare that Jamie actually thought Mick had aspirated on a Malteaser and was fighting for air; until he realised that the snort/wheeze was his best version of an amused giggle. *Giggle.* From Mick? Insane.

Jamie caught the SHO that Libby was supposed to be working with staring at her arse the day after that, so he kept her with him again. This was a little irrational seeing as Doug was a great bloke and would never make any woman he was working with feel uncomfortable. But for some reason the thought of thoroughly amiable and inoffensive Doug having a jolly old time with Libby, whilst intermittently staring at her arse, was not acceptable. So Libby stayed with Jamie for another day, and a day slid into a week, then into another. He started to relax around her and to get used to the low hum of almost painful physical attraction in her presence. She was on time every day and there were no more drowsy episodes. Indeed, she was one of the most attentive and quick students he'd ever come across. He was sure that when he and Pav were in their first year clinical they didn't know their arses from their elbows, leave alone the appropriate vertebral level for a spinal anaesthetic.

He met her small, outrageous friend Kira again that week. She plonked herself down at the table he was sitting at with Pav for lunch, turned to Jamie, and pouted her lips, saying: "Well, hello there, Dr G. Care for my spongy fingers... or maybe a custard crème?" The way she breathed the words, her eyelids half-mast and the hand that wasn't holding the plate of biscuits pushing her hair up off her neck, it was like she really was asking him to perform something sexual right there in the canteen. When her hand fell from her hair and onto his knee, giving him a firm squeeze, he nearly jumped up from the table, and caused Pav (a man not easily shocked) to drop his fork. She pulled her hand away and laughed in a maniacal way that suggested mental ill health, then slapped Jamie on the back.

"I told you I could make him blush," she said, turning to look at a horrified Libby, who was standing next to the table, holding her tray with a white-knuckled grip. "Oh, for badger's sake, close your mouth and sit down before you catch a fly, Hot Mess. My spongy fingers are going stale as we speak."

"Kira," Libby said through gritted teeth, her own face flushed bright red. "Get. Up."

"Sure now, these here fellas don't mind us squeezing on here – do you?"

Pav barked a laugh and slapped the table. "That's it," he said. "I'm in love. And I *definitely* want one of your sponge fingers, baby – custard creamed or not."

"That's what they all say, darling," Kira told him, blowing him a kiss across the table and pushing the plate towards him, before taking one of the sponge fingers herself, closing her eyes and moaning as she bit it in half.

"Awesome," Pav whispered, and Jamie looked at the ceiling.

"It's fine," Jamie said to Libby, who was making big eyes at her friend and jerking her head to the side to get Kira to follow her. "You ladies are welcome to sit here."

He ignored Pav's raised eyebrow as he waved Libby to sit on the opposite chair; Jamie had never sat with any students before, or encouraged any sort of friendship he felt was inappropriate, despite some of the less than subtle approaches made over the last two years since he'd been put in charge of simulation training. It wasn't as if he was a teacher and they were in school, but it was unethical. Not to mention they were practically teenagers. Jamie had always done everything by the book. No exceptions.

"I'm sorry," Libby muttered, reluctantly taking the chair

and glaring at Kira as she did. "I'm afraid I have no control over her."

"Well, any woman who eats sponge fingers and custard crèmes for her lunch, succeeds in making sexually based jokes around them, and uses 'badger' as a swear word, is a genius in my book. I'm Pavlos." Pav reached across the table to shake Kira's hand, but she offered him a closed fist instead. "And she fist-bumps," he added as their knuckles made contact. "Where have you been all my life?"

"Hello, Kira," Jamie cut in. "I think we've met in teaching."

"Indeed," Kira said around a mouthful of sponge finger. "Loved the partial pressure co-efficient calculation by the way. Riveting stuff." Pav snorted and Jamie's mouth pulled up into a reluctant smile. "And this one," she indicated Libby with a sponge finger, "has been on about you non stop. "Dr Grantham says ...", "Well, Dr Grantham doesn't think ...", "Dr Grantham told me to ...". You've made quite the impression, my man. She makes you out to be some sort of medical Einstein-slash-Terminator, totally unfazed by any situation, ready with your healing hands whenever the need arises." Kira's eyes flicked down to Jamie's hands and then she looked back up to wink at him.

"Kira. Shut. Up." Libby hissed, her face glowing now, with red spreading from her cheeks down her neck to her chest – another goddamn adorable trait which Jamie strove to ignore. He stifled a grin at Kira, ridiculously pleased that Libby had talked about him.

Pav groaned. "Please don't inflate his ego any more than it already is. Now, let's get back to the use of the word badger and the sexual nature of custard crèmes."

Once Libby had managed to control the blood flow to her face and stopped glaring at Kira, lunch was... fun. Unlike Jamie, Pav had never cared about convention or blurred lines, and he had always been effortlessly charming. Seeing Libby relaxed (well, as relaxed as anyone could be at a table with a loose cannon like Kira) added yet another layer to her attraction. Thanks to Pav, Jamie learnt that Libby was not in fact a teenager. Both she and Kira hadn't started their medical degrees until they were twenty, making them both twenty-two. Kira had done a science conversion course to apply for medicine, followed by a year out to "find herself": this spent "communing with my spiritual side and rearranging my chakras". Jamie presumed that Libby must have followed that same sort of path, as Kira had told them they'd been best friends since school – although she deftly changed the subject when it arose.

By the time they left, Pav was staring at Jamie with a smug smile on his face. It took a punch in Pav's stomach in the safety of Jamie's office before he would tell him why he was smirking.

"You like her," he told Jamie, his voice still smug despite being winded.

"Bugger off," Jamie muttered, his ears feeling hot, the traitors.

"You do! You like her!" Pav said, his eyes wide and his finger pointing at Jamie's ears. "The bloody ears are going – I knew it!"

Since he was a child Jamie's ears had had a ridiculous tendency to turn pink when he was embarrassed or angry. Pav, who from the age of eighteen had made it his life's work to embarrass Jamie at every available opportunity, discovered this foible early on at medical school. He loved the fact that Mr Control was never able to hide it when he fancied a girl or when he was riled.

"I'm not in the mood for this shit today, Pav," Jamie snapped, his hands closing into fists.

"Look, mate," Pav said, his tone now far more cautious

given the mood shift in the room. "I think it's great. Your ears haven't pinked up in years. This could be–"

"She's a fucking *student,* Pavlos. She's *my* student."

"Only for the next few–"

"She's a baby, practically a teenager. Grow up. She still parties so hard that she can't stay awake mid-conversation. What part of that do you think is appropriate?"

"That was only the one ti–"

"Twice, Pav. She fell asleep twice."

"You don't know wh–"

"Look, if she's not in scrubs, she dresses like a hobo at work. It's clear that she's a long way off adulthood. I'm not into little girls."

"Ugh!" Pav threw up his hands in disgust. "Sometimes I don't know why we're even mates. You're *so* judgmental. So what if she parties? So what if she turns up to work less than your quite frankly anal level of smart? At least she seems like a laugh. And anyway, you wouldn't let her explain about the whole sleeping thing. Maybe she works... nights... or something."

"Nights?" Jamie frowned at Pav in confusion. "What do you mean nights? The students aren't on the on-call rota."

"I mean work for money. You know, to live? Ever heard of that?"

"Why would you think she's working nights?"

Pav looked away and cleared his throat. "I just don't think you know the whole story," he muttered.

"She's had plenty of opportunity to explain since I cut her off."

Pav put his hands on his hips and rolled his eyes. "Come off it, you tosser. Would anyone bring it up again after you'd been that much of a dick about it?" He shook his head and turned to leave. "Trouble with you is you're too fucking straight. Loosen up, for badger's sake, or you'll end up a miserable self-righteous old git, alone with your Sim-Man and your *Oxford Textbook of Anaesthesia*."

Chapter 5

Gwown-up cwying

"Okay so at this point we would normally hand over to the incoming team, but since the patient hasn't been stable and I've been with them from the beginning, I'm going to stay," Dr Grantham told them as the surgeon was putting in the last of the stitches.

What should have been a simple procedure had been complicated by a run of ventricular tachycardia. The surgeon had had to step away whilst Dr Grantham stabilised the patient. Libby was starting to see what he had meant the other day when he said anaesthetics was ninety-nine per cent boredom and one per cent sheer terror. The surgeon had totally lost his cool: why he thought that the repeated use of the f-word and waving his hands in the air would flip the patient back into sinus rhythm was a mystery to the rest of the theatre, but that seemed to be his chosen technique.

In contrast, Dr Grantham was completely calm. He attached the defibrillator paddles, went through practiced motions, and shocked the patient back into a normal heart rhythm within a couple of minutes. Despite his efficiency, though, the list had now overrun and it was already five thirty.

"You guys are of course free to go but medicine is unpredictable, and this *is* a learning opportunity," Dr Grantham said.

"I'm staying," Toby replied at warp speed, and Libby closed her eyes slowly. "Got to take advantage of every learning op we've got, haven't we, Libs?" He turned his smug face towards her, and she sighed. He knew she wouldn't be able to stay, not at short notice. Toby was on the surgical team, but Dr Grantham often ended up teaching the surgical students as well if their allocated consultant was ignoring them.

"I..." She glanced at the clock on the wall of the theatre before squaring her shoulders. "I can't stay. I'm sorry but I–"

"No need to apologise," Dr Grantham told her, his voice tight as he turned back to the monitors and made an adjustment to the pressure on the ventilator. "It's *your* learning, Libby, not mine. If you've got somewhere more important you've got to be, then you're free to leave."

Libby felt a flash of anger shoot through her. If she were four, she would have stamped her foot. But she was not four; she was the adult. The familiar weight of heavy responsibility settled on her shoulders, chasing away her anger and leaving only the all-too-familiar feeling of defeat in its wake. "No, you don't understand. I would stay but I *have* to–"

"Libby," Dr Grantham snapped. "If you hadn't noticed, I don't exactly have time to chat. If you need to go, *go*. Right, Toby, we're going to prepare the patient to transfer to ICU and once we're there I'll need to insert a central line; you can assist."

Libby stood for a moment, her mouth slightly open, ready to defend herself, ready to make him listen to her explanation. But as she watched the two men turn away from her, dismissing her completely, her shoulders slumped.

What was the point? He had proven again and again that he was a judgmental piece of work. She had to accept that until things changed she had other commitments.

Beg, borrow or steal, she repeated to herself in her head. She always knew that it wouldn't be easy. The first two years in lecture theatres and labs were a world away from this – but she would not give up. She would do anything to achieve her goal, and for now she *had* to leave. If this big idiot didn't want to hear her explanation, then he could bugger off. She blinked away the stupid pointless tears that had gathered as she stood there. Before she could swipe one that had escaped, she noticed Mick staring at her. He frowned and shifted as if to make a move towards her, but she turned on her heel and was out of the double doors before she could see his intention.

Jamie rubbed his neck as he pushed his way into the anaesthetic office. It had been a long night but the patient was stable, for now. The annoying jumped-up little twat shadowing him had made the extra hours particularly painful, and Mick's inexplicably surly attitude had been bloody annoying. In his irrational, tired brain Jamie decided that he blamed Libby. If she had been there to dilute her compatriot's arseholerly the whole thing would have been a lot less irritating. He also knew that the conversation with the patient's family would have been smoother had Libby been there. Some people are like that, they have a calming influence, and they know what people need in those situations.

Only yesterday he'd been discussing the prognosis of a man with an ischaemic brain injury with his family, and the wife had started crying. Libby had leapt up – not to the woman but to the terrified-looking three-year-old sitting next to her. She'd asked him if he liked ice cream. This got his attention away from his upset mum and before Jamie knew it the child was following Libby out of the room. They came back to the family room twenty minutes later, the kid covered in chocolate and Libby with a smudge in the corner of her mouth. (Jamie very nearly reached up to wipe it away, totally inappropriately.) By that stage things had calmed down considerably and the lack of a high-energy three-year-old during the breaking of bad news had been a godsend.

Toby had been about as much use as a chocolate teapot when they'd talked to tonight's family; he'd sat so far back into his chair he looked like he was attempting to fuse with it, and kept his gaze firmly locked on his huge, annoying feet.

"Gah!" Jamie shouted as a sharp pain speared his shin, then jumped back when he noticed a small child standing in front of him. She had somewhat familiar bright blue eyes, and dark hair in two uneven bunches with ribbons tied around each one, matching her purple and pink corduroy skirt.

"Get off my Alan," she said, frowning up at him and pointing at his foot. He stepped back to reveal a now slightly squashed, large, fluffy toy... spider? What kind of little girl carried around toy spiders? The child snatched it off the floor and cuddled it into her chest protectively. "You," she said, pointing at him with the hand that wasn't holding the toy in a death grip, "are *too big*." She made it sound as if this was something he should be able to remedy immediately, and the failure to do so was offensive to her and anyone else under six foot.

"Um ..." he said, searching the large admin space filled with desks and computers for an adult and coming up empty. "Well, I just look big to you because you're small." He watched with growing alarm as her face flushed bright red and she stamped her foot; if it was possible for steam to come out of her ears he was sure it would have.

"I am *not* small – I'm taller than Mary Reynolds and she's at *big-girl school*. So there!" Jamie wasn't sure what frame of reference "Mary Reynolds" gave him for height, or any idea what age children were at "big-girl school", but the little tyrant in front of him couldn't have been much more than four years old.

"Uh... okay, my mistake," he said, squatting down in front of the little girl and forcing a smile onto his tired face. "I'm sorry for stepping on... Alan."

"Humph."

"Right... so, are you here on your own?"

"Course not, you wally," she told him, rolling her pretty blue eyes. "Mummy's in the loo." Her voice then dropped to a whisper and she leaned forward as if telling him a secret. "She cwying; she hides in the loo when she wants to do gwown-up cwying."

"Oh." Jamie did not know what to say to this heartbreaking piece of news.

"She's sad cause Bwian is bwoken and her bossman is a big fat meanie-poo-poo head."

"Uh..." Jamie muttered, trying to decipher some sort of meaning from what she was saying. They both turned towards the creaking of the toilet door across the office and, to Jamie's shock, Libby stepped out. She froze when she caught sight of the pair of them, her red-rimmed eyes wide in her pale face.

"He," the little girl said, pointing in Jamie's face and scrunching her nose, "*stepped* on Alan with his humongous feet." Libby's gaze dropped down to a now loosely held Alan, then moved up to Jamie's face, and if anything she grew even paler.

"She kicked me," was all Jamie could think to say as he straightened up.

"Tattletale," the little girl whisper-shouted at him.

"Rosie," Libby said as she jerked out of her trance and strode across the room to them. "Say sorry."

"But... but he *stepped on* Alan! And he's *too big*... and... and... I'm hungwy!" With that Rosie dissolved into floods of tears. Libby bent to gather the child into her arms, and then sat down heavily in one of the office chairs whilst the little girl buried her face in her neck and hair.

"Okay, Little Louse," she cooed, rocking the little girl on her lap, "it's okay. Mummy will take you home now."

"B-b-but we can't go home cause Bwian bwoken," Rosie sobbed.

"We're going to get the bus," Libby told her in a voice laced with false cheer. "Won't that be fun?"

"I... I... I'm gonna cwy *all* the way home."

Libby looked up at the ceiling and blinked away the tears Jamie could see forming in her own eyes. She then shook her head as if to clear it and looked across at him over the top of her daughter's head, giving him a weak, apologetic smile.

"Dr Grantham, this is Rosie. She's very sorry for kicking you; *aren't you* Rosie?" The only response from the tear-stained bundle in Libby's lap was a brief scowl in his direction and a small snort. As an apology it was not altogether convincing.

"Is...?" Jamie cleared his throat. "Is she yours?"

Libby lifted her chin and tilted it at a stubborn angle, her eyes flashing. "Yes. She's my daughter."

"You never told me you had a daughter."

"Well, I did try a couple of times, but you didn't–"

"I cut you off." Jamie ran his fingers through his hair, his mind going over the past two weeks and both of the times she had tried to explain, only to have him close the conversation down. Pav's words came back to haunt him as he took in the two females huddled in a soggy-looking mess on the chair:

Everyone's fighting their own unique war, man. "Shit, I'm sorry."

Rosie stopped crying for a moment, her head popped out from her mother's neck and she turned wide eyes to him. "What's 'shit'?"

Libby rolled her eyes to the ceiling again and she groaned. "He said ship honey, *ship*, with a p."

"Why'd he say ship?"

"Because I've got a ship," Jamie told Rosie, his face heating. When he glanced at Libby she had widened her eyes and was shaking her head frantically for some reason.

"Really?" Rosie breathed, all her hunger and tears forgotten at this news. "Can I go on your ship?"

"Ah... I... well it's more of a boat than a ship to be exact and..."

"I wanna go on your boat." She was bouncing up and down now; poor Alan fell to the floor forgotten.

"I don't think..." Jamie trailed off as Rosie's eyes started to fill with tears again and her bottom lip started trembling. "Of course, you can come on my boat," he told her helplessly and watched as Libby closed her eyes and shook her head.

"Right, come on, Little Louse," Libby said as she stood up from the chair, the child still clinging on to her like a barnacle. "Let's leave Dr Grantham alone and get you home. It's way past your bedtime."

"I'm gonna be a pirate when I get gwowed up," Rosie told him. "So I *needs* to go on a boat. I never been on a boat before."

"Yes... um... that makes sense," Jamie said as Libby started heading towards the door. On instinct he moved to block her path. "Are... are you guys okay? Rosie said something about 'Brian' being broken? Do you have another kid?"

Libby huffed and stepped to the side but Jamie mirrored

her movement. "Brian is a car and he won't start. I only have one child."

"That's why you couldn't stay," Jamie muttered, running a hand down his face and breathing out a sigh as he blocked another move by Libby to get past him.

"Yes," Libby told him through gritted teeth. "She goes to the hospital nursery but I have to pick her up by six. I don't have anyone else to..." She took a deep breath and blinked a couple of times as her eyes grew suspiciously wet. "My family live across London and they can only do so much; most of the week it's just me and Rosie."

"And Bwian," Rosie chipped in.

"Well, yes, and Brian... when he's not conking out on us."

"And Alan... where's Alan?" Rosie twisted in Libby's arms to look for her spider, her voice growing panicked. Jamie, fearing the return of the lip quiver, moved quickly to retrieve Alan from under the office chair and deposited him in Rosie's outstretched arms. Libby gave her a look when she didn't say anything.

"Thank you," he eventually heard the child whisper at record speed. They started towards the door again, but Jamie couldn't let them go. He moved to block the doorway.

"How long will the bus take?"

Libby looked from the doorframe to his big body blocking the way and frowned. "Not long, it's fine."

"Mummy! That is a porky pie!" Rosie shouted. "The bus takes *years*!"

"I can give you a lift," Jamie told her, surprising both of them.

"I don't think that–"

"I'm hungwy," Rosie moaned, and Libby closed her eyes in what looked like defeat.

Chapter 6

"Why's Mummy all jerky?"

JAMIE STARED AT THE ANCIENT RUSTED DENTED LIGHT-blue Polo as Libby rummaged in the back seat, retrieving various bits of kid detritus that Rosie claimed she *had* to take home with her. Brian it seemed was a tin can on wheels. Jamie wasn't surprised the bloody thing wouldn't start; he was more shocked that it even managed to get them to the hospital in the first place.

"Does this thing have an MOT?" he asked, watching the way Libby had to slam the back door and then lean against it for a full minute before it would click shut. She shot him an annoyed look.

"Of course it does. I wouldn't be driving it if it weren't taxed. It's all surface stuff."

"Clearly, it is not 'all surface stuff' given that it won't actually start."

Libby shifted her huge backpack onto her shoulder and grabbed Rosie's hand.

"Where's your car then?" she asked, ignoring his unhelpful comment.

"I'm on the next level," he told her, leading them to the car-park stairs.

"When's it getting towed?" he asked when they made it up to his car (Jamie had had to wrestle the backpack and car seat out of Libby's hands so that she could carry a nearly-asleep-on-her-feet Rosie). Libby shrugged and made a non-committal sound but carried on walking. Jamie beeped the locks on his black pristine BMW estate, pulled open the back door and pushed the car seat inside. When he turned back to Libby he saw that Rosie was now fully asleep, and he held out his arms to take her. Libby hesitated but then handed her over, surprising Jamie with how heavy the dead weight of a sleeping four-year-old could be. He sat her gently in the chair, tucking Alan next to her, and then stepped back to let Libby strap her in.

Once Libby had typed her address into Jamie's sat nav and they had driven out of the car park, she laid her head on the passenger window and closed her eyes. Some of her hair had fallen out of its confines, there were dark smudges under her eyes, and her mouth was set in a tense line.

When they eventually pulled up in front of a dilapidated block of flats a fair way out from Tooting, both the beautiful adult and child females in Jamie's car were out for the count. Living in London was not cheap. Jamie winced when he remembered the large house his parents had bought for him and Pav to share during their student days. Sometimes he forgot what an over-privileged bastard he really was. Feeling a little creepy but unable to stop himself he just sat and watched Libby's face relaxed in sleep as she took slow, steady breaths. After an inappropriate amount of time he cleared his throat.

"Uh... Libby?"

She stirred in her sleep and her eyelids fluttered but quickly settled again. He leaned over the centre console to her and was engulfed by the clean smell of her shampoo.

"Libby?" He didn't want to shout and risk waking up Demon Child, so he decided to give her shoulder a gentle shake. Wrong decision.

"Get. Off." Libby growled, grabbing his wrist in a surprisingly strong hold and throwing his hand off her shoulder. Her eyes flew open and she instinctively pulled away from him, flattening herself against the passenger side door.

"Hey," he said, holding his hands up in surrender. "I'm sorry. I was just trying to wake you up."

Libby blinked and looked from Jamie to the sleeping child in the back seat. Colour swept high over her cheekbones and her shoulders relaxed. "God. I'm sorry. You must think I'm a lunatic."

"Do you... I mean is there..." Jamie trailed off. He wanted to ask why she'd had such a violent reaction – if there was a reason behind it. Was there someone at home she was scared of?

He glanced around again at the rough neighbourhood and rubbed the back of his neck. Other memories invaded his consciousness to add to his concern. He thought back to the state of Libby's car, and then his mind flashed to a glimpse of the sole of Libby's shoe he'd seen the other day, with a hole right the way through to her sock. What had seemed a baffling but charming disregard for her appearance took on a rather more desperate tone. He turned to Libby who already had her hand on the door handle, ready to spring out of the car.

"You can't afford to have Brian towed, can you?" To be honest Jamie was starting to be surprised that Libby could even afford Brian full stop.

"Look, this is really none of your business," Libby muttered, pulling the handle, then freezing when Jamie leaned right across her to lay his hand on hers and prise her fingers away from the door.

"How will you get in tomorrow?" he asked.

"That's none of your business either," she whispered, her eyes now wide and her breathing shallow. He took a deep breath in of her clean scent and for a moment felt a little dizzy.

"Will you get the tube?" he asked, noting the station just down the road.

"Phobia," Libby muttered, her breath fanning against his cheek. She shook her head as if to clear it, then spoke quickly. "I mean Rosie has a phobia, of the underground. It's the reason we got that stupid car in the first place. But we can take the bus."

"You can't go on the bus – it's too far. There won't be a direct route," he murmured, staring at a freckle on her upper cheek, unable to take his eyes off it.

"Hungwy!" Rosie's weak, strangled cry came from the back seat, forcing Jamie out of his trance and making him realize what he was doing. Libby's back was against the passenger door and his body was caging her in. Their faces were inches apart and his hand was still covering hers on the handle. Her pupils were dilated and her breathing was shallow.

"Shit," he muttered under his breath, jerking away from her and sitting back in his seat.

"Why you talkin' 'bout ships again?" Rosie asked, her swear-word-detecting, eagle ears dragging her fully back from unconsciousness.

"Right, young lady, let's get you out of the car. We're home," Libby said, yanking the passenger door open and then slamming it shut.

"Why's Mummy all jerky?" Rosie's sleepy voice asked as they both watched Libby walk around the front of the car. Jerky was a good description: Libby's shoulders were hunched and her body tense, making her movements seem sharp and angry.

"Maybe she's hungry too," Jamie said as the back door was yanked open.

"Come on, Little Louse, you're going to have to walk up the stairs. The lift's broken and Mummy's too tired to carry you up four floors." Jamie jumped out of the car and slammed it shut. Libby had extracted Rosie from her car seat and deposited her on the pavement and Rosie's bottom lip had started trembling yet again.

Libby turned to face Dr Grantham and let out what might have been her hundredth sigh of the day. There he stood on the pavement in front of her crappy block of flats, next to his stupid fancy penis-extension car, looking way more attractive than was fair given her own bedraggled state, his pristine tailored suit making him seem even more intimidating than his scrubs and his white open shirt-collar a sharp contrast to his tanned throat. The hospital infection control banned ties, otherwise Libby knew he would be sporting one of those as well. There was nothing casual or relaxed about this man.

After picking Rosie up from the nursery, she and Brian had engaged in an epic hour-long battle of wills, which of course he won. He would only splutter briefly when she turned the key in the ignition, and even when she'd managed to find someone to give him a jump start he'd roared to life for about ten seconds before letting out a sort of death rattle and wheezing his last. Then, stubborn, stubborn arse that she was, instead of phoning Kira for help, and after realizing she had no data left on her iphone, she'd gone back up to the deserted anaesthetic offices to go online and plan which bus routes they should take home.

It wasn't as if Kira wouldn't have come to fetch them, but Libby was careful about how many favours she asked of people.

She knew she had nothing to give in return and she didn't want to use them up. She'd been struggling for so long it was almost ingrained in her to fight her own battles, sort out her and Rosie's problems by herself. When she'd seen how complicated the route home was though, it had been too much. That's when she'd retreated into the small toilet to have a quick self-indulgent cry where Rosie couldn't see her.

So now, not only did Mr Perfect know that she was a single mother, but he had been kicked in the shin by her offspring, seen Brian – the crappiest car in the history of crappy cars – and was currently eyeing her block of flats like it was the black hole of Calcutta. Rosie gave her a mutinous look and Libby gritted her teeth in preparation for the tantrum of the century; her daughter was a force to be reckoned with on a good day, but a tired and hungry Rosie, faced with climbing four flights of stairs, would not be pretty.

"Thanks," she told the big guy in front of her, who was – yet again – blocking her way. "I'll see you tomorrow."

He just stood there, his eyes bouncing from mother to daughter. Then, to Libby's complete and total shock, he reached down and swept Rosie up in his arms as if she were as light as a feather. The tears that had formed in Rosie's eyes suddenly dried up and her small mouth fell open.

"I'll carry you up, okay, kiddo?" he said to her through a wide smile. She blinked, then nodded; Libby doubted that any female, be they four or forty, would say no to Dr Grantham when he smiled like that.

"Your face is furry," Rosie told him, squeezing his cheeks together as Libby fumbled with the front door. Jamie's deep chuckle echoed through the urine-smelling corridor.

"I can take her from here," Libby lied, shifting the car seat in her arms and wanting to get rid of him as quickly as possible. Dr Grantham just looked at her, raised one eyebrow, and then stepped through the door she had opened, with Rosie still wrapped around him like a little octopus. He looked briefly at the defunct lift and shook his head before taking the steps two at a time up to the fourth floor. Libby shuffled after him as fast as she could. On the first floor he took the car seat off her, leaving her with just her backpack. By the time she caught him up on her landing she was wheezing for breath and cursing the fact that she hadn't bothered to get a new inhaler. He still had Rosie secure on his hip, totally and annoyingly unaffected by the climb. It wasn't the physical exertion that triggered her asthma so much as the stress.

"Okay," she managed to get out in between breaths, "thanks... again. We'll just..." She trailed off as she held her arms out for her daughter, but Rosie's attention was still fixed on Dr Grantham.

"You pwomised about the boat," Rosie told him, continuing to drop her Rs now that she was tired. "It's vewy naughty to lie. I told Mrs Wilkinson that I had put a big beetle in her bag when I hadn't and I lost Golden Time *and* I went on the Thunder Cloud."

To be fair to him Dr Grantham managed to keep a straight face throughout Rosie's dire warning.

"Well, we'll have to see what your mummy thinks about–"

"Wemember: *Golden Time...*" Rosie told him, her voice rising in indignation and her little hands squeezing his cheeks together again.

"Okay," Dr Grantham said, his voice distorted as Rosie forced his lips into a pout. "We'll go out on my boat." Rosie released his cheeks and then gave one of them a pat as if rewarding a wayward toddler after a tantrum.

"You can put me down now," she told him imperiously, wriggling around to hold out her arms for Libby. "I'm ready for my supper, Mummy."

Libby rolled her eyes as she swung Rosie away from Dr Grantham and onto her own hip. "Do you think Your Highness would consider walking to the kitchen?" Rosie snuggled into her mother's neck and shook her head. The flat door was wide open now and Libby was aware that she hadn't had time to transform her bed in the living room back into a sofa. They only had one small bedroom, which Rosie used when she wasn't sneaking in to sleep with Mummy. Dr Grantham's gaze had moved past Libby's shoulder and she knew he was taking in the disarray of the cramped space. She turned as she set Rosie down on her feet, making big eyes at her when the pout threatened, and pointing sharply towards the tiny table and chairs squished next to the kitchen counter. Rosie huffed but moved away, allowing Libby to turn back to Dr Grantham.

"Thanks for lugging her up," she said as she started shutting the door. "See you tomorrow. I'll be–"

The door was inches from closing when his foot shot out and blocked it. Libby looked down at his large shoe, then up to his frowning face, in confusion.

"I'll pick you guys up tomorrow," he told her, and her mouth fell open in shock.

"Uh... no really, you don't–"

"You two are not getting the bloody bus at God knows what time in the morning after hardly any sleep."

She growled. Libby actually growled in frustration. She was so shocked by the sound that her hand went up to cover her mouth and her wide eyes flew to his. The bastard was smiling (but who wouldn't when confronted by an adult human female that growled). Maybe she and Rosie weren't so different after all.

"See you tomorrow," he said through his smile. "Phone?" He held out his hand and Libby automatically handed her unlocked iPhone over. After tapping away on the screen for a few seconds he handed it back.

"Right, my number's in there. I'll see you both in the morning," he said. She started to reply, but he moved forward, crowding Libby back, away from the door, and pushing his head round, shocking her out of what she was about to say. "Bye, Pirate Rosie," he called, giving the little girl a wave and another smile; then he quickly withdrew, and turned on his heel for the stairs.

Gah! He was so bloody bossy.

Libby shut the door and flicked the latch closed, then banged her head against the solid wood once. She hadn't missed the way his eyes had flashed around her living space a moment ago, or the tightness in his jaw once he'd taken in the chaos. She straightened her shoulders and lifted her head: maybe her car *was* bollocks and her flat *was* tiny, but, against the odds, they were hers. She'd done what she had to do to hold onto what little she had. Pride was not something you could afford when you were desperate.

Chapter 7

Frightfully thorough

"Okay, Little Louse," Libby said as she squatted down in front of Rosie. "This will only be a few minutes. All you have to do is be quiet as a mouse and stay behind me, then you can have a–"

"Kinder Egg!" Rosie shouted, jumping up and down on the spot. Libby sighed and gently put two fingers over Rosie's lips.

"Quiet, remember, honey? Just like a little mouse who's lost his voice."

"Okay, Mummy," Rosie said in a stage whisper that for some reason managed to be louder than her normal volume. "I'll be as quiet as a slug."

"Um... great. Let's–"

"A slug whose been stepped on and all his insides have shot out... so he's *dead*. As quiet as that."

"Right... well, that *is* quiet. Let's go." Libby straightened and grabbed Rosie's hand to lead her into the radiology department. They stopped outside Dr Morrison's office. Libby positioned Rosie out of sight next to the doorframe, then widened her eyes at her and put her finger to her lips before knocking.

"Hello?" she heard a male voice from inside the office and felt relieved that Dr Phillips was in there too – at least he bothered to acknowledge her existence. "Come in." She pushed open the door, giving Rosie one last warning look. Rosie nodded enthusiastically and made a zipping motion with her lips.

"Uh... hi, Dr Phillips, Dr Morrison," Libby said, flashing them a nervous smile that was only returned by Dr Phillips. Dr Morrison hadn't even bothered to turn around in her chair to make eye contact. "I'm not here to request a scan, just to get some clarification on a report if possible." Still no response, and no attempt at a greeting. "Sorry," Libby added, shifting uncomfortably on her feet and chewing the side of her lip.

"I'm not on call," Dr Morrison said sharply to her computer terminal as she carried on flicking through the images.

"But... I thought."

"Sorry, young lady; Camilla finishes her on-call at five today and then hands over to Dr Ford," Dr Phillips explained. "She's only here because she's a workaholic." Dr Morrison flashed Dr Phillips a brief, annoyed look, then focused back on her screen, still managing to avoid eye contact with Libby.

To Libby's horror she felt her eyes fill with stupid tears. Her day had been an uphill battle from start to finish and now, just as she thought the end was in sight, there was yet another stumbling block. For the third day in a row Dr Grantham had been waiting outside her flat at seven to drive them to the hospital, despite Libby's protests. She wouldn't have the money to get Brian towed until after the weekend – and that was only if the club had some big players in and her tips were good. Sitting in his car, smelling his freshly applied aftershave and seeing the way he interacted with Rosie was slowly killing her – Rosie was now rushing out of the block of flats straight to his car every morning, demanding he pick her up and then squeezing his cheeks for as long as she had access to them, none of which Dr Grantham seemed to mind.

So Libby was actually pleased to be moving on in the rotation to a different department; less time with Dr Grantham could only be a good idea given her growing obsession with him. But unfortunately, whilst the urology team she was put with was great, she was still now paired with Toby – an unashamed, complete and total wanker.

Libby hadn't really had time to socialize at medical school and had decided to spend the five years either working or studying. What she didn't bank on was the force of nature that was Kira. Libby and Kira had been best friends since they were babies, as were their mothers before them. They decided to do medicine together, and when Libby had her little "hiccup" at seventeen, Kira hadn't wanted to start without her. She'd shrugged off Libby's protests, arguing that she needed to do the science conversion course anyway, and then delayed another year to backpack all over the world. Kira worked in Africa and India, doing everything from building wells to teaching English. She meditated in Nepalese monasteries and took the opportunity to do every other crazy Kira-esque thing she could think of, before starting at St George's with Libby. Libby had Rosie after her A-levels, then worked to save up before starting the course. That money, together with the grants and bursaries she'd fought for helped to cover her fees, but she'd have to pay most of it back eventually, and it certainly didn't cover living expenses.

Nobody at their medical school knew how Libby made her money except Kira. As Kira was incurably social she insisted that Libby's single-parent status was not going to mean all work and no play. She decided that Libby's social life would be her responsibility. She made her sit with everyone at lunch most days, and even, albeit rarely, managed to drag her out to the student bar a few times a year. (Kira, being pushy in the extreme, had somehow managed to enlist Libby's parents to extra babysitting duties in order that Libby could "have a life". As Libby's mum and dad were already worried that their bright and previously carefree daughter would never "have a life" again after getting pregnant at seventeen, they were the perfect targets for Kira's emotional blackmail. She even recruited her own mum as the babysitting contingency plan for if Libby's parents were busy.)

So, through Kira, Libby was involved in her year to some extent. A single teenage mother is a rarity at medical school and she was a source of fascination to the other students. Of course guys made passes at her – men had been interested in Libby to an unhealthy degree for many years by that point – but once her daughter's existence became widely known, and she had rebuffed any man brave enough to approach her, these approaches became much rarer, which frankly was a relief. The only really persistent bloke was Toby. He was another mature student, having done a degree in biomedical sciences before starting medical school, and very popular with the other girls in their year, despite his obnoxious personality. Libby could not stand him; he was always staring at her, sitting too close to her in lectures, and giving her significant looks whenever he mentioned: "The One" – a woman he would eventually settle down with after she had "tamed the wild beast" (his words).

Libby couldn't really understand his interest; it wasn't as if he didn't have his pick of the other, less complicated, students. One night a few months ago he had tried to kiss her, telling her magnanimously that he was "ready to be tied down now" and had "sown his wild oats". When Libby politely declined, things got ugly. He told her she was lucky he'd given her a chance, that nobody was going to want a "used-up slag who got herself up the duff as a teenager". Libby had shrugged and taken that on the chin. It wasn't the first time she'd been called a slut after turning a man down (always an ironic turn of events), and in her line of work she was used to people judging her.

The only problem was that the abuse didn't just stop with insults. Toby then made it his mission to show Libby up whenever he could. She was in the same dissection group as him and he deliberately sabotaged her in front of the tutors at every opportunity. A prime example being when he *threw* the brain at her across the table when the tutor's back was turned. Of course, not being prepared for an actual human brain to come flying towards her, and not even wearing gloves, she had dropped it. She was too shocked to defend herself when Toby had rolled his eyes telling her to "be careful" when the appalled tutor turned back around.

And the fact they were now working with live patients was not, apparently, going to deter him from his mission to make her life a misery. The very first morning on the urology ward Toby told her that the registrar had asked that she examine the prostate of one of the patients. Libby had no reason to be suspicious. After all, they were on a ward where prostates and external genitalia were their bread and butter. She went and gave the patient a rectal examination. He had looked slightly baffled when she asked for his consent prior to the procedure, but she forged ahead anyway.

"You're frightfully thorough at this hospital aren't you?" the patient had commented after she'd finished.

"No, honestly," she reassured him. "It's absolutely standard procedure."

When the ward round started and they skipped over the patient she had seen earlier, she tried to stop the consultant surgeon, who happened to be Dr Grantham's friend, Mr Pavlos Martakis.

"That's not one of mine," he'd told her. "He's a max fax case – wrong end I'm afraid."

Libby had shot Toby a furious look but he just smirked, saying: "Oh well, you must have misheard the bed number."

Then today the patient list went missing after the ward round. It had all her jobs written on it and she knew Toby had taken it. She'd had to go back through all the notes to find out what needed to be done, and had been late to pick Rosie up.

After getting Rosie from the nursery and hurrying back to the ward she had found Toby sauntering down the corridor, having finished up for the day, and swallowed her pride to ask him if he would discuss the results of the scan for her. He owed her that, seeing as she wouldn't be late if it hadn't been for him stealing her list, and he had been the one to insist they sort out the report for the registrar anyway, proclaiming it to be "a valuable learning opportunity – don't you think Libby?" All she could do was nod, even though she knew from experience that it was totally inappropriate for a medical student to attempt something like that. But when she practically begged him to go down to the x-ray department instead of her he'd just sneered down at her and Rosie.

"I've done *my* fair share of the work today thanks," he said. "If you can't manage to get everything done at this stage then maybe..."

"It's fine," she'd snapped, pulling Rosie away before the little girl could kick him in the shin (it wouldn't be the first time). "I'll sort it."

However, it would seem she was a long way from "sorting it", and the entire day of frustration crashed over her as she swiped furiously at her cheeks – which was why she missed the flash of pink streak pass her into the office.

"Why did you make my mummy cry?" asked Rosie. Her hands were planted firmly on her hips and her head tilted to the side – both danger signs, warning Libby that she'd better remove Rosie from the situation pronto.

"I..." Dr Morrison turned around in her chair and jumped when she saw the angry little girl standing right next to her. Her eyes went from Rosie to Libby and she frowned in confusion.

"Are you okay, dear?" Dr Phillips asked Libby, his wrinkled face frowning as he got up to shuffle over to her and put his arm around her shoulders.

"I'm sorry," Libby said in a broken voice as the tears continued to flow. "I don't know what's the matter with me; I didn't mean to disturb you." She gave him a watery smile. "Come on, Little Louse," she said to Rosie, trying to take the little girl's hand; but she wriggled out of her grip.

"I didn't mean to make your mummy cry," Dr Morrison said to Rosie, staring at her in fascination.

"Well, you did," Rosie told her.

"Yes... I did," Dr Morrison agreed, much to Libby's shock. "And I'm very sorry." She flashed Libby a very brief look as she said the word sorry; regret and confusion were all Libby could see in her expression, not the anger she might have expected. "Sometimes... I'm not very good with... people."

"Why not?" Rosie asked.

"Well, I... um," Dr Morrison's voice dropped to a whisper. "I guess they... I guess they sort of scare me."

Rosie's hands dropped from her hips, much to Libby's relief, as this meant they were out of the Danger Zone, Rosie-temper-wise. "But my mummy's not scawy."

"Rosie," Libby said, her voice stronger now that she had some control over her tears, "what happened to the little mouse that lost his voice? Come on, we've got to go."

"I was *not* a mouse – I was a squashed dead *slug*. But I decided to come back to life."

"Right well come on, slug. Let's–"

"I'm going to stay with the grumpy lady, Mummy. You go and finish your work. I'm tired of being a squashed dead slug."

Libby made a grab for Rosie's hand again but she darted further into the office to stand on the other side of Dr Morrison.

"Rosie," Libby whisper-shouted, now beyond mortified that she had not only cried in front of two of the hospital's radiologists but was also demonstrating how little control she had over her own daughter. "Come here, *now*."

"She... um..." Dr Morrison flashed Libby a very brief glance before looking back at her computer screen, which seemed to be her default. "She can stay here if you... I mean, if you have things to do before you leave. I don't mind."

"But I thought you finished at five? It's past six, don't you want to–"

"You go and sort what needs sorting, young lady," Dr Phillips said, patting her on the back. "Millie'll keep an eye on her. We'll take a look at that report, you get your stuff together and finish up what needs to be done." He was smiling broadly as he watched Rosie and Dr Morrison together – for some reason bizarrely happy at this turn of events. Libby pushed her hair behind her ears and puffed out a frustrated breath. If she was honest the prospect of not having to cart Rosie around with her to grab her stuff and finish up on the ward was very welcome.

Jamie ran down the last of the stairs into the radiology department to the office he was after and knocked loudly on the door. When there was no answer he breathed a sigh of relief and shoved the envelope under the office door. Whatever communication Pav needed to have with Nuclear

Winter (the name, one of Pav's creations, had been adopted by most of the hospital for Dr Morrison, seeing as she was ice cold and worked with radiation), Jamie really wished he wouldn't ask him to run things down to her office. Today it was: "You've got to help me out, mate. She seriously gives me the creeps but I need to get her on board with presenting her project at the Grand Round."

He was about to turn and leave when he heard hushed voices from inside the office. He frowned and put his ear to the door – the louder of the two voices was almost certainly a child's. Nosey bastard that he was, he knocked again and the voices fell silent, so he turned the handle and pushed. Nuclear Winter was kneeling on the floor, with Rosie sitting cross-legged in front of her. Rosie's head was covered in an intricate series of French plaits and Dr Morrison was securing the back of them with a hair band.

"Jamie!" Rosie shouted, jumping up from the floor and barrelling into his legs to give them a bone-crushing hug. "Have you come to take us home now?"

Jamie stared down at Rosie's happy upturned face, then over to Dr Morrison, who was awkwardly getting to her feet. He had never seen the woman in anything less than perfect order; it was weird to see her skirt wrinkled and her face flushed.

"Why didn't you answer the door?" he asked Dr Morrison, who was now back to her annoying habit of zero eye contact.

"Millie doesn't like people," Rosie told him. Dr Morrison's horrified eyes flicked to his and then away, and her face flushed even redder.

"I'm not on call, Dr Grantham," she told him in her little robotic, ice-cold voice. "I finish at five today."

"That doesn't mean you can't open the door."

"She didn't know it was you looking for me, silly," Rosie

chipped in. "I told her to open it. I told her it might be someone she *wants* to see, but she said there was nobody she *ever* wanted to see." Her voice dropped to a whisper. "She's a bit weird."

"Okay," Jamie said slowly. Dr Morrison's movements were sharp as she collected her things into her handbag. "Well, shall I just take Rosie and find Libby so that–"

"I ..." Dr Morrison took a deep breath and turned towards him, but spoke to his shirt collar. "I was entrusted with the child. I can't let you take her." She was gripping her handbag so tightly that her knuckles had turned white and her other hand was balled into a fist at her side.

"Hey," an out-of-breath Libby said as she came running round the corner, stopping dead when she noticed Jamie holding Rosie's hand. "Oh, uh ..."

"I was just dropping something off for Pavlos and I found this." He lifted Rosie up and she immediately started squeezing his cheeks. Meanwhile Dr Morrison slipped past him, muttered a goodbye to Rosie, and practically ran out of the department. "So weird," Jamie muttered under his breath as he watched her leave.

"Dr Morrison," Libby shouted, running a little way after her, "thank you ..." She trailed off, realizing Dr Morrison had disappeared; that woman could move surprisingly fast given the height of her heels. Libby turned back to where Jamie and Rosie were standing, pushed her hair out of her face, and put her hands on her hips.

"Rosalie Penny, I've told you before: *stop* squeezing Dr Grantham's cheeks."

Rosie huffed and scrambled down Jamie until she was on her feet again.

"Look, Libby, I've been driving you to work every morning for a week now – I think you can start calling me Jamie," Jamie said with an edge of impatience. He'd actually grappled with the idea of letting her use his first name – the whole "Dr Grantham" thing was a good and sorely needed reminder to keep his distance. And it appealed to his sense of order and propriety. But after he cracked and told them both to call him Jamie a few days ago, he was growing more and more frustrated that Libby had yet to actually say his first name.

"Right," Libby replied, giving him a cautious smile as she took Rosie's hand. "Okay, well; thanks for the lift this morning. We better get going. And... um, Brian will be fixed after the weekend; so don't worry about picking us up on Monday.

Jamie raised his eyebrows. "Oh? How have you... I mean, I thought you didn't have the..." He glanced at Rosie, then back at Libby. He'd actually decided to get Brian towed himself this weekend and fixed at his local garage. The plan was to be a little creative with Libby about the price of the repairs and tell her there was no time limit on paying him back. After he'd formed this plan he was strangely looking forward to his knight-in-shining-armour routine. He was a little sad that it had been scuppered.

"Mummy's working this weekend," Rosie chipped in. "She gets *lots* of money when she works. I'm going to stay with Gwanny and Bumpa."

"Oh, right." Jamie smiled at Rosie, suppressing his frown of confusion. "That's great." He looked up at Libby and opened his mouth to ask what she did for work, but she had spun around and was walking away. Jamie watched them leave, then shook his head to clear it. What Libby did and where she went were none of his business. How they were getting home was none of his business. Plus, taking an unhealthy interest in a student was inappropriate and beneath him.

But when he drove his car out of the multistory and saw the two dejected figures sitting at the bus stop, what was or wasn't his business went out the window.

Chapter 8

"Pinky pwomise?"

"Get in," he shouted out of his window.

"We're fine thanks," Libby shouted back, managing a feeble smile and giving him a pathetic thumbs up. Rosie gave her mother a disgusted look and slid off the seat to run over to Jamie's car through the rain. Libby looked down at her feet for a moment; her shoulders slumped before she followed her daughter across the pavement and into the back seat at a much slower pace. Jamie glanced behind him and took in the two beautiful drowned rats dripping on his upholstery. For once he didn't care about the state of the Italian leather. Their dark hair was plastered to their heads and they were both shivering. "You really didn't have to–"

"Your flat is on my way home," he lied smoothly, cranking the heating up as high as it would go.

"Well... thanks. But if you drop us at the next bus stop along I can get a direct one to–"

"Why was Rosie in Dr Morrison's office?" he cut in, glancing back at her in the rearview mirror.

"Oh, I had some stuff to finish and the nursery closes at six so I–"

"Well, it's not exactly ideal," Jamie pointed out. He didn't like to think of Rosie being palmed off on anyone who was available, and Dr Morrison had the ability to scare grown men; he dreaded to think what kind of company she would be for a child. "I mean, wasn't there any other arrangement you could make?"

His question was met with stony silence. He looked in the rearview mirror and could see Libby's profile as she looked out of the window; her jaw was clenched and her mouth was set in a grim line.

"Who's Dr Morrison?" Rosie asked.

"The lady you were with when I found you," Jamie explained.

"Oh! *Millie*. But she's not a grumpy crabby-pants," Rosie explained. "She just scares easy. And she didn't *mean* to make Mummy cry."

"She *what*?" Jamie said, his hands tightening on the steering wheel. He'd never particularly liked Dr Morrison but for some reason when he thought of her making Libby, who had been stoic in the face of some pretty harsh criticism (most of it, unfortunately, from him), cry he felt murderous.

"Hey!" Libby snapped as the car swept past the next bus stop at speed. "What are you doing? You've gone past the–"

"You two are not getting on any bus in that state," Jamie told her as he pulled out onto the main road. Libby groaned.

"Dr Gr–" Jamie gave her a sharp look and she swallowed. "I mean, Jamie. You can't do that again. The bus from that stop is a direct route to our street. I can't let you–"

"You're not *letting* me do anything. I refuse to drop you off to get on a bus, soaking wet."

"But I–"

"Now, what I want to know is exactly what that bi… " Jamie broke off and glanced in his mirror at Rosie sitting in the booster seat he had bought for her. (He'd told Libby he'd borrowed it from his sister. She didn't have to know that he ran out to buy one after that first day when he'd seen Libby struggle up the flight of stairs with hers). "… what *Millie* said to you."

"It was nothing," Libby said in a tight voice. "Long day, that's all. Mummy was just being a wally, wasn't she, Little Louse? Nothing to worry about."

"Well, you *are* a wally, Mummy," Rosie agreed happily.

"Any more run-ins with her, you phone me," Jamie said. Nuclear Winter a.k.a. Camilla Morrison was not going to intimidate Libby. She could find somebody else to sharpen her claws on.

"It's fine," Libby told him in a tight little voice. "I can fight my own battles, thank you." An extremely uncomfortable silence followed for the next ten minutes, broken only by Rosie's out-of-tune singing to bloody Justin Bieber, who was playing on the radio purely to torment Jamie.

"Hey!" Rosie shouted as they were finally nearing their address. "Stop at the chippy!" Rosie's voice was so commanding and so full of urgency that Jamie automatically slowed and then pulled into a free space in front of the Golden Fish Bar.

"Rosie, no," Libby said. "We'll get something at home before we leave."

"But it's Friday," Rosie whined. "I get to have fish and chips on Friday and no stupid broccoli. It's the law."

"Okay then, we can get something on the way to Granny and Bumpa's, broccoli-free, I promise."

"I'm calling the police," Rosie said, a telling little wobble to her voice that Jamie was a complete sucker for.

"I don't mind–" he started, but Rosie had already opened the passenger door. Libby sighed.

"This is why I always use child locks," she told him as Rosie scrambled over his lap, undid his seatbelt and started tugging his arm.

"Rosie! Stop," Libby snapped, following her out. Mother and daughter went into stare-down, during which Rosie crossed her little arms across her chest and stamped her foot.

"Honestly, it's fine. I'm not in any rush," Jamie told them both, happy to have the strained silence at an end and smiling at the two soaking, furious, stubborn females. For some reason appropriateness and what was or wasn't his business was long forgotten. He held his hand out to Rosie and she gave her mother a smug smile before skipping over to him.

Libby pushed the rest of her chips away with a sigh of regret. She was lucky her metabolism allowed her to eat relatively well and still earn the same money, but even she couldn't gorge on heavy takeaway food on a night she was working – nothing hid that kind of bloating, and the last thing she needed was to get a cramp.

"He deserved it," Rosie muttered darkly around a mouthful of battered cod.

Libby shuddered. "Nobody deserves to have woodlice put in their pencil case Rosie."

The three of them were sitting around the coffee table, Libby and Jamie squeezed onto Libby's ancient sofa and Rosie sitting facing them on a cushion on the floor. After Jamie had insisted on buying them all fish and chips Rosie had practically dragged him upstairs to their flat to eat with them. It was becoming clear to Libby that Jamie was a sucker for a four-year-old girl with a serious amount of attitude.

"You are *way* too big," Rosie had told him accusingly once he'd squeezed onto the sofa.

"Sorry," Dr Grantham... *Jamie*, said through a chuckle. "I'll work on that, okay?"

Rosie was right really: Jamie did make their tiny flat seem even smaller; and his bulky frame on their small sofa looked ridiculous. Libby cursed the fact there was still low-level chaos reigning in her living area. The contrast between that and Jamie's appearance, with his tailored suit and perfect... everything, was stark. He looked completely out of place in their tiny home.

"Do you like minibeasts?" Rosie asked him; then before waiting for a response she shot to her feet and ran out of the room. Jamie looked at Libby and she just sighed, shaking her head. A moment later Rosie dashed back in and dumped her plastic toy medical case on the middle of the table. That would have been fine if the case only contained the fake stethoscope and other toys it was meant to, but through the clear plastic lid you could clearly see soil, leaves and about ten of Rosie's "friends".

"See," Rosie said, beaming up at Jamie. "Aren't they cute?"

He peered in through the lid, blinked, then surreptitiously moved his food away from the case. "Uh..."

"You can take one of them home if you like," Rosie offered.

Libby glanced over to see his eyes dance as he pressed his lips together. "I've never had a pet woodlouse," he told her, his voice shaking with suppressed amusement. "And although they are... cute... I better not – it might upset my dog."

Rosie's mouth fell open and her eyes went wide with wonder.

"You have a doggie?" she asked, the longing painful to hear in her voice. She carefully lifted her woodlice container up off the table and hugged it to her chest. "Is it a girl or a boy doggie?"

"She's a bi– I mean, she's a girl. She's called Beauty. Look, I'll show you." Jamie pulled his phone from his back pocket, tapped the screen, and then handed it to Rosie.

"She's bootiful," Rosie said, holding the phone right next to her face, her eyes roving the screen reverently.

Jamie laughed. "I'm not sure many people would agree with you there, sweetheart. She's a bit of an acquired taste." Libby leaned over the table and peered round to look at the phone. A massive slobbering obese black and white dog was looking out of the screen. One ear stood up, the other was floppy, and she had a ball in her mouth, with a good amount of drool hanging from one side. "I got her from a rescue centre. I was supposed to just be helping my nephew pick out a kitten, but I couldn't leave her there once I saw her."

"She *is* bootiful," Rosie told him fiercely, still gripping the phone. "Can I meet her?"

"I..." Jamie's eyes slid to Libby and he flashed her a brief apologetic smile. "Of course you can."

Rosie's face lit up and before Libby could stop her she had administered a soggy kiss to Jamie's screen. Then she handed it back to him, saliva and all, before dashing back to her room with her woodlice. Libby could hear Rosie telling them about the "bootiful doggie" through the thin wall.

"Sorry," she said, tearing her eyes away from Jamie's mouth to look at his eyes. The sofa was so small that their arms and legs were touching. He felt warm and solid next to her and for some reason her hand was twitching to touch him, so much so that she had to shove them both underneath her thighs. "She loves animals, always has. We can't have pets here so she hoards the woodlice instead. She's named them all." Libby bit her lip and looked at the coffee table. "You don't have to show her your dog. I'm sure she'll forget about it in a few days," she lied; there was no way Rosie would ever forget about that dog.

"I wouldn't have said it if I didn't mean it," he told her. She lifted her eyes to his and smiled but it fell slowly as she saw how close he was. He'd turned towards her in the small space and was watching the smile fade from her mouth with what looked like intense concentration. His gaze then moved to lock with hers and his large hand came up to the side of her face, where it slid across her cheek and pushed a chunk of her dark hair behind her ear. Some sort of invisible force pulled her forward until her mouth was millimetres away from his and she could feel his breathing against her face.

"I'm ready to go meet bootiful doggie now!" Rosie's shout made them both start in surprise, yanking them out of their trance. Jamie's hand dropped back to his lap and he jerked away from Libby, muttering "Shit" under his breath.

"And your ship!" Rosie added, proving that her bat-like hearing was still very much intact. Her arms, one clutching the woodlice case and the other her Dora the Explorer backpack, shot straight up in the air. "We can go sailing on your ship with your doggie!"

"Rosie," Libby said, walking over to her and gently pulling both the case and the backpack from her grip, "we're going to Granny and Bumpa's tonight, remember?" Rosie's lip wobbled and her face grew red, then two fat tears fell down her cheeks. Libby sighed and turned to dump the bags behind her, but before she could bend to hug her dejected daughter Jamie was squatting down in front of Rosie, swiping away her tears.

"I promise you can meet Beauty and sail on my boat soon," he told her solemnly.

"You pwomise?" she asked, her voice wobbling and her Rs disappearing in her distress.

"Yes."

"Pinky pwomise?"

"I..." Jamie trailed off as Rosie grabbed his large hand in her small ones, pulled his little finger out and linked it with hers, then looked up at him expectantly.

Jamie smiled. "Pinky promise," he said, and she threw her arms around his neck, burying her face into him. After a moment she pulled back, holding onto his little finger with both hands.

"If you break a pinky pwomise you gets killed... by an alien," she told him solemnly, and Jamie nodded, rearranging his features into a grave expression rather than the amused one he had to suppress.

Libby's chest felt tight. Other than her Bumpa, men were few and far between in Rosie's life. Maybe that was why she attached herself to Jamie with such fervour. It was definitely why she named everything the most boring male grown-up names she could think of. Libby could taste the familiar guilt in her mouth. Rosie should have a father. And a mother who didn't put her in full-time childcare. She should have a bloody dog, not have to resort to keeping woodlice. Libby shook her head and fought the constriction in her throat.

No fate but what you make.

She repeated the *Terminator* quote in her head. *The future is what I make it.* She moved forward to a Rosie-wrapped-Jamie and laid her hand on his shoulder.

"Thanks," she mouthed when he looked up at her.

"We've got to get going now, Rosie," she told her daughter, stroking her soft curls.

"K," Rosie muttered, her face still buried in Jamie's chest. Libby waited a few more seconds before gently prizing Rosie's surprisingly strong arms from Jamie's neck. "Come on, Little Louse," she said, pulling her out of his arms and into her own, "we'd better get a wriggle on."

"It's late," Jamie told her, frowning at both of them as Libby stood with Rosie in her arms. "Why don't you go in the morning?"

"I... um... I work at night."

Jamie's eyebrows shot up and he glanced at his watch. "But it's nearly seven. By the time you get to..."

"My folks live in Elephant and Castle but I work at Covent Garden."

"Covent Garden? It'll be insanely late after you've made it to your parents and then on there."

"Yes, well. Rosie can sleep on the way so–"

"When are *you* going to sleep?"

Libby huffed and narrowed her eyes at him. "I'm fine. It doesn't–"

"You've been up since six. You shouldn't be working at this hour, it's–"

"Go to your room, Rosie," Libby said, cutting Jamie off. "Get Alan packed, okay?" Rosie wriggled down her mother and started toward her room, but before she made it there she stopped and turned to face Jamie. One hand went to her hip, which she cocked to the side and the other pointed in his direction.

"Doggie. Boat," she said, punctuating each word with another point of her finger. Jamie pressed his lips together again and nodded solemnly.

"Yes," he told her. She narrowed her eyes at him for a moment before nodding, spinning on her heel and flouncing through the bedroom door. Rosie gave good flounce. Jamie watched her go with an amused expression, but sobered when he turned to Libby.

"Listen, I appreciate all you've done for us. I really, *really* appreciate it. But I've been looking after Rosie and myself for a long time. I know what I'm doing, I–"

"Is that why you fell asleep in teaching, even in theatre?"

"Listen, I was working night shifts before we started the rotation, and then Rosie was sick. I didn't get more than a few hours sleep in the week before our induction. She never gets sick... it... it was an exception."

"You'll make yourself ill like this. Where do you work anyway? Why do you have to go to Central London to do it?"

"I work in a bar. I mix cocktails; it's a skill. Pays really well but has to be at night. And in the daytime I teach dance and gymnastics to some... women. Um... a sort of class I've set up." The practised lies spilt out with ease. Apart from Kira, nobody in her life knew how she earned her money.

"You teach dance?"

"And gymnastics. I was a national champion when I was a teenager." That much at least was a true, if now irrelevant, fact.

"And at night you *mix cocktails*?" One of his eyebrows crept up his forehead. Libby got the impression he wasn't buying that particular lie and she was beginning to hate that damn eyebrow which went perfectly with his superior bloody attitude.

With a sudden movement he threw something in her direction. Libby was never very good at catching. She fumbled the object and it fell to the floor. When she looked down she saw it was his wallet. "What...?" she started, as she bent down to retrieve the square of brown leather.

"You're lying," he told her. "Why are you lying?"

Libby gritted her teeth and shoved his wallet at him. "You can leave now."

He crossed his arms over his broad chest and planted his feet wide; weirdly, his stubborn pose reminded her of Rosie at her most difficult.

"I'm driving you to your parents." She stared at his pose and the tension in his jaw and sighed, recognizing that there was no point arguing with a two hundred pound, over six-foot tall man with a stubborn streak a mile wide.

"Arrogant Nerf Herder," she muttered as she turned and moved to the bedroom, unaware that it was more flounce than walk, and nearly identical to her daughter's exit moments ago.

Nerf Herder?

Jamie uncrossed his arms and watched the beautiful woman follow the beautiful child out of the room. Then he smiled.

Chapter 9

World famous

Jamie smiled down at his pint glass. The loud noise of the pub and the banter around him faded into the background as he pictured Rosie's earnest little face when she ran back to him before going into her grandparents' tiny, terraced house in Elephant and Castle. She'd told him to hold his hand out, and had deposited a woodlouse into his open palm, grinning at him like she had just given him a rare diamond.

"That's Arthur," she'd told him. "He wants to meet Beauty. I'll come and get him when I come over, okay?" Jamie had swallowed and managed a weak smile (he hated creepy crawlies). Rosie patted him on the cheek and flounced off after her mother. He'd had to endure Arthur crawling around inside his closed fist until he could make it back to the car and deposit him in an empty water bottle. The memory still made him shudder.

"Drink! Drink! Drink!" the loud chanting around him broke through his mental fugue and he looked up from his pint. The whole table was pointing at him. He shrugged and downed his beer, not bothering to ask why – he knew that would be pointless.

"What's wrong with you?" Pav shouted in his ear. The stupid bastard lost all ability to regulate volume after a couple of drinks. "You're always king of Thumb Master – weaselling your way out of drinking any way you can."

"I'm fine," Jamie muttered.

"And why are you smiling all the time? It's weird and it's starting to freak me out."

"Fuck off, mate. I smile."

Pav scoffed. "Er... no – no, you really don't. You were grimacing in our graduation photos and don't even get me started on your thirtieth birthday."

"I don't like surprises."

"You looked like a constipated goat the whole night. I nearly punched you in the face."

"You did punch me in the face."

"Oh, did I?"

"Yes, you said it was to cheer me up."

"Ah..."

"I had a black eye for my consultant interview."

"Yes, well... Look, stop trying to put me off! Tell me what's got you so goddamn happy all of a sudden."

"I repeat: Fuck. Off."

"What are you two ladies banging on about?" Dan shouted across the table at them.

"Chopper's smiling like a weirdo and he won't tell me why."

"Smiling? You're normally a miserable fucker, Chopper – what's tickled your giblets?"

Jamie sighed. Weren't they all too old for these bloody stag weekends? Endless rounds of drinking games, reverting back to their student days. He loved his friends but it seemed like there was one of these endurance tests every five minutes at the moment. This was the fifth stag he'd been on that year. Practically all his spare time was swallowed up with other people's nuptials, be it stags, stens, rehearsal dinners, and of course the actual weddings themselves. It was exhausting. And why did Dan have to come along to all these things? Jamie's brother hadn't even gone to medical school with them all, but somehow they'd adopted him as "the Fun Grantham Brother". Annoying. And this time he was actually the best man.

"Maybe he's found out where we're off to later," Dan said. "That would cheer even the most grumpy article up."

"Please not another casino," Jamie groaned. Those places blocked all natural light, had no clocks and fed you endless drinks so long as you kept gambling. Last time he'd been dragged to one he hadn't emerged until the next morning, with someone else's vomit on his sleeve, a heavy head and a considerably lighter wallet.

"Uh-uh," Dan said, his face lighting with anticipation. "Much better than that, brother dearest. *Much* better. Pavlos knows all about it, don't you mate?"

When Jamie turned to Pav he was frowning down into his drink, an uncharacteristically pensive expression on his face.

Libby looked up at Claire, who tutted and swatted her with the brush. "You're smiling like a badger watching a car crash. Go back to your normal exhausted, slack-jawed face – it's easier to do your make-up."

"Sorry, hun," she said, trying to rearrange her expression.

"What's perked you up?" Claire asked, narrowing her eyes at Libby's lips, which were pressed firmly together to suppress another smile. "I thought this new fancy-pants medicine was getting you down."

"It's not that it's 'fancy-pants', it's just that I can't sit in the back of lecture theatres anymore if I'm tired. I've got to be *on it* all the time." Libby's shoulders slumped and her smile faded. She'd always known that this half of her training would be tough, but she'd come too bloody far to give up now.

Claire pushed some of Libby's thick hair back from her face and took in the shadows under her eyes with a small frown. "You're a determined little shit, aren't you?" Libby shrugged. "You know," Claire fiddled with the brush for a moment, shifting uncomfortably on her feet, "the girls and I, we've been talking about you and your little one, and if you need a loan or... well... we'd be happy to club together. Give you a break."

Libby's throat closed over and she felt her eyes fill with tears. Claire was the very definition of hard-nosed bitch. Libby was guessing that genuine expressions of concern and offers of help from her were few and far between.

"We're fine," she said as one of her tears spilt over, no doubt ruining the perfectly applied eyeliner. "Thank you."

Claire huffed and rolled her eyes and she wiped away the tear with a cotton-wool pad. "You're not fine," she muttered, applying concealer under Libby's eyes.

"You're a stubborn bugger, that's what you are," Tara put in as she adjusted her white bra in the mirror. "Get yourself a sponsor, for Christ's sake."

Libby smiled and suppressed a shudder. She knew exactly what Tara meant by "a sponsor", but there was no way that was an option. Men could watch her, they could take that from her; she accepted that that was a sacrifice she had to make. But that small part of her soul was all they were getting.

~

"This place is insane," Jamie said in Pav's ear after they had finally made it to the booth that had been reserved. Dan had organized this stag for their friend Jonty. Jonty was one of the few defectors over to the dark side. After finishing medical school and realizing quite how much the NHS was going to expect of him, he jacked it all in and went into the City, with Dan's encouragement. Now he was a management consultant at Dan's firm and earning an unspeakably high salary. The kind of industry he was in was work-hard-play-hard, so coming out to a place like this of an evening was in no way out of the ordinary (although Jamie knew for a fact that Dan's wife Amy had put an all-out ban on strip clubs after some unfortunate lap-dance photos leaked their way onto Facebook. Jamie was under strict instructions not to breathe a word to his sister-in-law).

Jamie's salary and private practice income was nothing to be sniffed at, but he had nearly choked on his beer when he heard the cover charge to get into the club Dan had booked. On top of that, as soon as they sat down three scantily clad, incredibly beautiful women delivered three bottles of Cristal to the table. They were so perfect that it was almost unreal: shimmering gold and silver backless dresses, flawless make-up, smooth, tanned skin, incredible long legs; it was like stepping into another universe.

"Bugger me," whispered Pav as he watched their retreating backs with his mouth hanging open.

Dan rubbed his hands together. "That's *nothing*," he told them all. "Just wait till the show. I swear your wank banks will be topped up for life after you see the main attraction. This place is fucking world famous. We come with clients all the time. Better than anything else in London. Isn't that right, Pavlos?"

"I've only been here once before," Pav said, for some reason shifting in his seat with discomfort and flicking Jamie a nervous look. "Dan made me come on a "recce" before the stag to make sure it was okay. I–"

"Oh come on!" Dan shouted. "You bloody loved it! Right, who wants more champagne?" As Dan started obnoxiously signalling the waitress, Pav leaned across to speak to Jamie.

"Jamie, mate," he started, then chewed his lip for a moment. "I just want to say that... I mean, I–"

"Come on, you boring bastard." Dan shoved a shot of tequila into his hand. "This is supposed to be Jonty's last night of freedom – no time for serious convos."

As Jonty and Pav choked on the spirits, Jamie's eyes moved over the lavishly decorated interior dotted with other booths and tables, all full to capacity, to the stage in the middle of the room. There were two huge guys in dark suits stationed next to it, wearing earpieces and intermittently making eye contact with the further twenty-or-so suit-clad men around the perimeter. It was like they were expecting some kind of riot.

Two raised walkways led from two sets of double doors and cut through the tables to the central stage. But the most obvious, glaring detail on the stage was of course the three poles. They could tart this place up as much as they liked, make it look like an up-market boutique hotel, charge an exorbitant admission fee, but as far as Jamie was concerned nothing could change the fact that it was still a strip club. The clients Dan brought here might be billionaires – but to Jamie they were still seedy little men in a seedy little titty bar. The whole set-up gave him a vague feeling of disgust.

A couple of tequila shots and a glass of champagne later he was leaning over to look at a picture of his five-year-old nephew, thinking to himself that he was nowhere near as cute as Rosie, and asking Dan if he liked woodlice – which earned him a confused stare. Just as he was about to explain, the lights went down and a hush fell over the audience. Pav chose that moment to try to get Jamie's attention again but was silenced by the rest of the table.

Jamie looked up to see spotlights focus on the two sets of double doors. After a moment "Uptown Funk" started blaring through the club and both sets of double doors burst open, revealing two women, one at each door. They were wearing white broad-rimmed fedora-style hats, white low cut, fitted suit jackets which ended high on their thighs, paired with toweringly high white stilettos. They strutted down the walkways in perfect unison. Halfway across they both reached up to their hats and snatched them off their heads with a flourish to reveal huge amounts of long, blonde, glossy hair, which cascaded over their shoulders and down their backs.

The hats were thrown into the cheering crowd and the blondes continued on to the poles at the centre of the stage. After a beat they swung up onto the two outer poles and spun round together, hair flying, low-cut jackets opening to reveal the white lace underwear beneath... it was almost beautiful. Although it was not Jamie's first rodeo in a strip club, he had never seen *anything* like this before. These women were so polished, so stunning; it was like they were on a Victoria's Secret catwalk. Their shimmering make-up made them look almost ethereal, not like strippers.

As the initial shock of their entrance faded, the whistles and whoops started rumbling through the crowd and the atmosphere in the room turned electric. An obviously drunk man sitting next to the stage leaned forward as if to touch one of the women with a glazed expression on his face. But a huge, dark-suited bouncer was there in a flash, giving the man a hard shove in the middle of his chest so that he went flying back into his chair, clearly winded. The women did one final spin on the poles, fell to the ground and their spotlights cut off, plunging the club into darkness and silence.

Jamie felt the atmosphere in the room change again; this time, instead of just the electricity crackling through the crowd there was an almost explosive anticipation. A third spotlight shifted to a set of double doors he hadn't noticed before at the back of the room. These doors led out onto a short raised platform. As the opening chords to David Guetta's "Titanium" sounded a single chair shot out into the light. After a moment another woman walked out to the chair and leapt up onto the seat. In contrast to the blondes this woman was all in black: black hat with the brim set low over her eyes, black jacket, and black stilettos.

One of her stiletto-clad feet came up to the back of the chair and she tipped it back so that it was balancing on just two of the wooden legs. She then lifted her other foot so that for a moment she was suspended above the chair but jumped off just as it was about to fall, landing behind it and catching it before it hit the ground. The crowd went wild as she spun the chair to face her and sat down. One hand went to the top of her hat and the other gripped the chair at the side. She flicked both her feet up one after the other and her stilettos went flying back through the double doors, then she flipped over in a sudden movement to stand facing the chair, before launching herself forward to spring over the back of it into a front flip which took her to the edge of the platform.

Jamie frowned, noticing that there was no raised walkway for her to get to the central stage, but then his mouth dropped open as she went up on her toes before soaring through the air in a graceful flip, springing off her hands on one of the benches to land on her feet on the table in front of her.

The men sitting around the table she'd landed on were gaping up at her with awestruck expressions. She smiled and took a couple of steps across the wooden surface, gracefully avoiding various drinks and other detritus before springing again, this time using the back of one of the men's chairs as leverage, and landing dead centre in the middle of the table right next to the booth Jamie and the rest of the stag party were sitting in.

She leapt from the table to the back of the bench that curved around their booth, and then flipped twice along the narrow surface until she landed in the middle of *their* table. Once there, she stopped and fell to a squat in front of Jonty, held two fingers against her perfect lips and kissed them before pressing them gently to his. Then she stood tall on the table, her hand flashed to her hat and a cascade of glorious dark hair fell from its confines. Her perfect features were highlighted with smoky make-up, and the jacket she wore revealed glimpses of a black-lace-adorned, truly stunning figure. She was the most strikingly, outrageously gorgeous thing Jamie'd ever seen in his life. Suddenly the cover charge started to make sense. The crowd cheered as she squatted again and planted the hat on Jonty's head.

Then she smiled.

One side of her mouth hitched up slightly further than the other, and Jamie felt a jolt of recognition. In that same moment he noticed a flash of panic cross her face as she looked at Pav sitting next to Jonty.

Then, as if sensing his presence at the table, her big blue eyes locked with Jamie's and went wide with shock. Before he could react she had leapt to her feet. Her arms went straight up in the air and she started falling backwards. On instinct he reached for her as she fell, shoving the other guys out of the way and spilling several drinks as he jumped up from his chair. But instead of crashing to the ground she sprang off the edge of the table with her hands, and landed on her feet at the bottom of a set of steps to the stage.

"What the fuck are you doing, you nutter?" Dan shouted, grabbing hold of Jamie's arm and trying to force him back to his seat. Jamie shook him off violently to watch Libby's back as she ascended the steps to the centre of the stage. The two white angels flanked her as she swung her leg round the pole and flew through the air, so fast she was almost a blur. Jamie stood fully upright, jolting the table so that several more drinks went flying. Pav had taken hold of his other arm, and both he and Dan were trying to drag him back to sitting. He could feel his face flushing with rage and there was a faint buzzing in his ears that blocked out the swearing of his friends around him.

Without thinking, and with his eyes fixed on the stage, he pushed Pav out of his way and stepped out of the booth. His nostrils flared as he saw her spin up to the top of the pole and hang upside-down, before ripping off both the other girls' white jackets by the collars and throwing them to the side amid cheers and whoops from the crowd. She then curled up to grip the pole at the top, and swung out to land on her feet between the now underwear-clad blondes. Jamie's fists bunched at his sides and he jerked forward towards the stage in a sudden movement that caught Libby's eye. She faltered for a moment in her routine. Both the blondes looked at her in shock and he saw her give a small shake of her head before she stepped forward to the front of the stage and lifted both her arms from her sides.

The blondes leaned forward in unison and grabbed an arm of her jacket each. After they ripped it off the crowd had a few moments to appreciate her perfect figure in the black lace underwear before a cascade of water fell from the ceiling, soaking all three of the women completely, followed by what appeared to be heavy rain, just on the stage where they were dancing. They all fell to their knees and slapped the ground in perfect synchrony, spraying the men directly around the stage and ratcheting up the cheering levels significantly.

In that moment Jamie lost his mind and pushed the man in front of him out of his way to get to the stage. Libby's shocked gaze met his furious one again and she froze. She was soaking wet, practically naked, every man in the room had his greedy eyes on her – he'd never seen anything more achingly vulnerable, and a surge of fierce possessiveness went through him. He reached for her and that was it. Two bouncers yanked him back so hard it felt like his arms would be pulled out of their sockets.

"Listen, fella," one of the bouncers shouted into his ear, "nobody touches the girls. You need to calm the fuck down." Jamie watched as all three women sprang to their feet. With superhuman strength he wrenched free of both the bouncers and made another lunge for the stage, but felt a fist collide with the side of his face, then another into his stomach, and everything went black.

Chapter 10

Mr High and Mighty Stick Up Your Arse

"How was I supposed to know he was your boss?" Barry muttered. "Crazy bastard was trying to get on stage."

Libby sighed and knelt down next to Jamie. He'd recovered consciousness but was still winded. "You didn't have to punch his lights out. Couldn't you have just held him back or something? What happened to non-violent restraint techniques?"

"Load of bloody bollocks," Barry muttered. "Non-violent, my arse. Anyone tries to touch you girls they're gonna be sorted out good and proper." Jamie groaned and his eyelids fluttered. "Aren't you supposed to be checking him over or something, mate?" Barry asked Pavlos Martakis, who had battled his way to the changing room after Libby had made Barry and Steve carry Jamie through and lie him on the sofa.

"What?" Dr Martakis said, flashing Jamie a brief glance before focusing back on all the activity around him. His apparent concern for his friend seemed to have evaporated as soon as he made it backstage. Libby was guessing that a room full of semi-naked, universally well-endowed women squeezing themselves into all manner of tiny outfits would do that to a man. "He seems fine to me. Told me to sod off so he can't be too bad. Don't worry; I know from experience that his head is pretty hard. I'm sure a cheeky tap to his temple won't do him much harm."

Libby rolled her eyes at Dr Martakis and he winked at her. "Fantastic job in there by the way. All that leaping about. I must say I thoroughly approve of your career choice. Stuff the NHS; you'd be doing far more good for humanity prancing about in your underwear. It's done me the power of good I can tell you."

"Pavlos," Jamie muttered, his eyes now blinking open as he swung up to a sitting position on the sofa. "Will you, for once in your life shut the fuck up." He rubbed the side of his face and winced when he encountered the bruising and swelling that was blooming across his cheekbone. Libby reached for him as he sat up, her hands fluttering uselessly around him, anticipating another blackout. Eventually she touched his forearm.

"Are..." she cleared her throat. "Are you okay?" She gave his arm a squeeze and he jerked it away, avoiding eye contact with her.

"I'm fine," he said. "Great cocktails you mixed there." Libby bit her lip and withdrew her hand to tuck her hair behind her ears. She was wearing her huge fleecy dressing-gown in the style of a Jedi Knight, which covered her from chin to feet, but somehow she still felt exposed.

"I have ice for the stupid bugger," Tara snapped as she strutted across the dressing room from the kitchen. She was still in her white underwear – never one to bother with a dressing gown, even when soaking wet. She stopped in front of them, threw her hip out and rested her hand on it as she chucked the ice pack onto Jamie's lap. Her eyes flashed to Dr Martakis. "What is this pervert doing in here? You after a free show?"

"I..." Dr Martakis looked Tara up and down, then smiled

slowly. "Will you marry me?" Libby saw Tara's lips twitch before she pressed them in a thin line.

"Got a bloke, mate, and he'd twist your dick into a pretzel before he let you anywhere near me. So hush your mouth."

"Wow," Dr Martakis said. "Sounds like quite the young man. Although, I must advise that from a urological perspective that would be ill advised. Tell me – are you always in that Big Spender get up? Ever switch things up? Naughty nurse maybe? Is there a suggestion box?"

"A *what* perspective?"

"He's a urologist," Jamie snapped, standing abruptly from the sofa, his face like thunder. "Pav, shut up. Jesus."

"Just complimenting the ladies on their craft and giving general encouragement," Pav told him, his eyes following a topless redhead as she walked past them in just a shiny g-string.

"I think they're doing just fine in their *craft* without your input." Jamie said *craft* with an unmistakable sneer in his voice, and his lip curled as he took in the rest of the room. "Where's Rosie?" It was the first time he'd looked at Libby since he'd regained consciousness; his expression was cold, clinical even.

"She's at Mum and Dad's," Libby told him, standing from the sofa to face him.

"Do *they* know what you're doing here? Or did you fob them off with the cocktail story as well?" he asked.

Libby pressed her lips together and looked away. She had been working last night till the early hours and then hadn't wanted to miss out on Saturday with Rosie, so over the last forty-eight hours she'd had very little sleep and the tight band of a tension headache was beginning to make itself known. She wasn't up to angry confrontations and men intent on making her feel like crap. *No fate*, she repeated in her head as she turned away from him. This was a means to an end and nobody was going to make her feel ashamed.

Jamie was fuming. He couldn't believe that Libby, *his* Libby... fuck, no, she wasn't *his* Libby. Clearly she didn't even trust him enough to be honest about what she did for a living.

A stripper?

This woman who wore no make-up, flat shoes, tied her hair up in a goddamn elastic band? *This* woman was making a living by tarting herself up and stripping off her clothes? He glanced again at her face, still hauntingly beautiful even caked with the make-up that had stood up surprisingly well to the drenching it had received. For a moment he felt like he was going to throw up.

"I can't even look at you," he muttered. "A stripper? What were you thinking?"

He watched as her skin paled beneath the thick camouflage and then flushed bright red. She squared her small shoulders and her eyes flashed.

"Maybe..." she paused for a moment. All the emotion drained from her face and her mouth hardened. "Maybe I was thinking that instead of having a baby at eighteen and dropping out to collect benefits, I would try and make something of myself. Maybe I thought: You know what? This," she pointed to her face, "and this," she swept an arm down her body, "and these," she grabbed both her breasts through the thick dressing gown material, "could actually *help* me instead of dragging me down. Could actually earn me enough money to take control of my life. Could allow me to carry on with my education *and* spend time with my daughter.

"It's not my fault that rich Hutt Spawn like you lot are dumb enough to part with your money just to watch women like me in my underwear. *You*," she poked him in the chest and moved into his personal space, "haven't been a scared, pregnant seventeen-year-old disappointment to your parents. *You* haven't been faced with the prospect of all your dreams going to shit because of one stupid decision you made when you were still a child yourself. So fuck you, Mr High and Mighty Stick Up Your Arse. Fuck you and the horse you rode in on."

"Well said, sweetheart," Dr Martakis put in. "Just to clarify: we didn't ride in on a horse exactly – more like Derek's Ford Focus; but well said all the same. Not sure what a Hutt Spawn is, so I'll take it as a compliment for now. I'm going to take Mr High and Mighty Stick Up His Arse – which by the way is *so* being logged in as your new nickname on the theatre rota, mate – and get out of your hair."

Libby was close enough that Jamie could smell her shampoo and see unshed tears swimming in her eyes. His chest felt tight and he had to clench his fists at his sides to stop himself from touching her. A loud clap in front of his face cut through his concentration. One of the white angels was glaring daggers at him.

"Out!" she shouted. "All of you. No men allowed in here."

They were ushered out of the room by the bouncers, but before the double doors closed Jamie looked back once at Libby only to see her eyes downcast and a single tear tracking down her cheek.

"So, MY JUDGMENTAL FRIEND," PAV SAID, SLAPPING JAMIE on the back as they walked down the road towards the others. "What exactly was that display of alpha male tomfoolery about?"

Not enough people use the word tomfoolery nowadays, Jamie thought vaguely as he tamped down his irritation, but that's Pav– always pushing the boundaries of what a straight man can say and get away with in this century.

"Leave me alone," he muttered, shoving his hands in his pockets and frowning down at the pavement. "You knew she was a stripper the first time you saw her, didn't you? I'm not in the mood for you being a glib twat at the moment."

"At least I'm not being an arrogant cruel fucking bastard, *mate*," Pav said, his tone still light, which somehow made the insults more shocking.

"I wasn't–"

"What do you think would earn an unskilled worker the kind of money it takes to support them and a child whilst being a full-time medical student?"

"Look, I don't–"

"No. *You* look, arseface." Pav drew to a stop and put his arm out to halt Jamie mid-stride. "I can think of one other option open to her. *One* thing, other than what we saw tonight. Can you imagine what that might be?"

Jamie winced and looked away from Pav's furious face.

"All those disgusting blokes looking at her," Jamie mumbled, rubbing the back of his neck and staring down at his shoes.

"Looking at her, Jamie. *Looking*. So what if a bunch of stupid horny idiots want to pay a fuckload of money just to look at this girl? Good for her. You experienced first-hand what happens when one of the natives gets handsy. Those big bastards in there don't let any of the punters get anywhere *near* the women on stage."

"I don't like it," Jamie muttered, shoving his hands in his pockets.

"Well boo-fucking-hoo, Mr Holier-Than-Thou. Remember, *you* were one of the disgusting pricks tonight."

Jamie gritted his teeth, clenching his jaw so tight he could feel the muscles ticking along his cheek.

"What were you doing in there, you tit?" Dan roared as he stormed down the pavement towards them. The groom-to-be was being held up between two of the other guys, his face looking a little green, but Dan's was a mask of fury. "We didn't even get to see the good stuff from that dirty bitch. And because of you we've all been thrown out." Jamie felt his fist bunch at his sides at the mention of Libby. Dan had always been a mean drunk. Jamie was normally able to overlook his brother's behaviour under the influence, but this was pushing his control.

"Ease up, mate," Pav said, stepping in between them and holding up his hands placatingly. "She's practically his Mrs. Give him a break, okay?"

Dan frowned in confusion. "What are you on about? The chick with the dark hair? I mean, she's the most fuckable thing I've seen for a *long time.* Don't get me wrong, but she's a goddamn whore, bro."

That was it. Jamie had officially reached breaking point.

She was Libby.

Not a dirty bitch.

Not a "fuckable chick with dark hair".

And *not* a goddamn whore.

He drew his fist back and let fly at Dan's smug, incredulous, self-satisfied face, and his brother, the best man, organizer of the whole night and payer of all cover charges, fell to the ground in a heap.

Chapter 11

Xena, Warrior Princess

"Ah," Kira sighed as she sank down into the seat next to Libby. "I never thought I'd say this, but I've seen me enough dick for one day. I'm totally over it. It's even leaked into my food choices." She waggled her eyebrows suggestively as she bit into the huge frankfurter hot dog she'd just bought at the hospital canteen. It was Kira's second week of urology and her initial excitement was waning.

Libby gave a half-hearted laugh. "Ki-Ki, I think you're the only one who actually buys those things. It shouldn't even be legal to sell something so unhealthy in a hospital." Kira's vegan kick had been shelved for the time being, leaving her free to eat any "cancer meat" she could lay her hands on.

"Pfft, you'd be choking back the dongs and you know it, if you didn't have to maintain that perfect bod of yours."

Libby's face fell and she looked back down at her own rather sad tuna salad. "Yeah, well, we all have to make sacrifices," she muttered as she took a half-hearted bite.

"Hey," Kira said, more softly now. "You okay? I didn't mean

to upset you. I know you have a secret love of dongs, but you don't usually take my junk food taunting *that* badly."

"It's not that, Kir," Libby said, trying for a smile and failing miserably. "I'm just tired I guess. Heavy weekend. And ..." she trailed off, fiddling with her tuna, "it's nothing."

"Okay," Kira said slowly. "Well, if you want cheering up, I could tell you about this monster co–"

"Kira, do you think I'm a slut?" Libby whispered, flashing a nervous look around the practically deserted mess.

Kira's normal amused expression dropped and her lips pressed into a tight line as she lowered her hot dog. "Who said that to you?" she asked in a tightly controlled voice.

"Nobody... it's nothing... just that..." Libby sighed and closed her eyes, renewed humiliation washing over her, "Dr Grantham and Dr Martakis were at the club on Saturday night. They saw me do my thing and... well..."

"Triple G and Dick Doc were there?" Kira semi-shouted, causing Libby to shush her furiously. Kira narrowed her eyes at Libby. "Did those overgrown weasels call you a slut? I swear I'll take their toothpick wieners and shove them right–"

"Kira!" Libby snapped. "Calm it down. I've seen Dr Martakis there before – he recognized me the other day but didn't say anything, so I think he's actually a decent guy. As for Dr Grantham... There'll be no toothpick wiener assaulting. He didn't call me anything, it's just... Look, forget I said anything. I'm being oversensitive. Must be–" Libby broke off to start coughing. The occasional dry cough she'd developed a couple of weeks ago was becoming more troublesome and chesty over the last few days. She'd needed her inhaler more than normal in between performances. Kira's face morphed from a mask of fury to one of concern.

"Hey," she said as Libby's coughing subsided and she

started rubbing her back. "That's been bad for a while. Do you think you should–"

"It's fine," Libby said, tucking her hair behind her ears and clearing her throat. "I'm fine. I don't have time to be sick."

"Uh, yeah, so Matt gave you this one to clean up – I've got the baby," Toby said, and Libby gritted her teeth. They had moved to A&E now, but they were still on rotation together. She looked over to the cubicle Toby had indicated and sighed. A large, tattooed man with a gaping wound on his forehead was lying up on the trolley. She could smell the alcohol on him from across the bay.

Toby and the A&E registrar were in the same rugby club together at uni, and so far that morning there had been a lot of backslapping and in jokes to contend with. It also seemed that the registrar was happy for Toby to cherry-pick his patients. Toby knew Libby liked paediatrics, he knew that she was good with kids, and he was making sure she didn't have the opportunity to shine.

They'd had their induction in emergency medicine yesterday and been shown around the department. The drill was that they were to take histories and make a start with patients that were waiting, and then present them to the doctors on the floor when it was the patient's turn to be seen. So far Toby had tried to trip Libby up anyway he could. She knew for a fact that Matt, the registrar, would not have allocated her the guy on the trolley across from them. She'd heard earlier that one of the male nurses had had to move areas to look after him as he was harassing the female ones. Toby raised his eyebrows in challenge, and she snatched the chart away from him, then walked quickly over to the drunken man before she lost her nerve.

"Hello, Mr... uh... Mr... Terminator?"

"The Terminator," he slurred, attempting a sloppy smile. "It's *The* Terminator, darlin'."

"That's your name?"

"Yup."

"You were born and your parents named you 'The Terminator'?"

"I wasn't born. I was made by SkyNet to destroy humanity's one hope for survival."

"Right," Libby said slowly. "So... anyway, it seems as though the flesh covering your exoskeleton is damaged. Can I take a look?"

"Are you Sarah Conner?" he asked suddenly, sitting up and stabbing a finger towards her.

"Nope," Libby said quickly, taking a small step back. "No, nope, definitely not Sarah Conner."

"Oh," he huffed, sounding disappointed as he slumped back on the trolley. "Go on then."

Libby got a tray ready with a sterile dressing pack, and then approached him at his side. As she applied the chlorhexidine-soaked gauze to his forehead he hissed, batted her hand away, and then in a sudden movement he grabbed both her upper arms and pulled her towards him.

"You're pretty," he told her, giving her a small shake, then dropping one hand down to grab her arse. Barry had insisted that all the girls learn some moves in case they ever needed to fend punters off themselves. Crazy really, as they were far more protected in the club than they were out here in the real world. Libby hadn't seen the point at the time, but when she'd protested Barry had crossed his huge arms and scowled down at her.

"If there's anyone who needs to be able to defend herself it's you," he'd told her.

"Why me?" Libby had asked, annoyed that the training meant she had to turn up an hour early for her shift once a week. He'd made a disgusted noise and thrown his hands up in the air.

"You know *exactly* what men think when they look at you," he'd growled, and she'd blinked in confusion. "You can't believe that the no make-up elastic-band bird's-nest hairstyle and hobo clothes disguise any of this–," and he'd swept his hand from her face and up and down her body in an annoyed jerky movement. "I'm sorry. I know it's annoying, but you have a responsibility to that little girl of yours to learn how to protect yourself."

Libby had grumbled and been a pain in Barry's arse, but she was going to kiss Barry right on the lips the next time she saw him.

Before The Terminator could pull her any closer she twisted one of her arms free, grabbed two of his fingers and pulled them backwards until he squealed. She was so intent on her mission and so angry that she didn't notice the entire emergency department fall silent and turn in their direction.

"Pay attention, Big Guy," she said, pulling his fingers even further back and causing him to shout out again. "I can make a man twice your size cry like a baby. You can either shut up and keep your hands to yourself whilst I clean up your cut, or I can snap your fingers in half, sedate you and *then* clean up your cut before I buddy-strap your broken digits. Choice is yours, Hutt Spawn."

"Okay, okay," he panted, writhing on the bed in pain. "I'll shut the fuck up."

"And...?" Libby snapped, not letting up on her grip.

"Sorry, sorry. I'm sorry, okay?" he squeaked out in desperation. Libby released his hand, turned back to the trolley and picked up some more chlorhexidine-soaked gauze. He flinched when she applied it to the torn flesh again but kept his mouth firmly shut and his hands to himself.

She finished quickly and found the registrar responsible for the patient gaping at her from the central island. Kira was standing next to him with a huge smile on her face.

"I'm no lesbian," Kira announced, and any eyes that hadn't been watching Libby after the commotion turned to her friend at that statement. "But even *I* found the whole Xena, Warrior Princess thing you had going on vaguely arousing."

Libby rolled her eyes. "Why are you even here? Shouldn't you be with the urology team?"

"I've saved enough willies for one morning," Kira said breezily. "I'm here to bring you lunch."

"Uh, thanks but The Terminator has agreed to let me stitch him up." Libby turned to face the registrar, who had been watching the exchange between the two women like some sort of tennis match. "Would you mind, Dr Ford? Supervising, I mean?"

He blinked and snapped his mouth shut before swallowing and nodding his head with a little too much enthusiasm. Kira nudged him lightly with her hip. "You might want to be more careful with patient allocation," she said, her tone light but an edge creeping into her voice. "Not sure the supervising consultant would have been too pleased if that had gone a different way. Libby should not have been allowed to see him without a chaperone."

"Right," the registrar said, pushing away from his half-finished paperwork and rounding the desk to stand in front of Libby. "Of course. Let's go. I'll teach you to suture."

Libby looked across the department and caught sight of a red-faced Toby covered in baby vomit and dealing with an irate mother. She smiled across at him, waved the suture pack in the air (he would hate the fact she was getting that experience under her belt) and followed the registrar back to The Terminator.

"THAT'S GREAT!" THE REGISTRAR SAID IN AMAZEMENT. Libby stood back and admired her sutures. They were small, neat, and the skin was aligned perfectly.

"I practice on oranges," she told him proudly.

"Well, it's paid off. Took me ages to be able to suture that neatly. Maybe you should think about a surgical career."

Libby smiled and shrugged. Surgery was not for her. All she'd ever wanted to do was be a paediatrician. A shrill ringing cut through the conversation just as she was about to answer, and the registrar frowned before turning towards the red phone on the wall next to them. After he picked it up his frown intensified. When he'd taken down some details he replaced the handset and started barking out orders.

He pointed to the nurse in charge saying: "Trauma team." Then started towards Resus. Libby wasn't sure whether to follow or not, but he paused mid-stride and turned back to her. "Come on," he told her. "Great learning opportunity."

In Resus the registrar briefed the team as they got ready. "Male, twenty-two, MVA, facial injuries, bilateral fractures." Everyone started putting on the heavy lead gowns, which had their position in bold letters on the back: EMERGENCY DOCTOR / NURSE / RADIOGRAPHER / ORTHOPAEDIC SURGEON. Libby was handed one with MEDICAL STUDENT on it. As she looked around at the others her eyes went wide when she realized that the man donning the ANESTHETIST gown was Jamie. She hadn't even noticed him arrive.

Everything was a flurry of activity for a minute or two whilst trays were prepared and equipment made ready, then they all fell still. Nervous anticipation filled the air as the team stood almost in suspended animation, waiting for the patient to arrive. Libby glanced over at Jamie, colliding with his hazel eyes for a moment before he looked away; his jaw was clenched and a muscle was jumping in his cheek. She found herself thinking that this silence was like the quiet before a Tsunami, almost eerie.

Then everything changed.

Men and women in red suits with AIR AMBULANCE emblazoned across the back pushed a patient on a trolley quickly through the department, bringing him into the Resus cubicle they were all assembled in. The paramedic in charge started talking through the history whilst the team moved as one to start working on the patient.

Clothes were cut off. Intravenous lines inserted. Jamie moved to secure the airway.

"Why is his GCS so low?" the ED consultant asked. GCS stands for Glasgow Coma Scale – a score below 8 means you are unconscious. The patient had an obviously broken leg and facial injuries, but that wouldn't necessarily mean he would have lost consciousness; if it was the head injury causing it, it was a bad sign – bleeding into the brain and swelling could both be responsible.

Toby had pushed his way in and managed to get a cannula into the man's arm. After he did it, in typical Toby style, he stood back and raised his arm, shouting, "Access here, guys. I've got the IV access." Everyone ignored him, seeing as the patient had two other wide-bore cannulas already secured.

Libby was not pushy, and she was gradually shunted into the background. But in all the activity and through the bodies in front of her, she caught sight of a metal bracelet on the patient's arm and squinted at it. The jewellery seemed incongruous with the rest of his attire. She darted around the registrar to get a better look and her eyes went wide. She swallowed, tamped down her shyness and straightened her shoulders.

"What's his blood glucose?" she asked. Everyone ignored her, having already wasted time listening to an annoying bolshy med student. She turned to the counter, grabbed a 50ml syringe of 50 per cent dextrose, and pushed into the patient's side again, attaching it to the drip.

"Libby," Jamie's sharp voice cut through the activity of the team. "What are you doing?"

Silence fell and all eyes turned to her. "What's his blood glucose?" she asked again, her voice steady despite her nerves.

"Well... I-" The paramedic frowned as he looked down at the patient's chart. "Shit, we don't seem to have... " One of the nurses moved quickly to pierce the patient's finger and ran the blood through the BM machine.

"It's unreadable," he said after a tense few seconds had passed.

"Go ahead, Libby," Jamie told her as he continued to ventilate the patient with the bag and mask. Libby injected the IV dextrose, and after another tense few seconds the patient's eyelids fluttered open. She breathed out a huge breath in relief as she stepped back to let the rest of the team in, and before the others could block her view she saw Toby scowling at her so fiercely she actually felt a flicker of fear go up her spine at the hate in his expression.

Chapter 12

Fair warning

Sweat trickled down Libby's back as she watched the now very much awake biker being wheeled away to the CT scanner.

"Why wasn't the BM taken before?" she heard Jamie ask the team and the paramedic crew. His question was met with blank stares and shifting feet. He sighed and threw his hands up in the air. "This is why we have protocols. The guy probably crashed his bike because he was hypoglycemic. He could have gone into a coma and come out with brain damage if Libby hadn't been thinking so quickly.

"We need to run some more simulated scenarios in this department. And where's the consultant in charge today?"

Libby backed away from the cubicle, keen to get out of his eye-line and maybe avoid interacting with him altogether. She shrugged out of the heavy gown and then pulled her cardigan off as she slowly retreated, feeling too hot in the stuffy environment of Resus after all the excitement; but she froze when she heard a loud hiss across the cubicle.

"What the *fuck* happened to your arms?" Jamie said as he

pushed through the team in Resus to catch up with her. Libby jerked round in surprise. The movement was the last straw for her hair band, which snapped, letting her mass of dark, wavy hair flow down her back and over her shoulders. She felt like Cousin It. Huffing in frustration, she grabbed all the hair she could and tied it in a knot at the nape of her neck. It was already falling out by the time she had finished. All she had achieved was allowing Jamie a better look at her bruised arms. His eyes flashed and he took both her elbows in his hands, turning them over to see her upper arms and the red fingertip bruising around them.

"Did this happen at the club?"

Libby's eyes darted around the department, and she shushed him before gesturing for him to follow her into the treatment room.

"Do you mind not mentioning Saturday, like, ever again? And especially *not* at work," she whisper-shouted once they were in relative privacy.

Jamie frowned down at her and crossed his arms over his chest, the muscles in them bunching – not helpful for Libby's concentration.

"*Please*," she added when he remained silent. She hated the pleading note in her voice, but if it meant nobody at work would know what she did outside the hospital she was prepared to beg even an arrogant small-minded twat like Dr Grantham (she decided in that moment that he was no longer Jamie, not to her). *Beg, borrow or steal* – her mantra since she got her A-level results the day after she'd given birth. She would do anything for the future Rosie deserved.

"God, Libby, I'm not going to tell anyone," he said, irritation lacing his tone. "Do you really think I'm that much of an arsehole?"

Libby stared at him steadily, her mouth clamped shut. He

might hold all the power in this situation, but she could not bring herself to lie.

He ran his hand through his hair, making the light brown strands stick up haphazardly in stark contrast to the pristine scrubs he was wearing. "Look, will you just tell me how you got those marks? Is this a regular thing? Do you always end the weekend looking like a punching bag after the bouncers let all sorts of blokes grab you willy-nilly? It's completely obvious to me that a place like that is not safe. You... you shouldn't put yourself at risk."

Libby almost let out a nervous laugh at the term willy-nilly coming from Dr Grantham, but managed to hold it in.

"*Of course* the guys don't let any punters come anywhere *near* us. You saw for yourself what happens when someone steps over the line."

Dr Grantham threw his hands up in frustration. "Then what? Do you have a beer-guzzling wife-beater-wearing boyfriend that knocks you about? Are you trying to live up to all the stripper clichés at once?"

Libby clenched her small fists at her sides and her face flushed red with anger. "Do you think I would *ever* allow anyone violent *near* my daughter?"

Dr Grantham stared at her and then let out a long breath. "Okay, but what–?"

Libby was so furious that she didn't think about what she was doing when she stepped into Dr Grantham's personal space and poked him in the chest. "You sanctimonious prick," she hissed. "You think a place like that – somewhere you consider *so* far below you, with people in it at the very bottom of the food chain – you think I'm in danger *there*. Well, I've got news for you, buddy, I'm a hell of a lot safer in that club than here in an NHS hospital with zero security and working with utter bastards."

"You got those bruises *here*? What happened?"

Libby took a deep breath in through her nose and let it out through her mouth as she shoved her arms back through the sleeves of her cardigan. "Look, I'm sorry but you are not my supervising consultant now, Dr Grantham."

He groaned. "Libby, please don't go back to that Dr Grantham bullsh–"

"I don't work for you anymore," she interrupted, and he frowned at her in frustration. "And quite frankly this is none of your business." She was surprised when he didn't stop her as she stalked out of the treatment room. As she crossed to the central island Matt, the registrar caught up with her and handed her a chart.

"Would you mind taking a history and examining the baby?" he asked. "Mum doesn't seem to have taken to Toby and we don't want a complaint on our hands."

"No worries," Libby replied, taking the chart with a smile as she caught sight of Toby's retreating back, practically running out of the department.

"Thought he could use a break," Matt explained. Libby smiled again and just before she turned to leave he blocked her way. "Good call with that biker," he said, and then shifted uncomfortably in front of her for a moment. "Look," he muttered, his voice dropping to a lower volume, "I just wanted to say sorry for not being the best teacher the last couple of days." He rubbed his neck, looking down at his feet. "I played rugby with Toby and I... well... he might have implied that... Look, I'm sorry. Won't happen again."

Libby waved her hand dismissively. "Crikey, don't worry about me. I'm no delicate flower, I promise you." She moved a little closer so that she could touch his upper arm to reassure him. "Thanks for saying something though," she said, her expression serious. The registrar looked up from her hand to her face and his eyes went unfocused, his jaw dropping slightly before Libby could realize her mistake.

"Go out with me," he blurted, and she had to fight the urge to roll her eyes. She took a small step back after giving his arm a friendly pat and withdrawing her hand. On balance it was probably better when he was ignoring her.

"I'm going to get back to work now," she told him, her smile still in place but now a little forced. "Okay?"

He blinked and she wanted to click her fingers in front of his face to pull his mind back to the here and now. A loud slam made them both jump a little and Libby looked over to see Dr Grantham scowling in their direction. They were close enough that he had probably heard the entire conversation. She heard him mutter what sounded like "fucking hell" under his breath as he swept past them and zeroed in on the consultant in charge. Libby gave the registrar another brief smile and made her way over to the island to read the patient file for the baby. Out of the corner of her eye she could see Dr Grantham take the consultant aside, who at first had a smile of greeting on her face, but the smile was slowly fading now with whatever Dr Grantham was telling her.

Libby could tell that Dr Grantham was angry, given the jerky way he was using his hands as he spoke. He nodded towards Libby and they both looked over to where she was sitting. Libby's face flushed red, and she wished the ground would swallow her up. When Dr Grantham had finished, Libby abandoned the file and moved quickly to cut him off in the corridor.

"How dare you speak to the consultant about me," she hissed. "I can look after myself. I'd sorted it all out. It's none of your business."

"Libby," he said, his jaw tight and his eyes narrowed on her. "I'm in charge of some aspects of training, and if those fuckwits in there are putting you at risk then it most definitely is my business."

"You–"

"*And*," he cut in, taking a step closer to her so that he was right in her personal space. "Fair warning, Libby. I'm making *you* my business from now on, so you better get used to it."

With that statement and without any warning he reached up, cupped her face and for a crazy moment she thought he was going to kiss her, right in the middle of the deserted corridor. His stubbled face hovered millimetres from hers and she was surrounded by his clean masculine scent, before he pulled away abruptly and stormed off. Her mouth fell open as she watched him leave and a hand went up to touch her lips. It may have lasted all of a few seconds, and he may be a total prick, but Libby thought that was the most turned on she had ever been in her entire life.

"You kissed her?" Libby heard Dr Martakis's voice through the door of Dr Grantham's office and she froze, her hand hovering over the door handle. "What the bloody hell are you playing at, mate? I thought you didn't touch the students?"

"I said I *nearly* kissed her," Dr Grantham groaned, and she heard a soft thump which was likely him collapsing into his office chair. "Christ," she heard him say, and held her breath. She had decided to talk to him in his office after her shift, before she picked up Rosie. Explain to him that she didn't want someone fighting her battles for her and that she was not interested in becoming any man's *business*. The last thing she wanted was to be cornered in front of Rosie or at work again; it would be better if they could talk alone.

It didn't matter that she couldn't get his smell out of her

head. The last thing she needed was any complications to her manic-enough life, and he'd already proved himself to be more than a bit of a tosser.

"I don't know what I'm doing. I don't know what came over me. I've never felt like that before. When I saw the bruises on her arms it turned me into this weird over-protective caveman. I went nuts at Rebecca for letting her get hurt and the poor woman wasn't even on the floor when it happened."

"Do you like her?"

"Of course I like her. Have you *seen* her?"

"Jamie, mate," Dr Martakis said, his voice more serious than Libby had ever heard it before. "You know what I mean. Do you *like* her? You don't fuck around with a single mother. Bad form." There was a pause and Libby assumed that Dr Grantham must have made some sort of non-verbal response, as Dr Martakis went on: "Well then, go for it, mate. Stop making everything so difficult for yourself."

"She's a student, and even if she weren't, she's not exactly a girl I can take home to Mum and Dad, is she?" Jamie said, and Libby jerked back from the door sharply, as if she had been slapped. "I mean, not even Dan at his very worst brought a *stripper* home." Tears stung her eyes but she blinked them away, refusing to let them fall. Before she could hear any more she gave his door a one-finger salute, and spun on her heel to run down the corridor in the direction of the crèche, but slammed into something as she turned.

"Oomph!" Libby heard, and watched in horror as Dr Morrison staggered back from the impact.

"Shit, sorry," Libby cried, her hands coming up to steady the other woman but withdrawing when Dr Morrison jerked away. The brunette straightened up and dusted down her still immaculate skirt.

"It's fine," Dr Morrison said, her eyes darting to Libby's for a moment before she looked away. But something must have caught her attention because she frowned, swallowed and looked back at Libby's face. "Are you...?" Dr Morrison looked like she was going to take a step towards Libby but then drew back again. "Are *you* alright?" The words sounded stilted and awkward but there was genuine concern in her expression.

"It's nothing," Libby said, moving round Dr Morrison to continue down the corridor. "So sorry. I wasn't looking where I was–"

"Why were you swearing at the door?" Dr Morrison asked, and Libby froze, forcing out a light laugh.

"Just a little joke," she said, moving away again. "Well, sorry. See you around."

She didn't wait for Dr Morrison's response. She needed to get her child, go home and forget about the hospital and all its stuck-up, judgmental occupants for a while.

"You are *such* a tool," Pav spat out, pushing up from Jamie's desk in disgust. "She's a fucking *medical* student. Your mum would bloody *love* her. The only one with a stick up his arse around here is you."

Jamie sighed. "I know, I know. I'm being a complete pillock aren't I? I didn't even mean that. Of course Mum would love her. I just feel like a creepy weirdo wanting to make some sort of move on her. She's too young for a start."

"She's twenty-two," Pav said dryly. "And she has a four-year-old daughter. You might be eleven physical years older, but personally I think her mental age is light years ahead of yours."

A light tapping came at Jamie's door and he frowned, barking: "Come in."

The door opened slowly to reveal Dr Morrison on the other side. She granted Jamie the standard millisecond of eye contact before focusing on his desk. "I've ..." she cleared her throat. "Dr Grantham, I've brought the list of procedures I think will benefit from pre-op CBT and a pile of consent forms."

Jamie had agreed to consent patients pre-operatively to take part in Dr Morrison's research study. Dr Morrison seemed to like lists. A lot. She moved into the office and reached out to put the pile of papers on the table, but when she caught sight of Pav she gave a weird little squeak and the forms went flying out of her hands, all over the office floor.

"Ah! The lovely Dr Morrison!" Pav exclaimed, smiling broadly. "I haven't seen you in weeks." He lowered his voice to just above a whisper. "It's almost as if you're hiding from me." Dr Morrison jerked back and then froze as she focused on the mess on the floor, obviously torn between not leaving it for them to clean up and her extreme dislike for Pav. Jamie had no idea what she had against him, but Dr Morrison seemed to have a very strong aversion to his best friend, which, in typical Pav fashion, he found hilarious. Jamie would admit that Pavlos wasn't everyone's cup of tea, but he'd never really encountered anyone who actively disliked him enough to make it as obvious as Dr Morrison did. "When are you going to start giving my patients the old mind-bending treatment?"

Dr Morrison had been running a study on the effect of preoperative CBT on postoperative recovery. So far it had just been for orthopaedic patients having joint replacements but Jamie had heard rumours that its success may mean expanding to other surgical specialities.

"It's not m... mind-bending," she muttered as she dipped down to pick up the papers, hovering over them in an attempt to keep her immaculate suit clean. "And I'm not the one doing the therapy. Anwar is a qualified psychologist." Throughout this Dr Morrison kept her eyes on her papers, not once giving either man any eye contact. Pav, who was never very good at being ignored, bent down next to her and the shock of it caused Dr Morrison to jerk to the side, falling onto the dusty floor. She straightened immediately and started frantically brushing off her skirt before patting her still perfectly styled hair.

"Bloody hell," Pav muttered as he finished gathering the papers. "Sorry, Dr M., are you okay?" Dr Morrison's left eye twitched at Pav's abbreviation of her surname but she still avoided looking at him, focusing instead on Jamie. She squared her shoulders, took a deep breath and her hands formed into tight fists at her sides.

"Have you upset your medical student?" she asked Jamie, and his eyebrows shot up.

"Why do you think th–?"

"I just saw her leaving and ..." she glanced away and bit her lip before taking another deep breath and looking back at him, "she seemed upset. I don't think ..." Dr Morrison trailed off, twisting her hands in front of her for a moment. "I'm not sure she's being treated very well and it could have an adverse effect on her training." With a short nod and a deep exhale after she'd said her piece, she turned to go.

"Dr Morrison, wait," Jamie said, shooting up from his chair to come around his desk towards her. "What do you mean? Where did you see Libby?"

Dr Morrison turned and frowned at him in confusion. "Well... coming out of your office, just now."

"What makes you think she's upset with me?"

Dr Morrison looked away and bit her lip again. "I don't want to get her in trouble," she whispered.

"I promise," he said, moving to block the door and watching a panicked expression cross Dr Morrison's face as she saw her path to escape from Pav cut off.

"She... she told your door to go and... well... have intercourse with itself, and she did ..." Millie trailed off as she lifted her hand but could not bring herself to actually make the gesture.

"Bollocks!" Jamie shouted, causing Dr Morrison to jump about a foot in the air and stumble to the side again. He rubbed his hands down his face and stood back to let her out. "Uh... thanks for telling me. I apologise for swearing."

"You won't... ?" Dr Morrison trailed off again as she made for the door and reached for the handle. "I mean, she's a good student. I don't –"

"Believe me, I deserved her abuse of my door," Jamie said in a dejected voice. "I will apologise and I promise it won't affect my treatment of her as a student." Dr Morrison breathed out a sigh of what seemed to be relief before she shot out of the door, and then Jamie heard the clicking of her high heels as she sped down the corridor.

"Hmm," Pav said, rubbing his chin and smirking over at a pissed-off Jamie, "doesn't look like you're going to have to worry about introducing Libby to your mum in the near future, does it?"

Chapter 13

Is he a Catholic?

"Yeah, we miss you too, Mum," Libby said as she dumped a big glug of milk into the mixing bowl, frowning down at the gloopy, stewing contents with the phone propped up under her chin. How hard could this pancake-making business *be*? Mum seemed to manage it fine every Saturday morning. Libby was determined not to be outdone by her mother and prove to Rosie that her cooking was just as good. "Bugger," she muttered under her breath as she rooted in the cupboard for the electric whisk, sending a couple of pans clattering onto the floor.

"Libby? You're not... *baking* are you? Unsupervised?"

"Mum," Libby growled, sticking the whisk into the mixture. "I am twenty-bloody-two years old, I think I can make a couple of sodding pancakes without too much of a palaver." With that she turned on the whisk full blast and was rewarded with great splatters of egg, milk and flour all over her and the kitchen.

"It's snowing!" she heard Rosie shout behind her, and she turned to see the little girl equally covered in egg and milk and spinning in a small circle with her face upturned to the flour that was still falling around them. "Granny," Rosie shouted, reaching up for the egg-covered phone. Libby sighed, wiped off the worst of it with her top and handed it over. "Mummy made it snow inside. She's magical." Libby looked around at her tiny, dripping kitchen, and then at Rosie's happy face; anger briefly warred with amusement, but Rosie's grin managed to tip her over the edge and she started laughing.

Rosie continued to spin while giggling down the phone to a most-likely laughing Granny when the doorbell went. Libby was used to Kira dropping in unannounced on the weekends when they didn't have to work, so she didn't think to grab a dressing gown before she answered the door. When she pulled it open she was still laughing, in only her pajamas, and covered in pancake detritus – only to find herself staring up at a large man filling her doorway. Her laughter died and her eyes widened in shock. Dr Grantham stared at her, taking in the full effect with a slow body-sweep of his eyes, after which he shifted uncomfortably and swallowed. Three thoughts went through her head simultaneously: number one, he could wear the shit out of a pair of jeans; number two, when he wasn't shaved for work his thick, dark stubble was a joy to behold; number three, she should never answer the door in her pajamas.

"Bloody hell," he muttered as he glanced behind him down her corridor. His eyes flicked down to her tiny shorts-and-T-shirt combination again before he started moving. He put a large, warm hand to her stomach to gently push her back, and followed her inside, shutting the door firmly behind him. She started to feel ridiculous: her shorts were covered in small Darth Vaders, and her ancient over-washed T-shirt, which had shrunk considerably, leaving her midriff bare, had an "I had friends on that Death Star" slogan stretched tight across her breasts, with a forlorn-looking Storm Trooper beneath. Her hair, which she hadn't yet had time to control, was falling free down her back and over her shoulders in thick, gloop-covered waves.

"Do you always answer the door like that?" he asked, dragging his eyes back up to hers, that frown and goddamn single-eyebrow raise very much in evidence.

She put her hands on her hips and stood her ground, squashing the urge to run to the bathroom and cover up. He'd already seen her in a lot less than what she was wearing now, she reasoned; but somehow the intimacy of him being in her flat and staring at her in her night gear made her feel unaccountably shy. In the club when she was performing she was someone else, not the Libby who wore *Star Wars*-themed sleep shorts and screwed up pancake mix on a Saturday.

"I thought you were Kira," she told him. "And how I answer the door is none of your business. In fact, *I* am none of your business so you can just–"

"Hi, Jamie," Rosie's excited voice called, and Libby closed her eyes in frustration. "Mummy made it snow inside, see?" She twirled on the spot and a cloud of flour was shaken off her clothes and hair. "Ooh!" she shouted as she came bounding up to him. "You can talk to my granny. She makes Porkshire Fuddins, and she don't ever get shampoos in your eyes when she washes hair." With that crucial information imparted, Rosie shoved the phone into Jamie's hand, complete with sticky congealed egg coating, and before Libby could make a grab for it he was talking to her mum.

"Hello, Mrs Penny? That's quite an impressive resume you've got there." Libby reached again for the phone but he leaned away from her. He was too tall to snatch it from him without some serious physical contact – something Libby was not going to risk, especially not when he was on the phone to her mother and with Rosie in the room. Dr Grantham chuckled at something her mother said on the phone and Libby rolled her eyes.

She could just imagine how excited Rita Penny would be at the prospect of her daughter receiving a gentleman caller, seeing as nothing had happened along those lines since Libby was seventeen. Thank God she hadn't let him meet her parents when he dropped her and Rosie off at their house last weekend. She'd even made him park two doors down so her mum wouldn't ask any questions.

"Yes, I work with your daughter. She's a very capable student, you should be very proud." Libby's hand, which had been outstretched for the phone, dropped to her side. For some reason his words made her chest tight.

Proud of her?

After the shame of a teenage pregnancy in the family, Libby was hoping that one day her parents would be able to feel that way.

"Well, Rosie and Libby are coming out with me on my boat today," she heard him say through a smile as he watched her narrow her eyes at him. "Yes, we're going to make a start on Rosie's pirate training – she tells me this is her career of choice. I'm hoping they won't mind if I bring my dog along as well."

Libby clenched her fists by her sides as Rosie gave out a loud, high-pitched squeal. It would be considered child cruelty if she turned down his offer now, and as she took in Rosie's excited face she knew that despite the fact it would be fun to tell this arrogant tosser where to go, it was going to break her daughter's heart to deny her both the boat *and* the dog experience. How on earth did he have a boat anyway? They were in London for varp's sake. Scowling up at him, she held out her hand for the phone, and after a little more banter with her mum he handed it over.

"Jesus, Mary and Joseph," her mother breathed, the Irish

accent filtering through more strongly in her excitement. "He sounds like a fantastic young man. What does his father do?"

Libby rolled his eyes. "I don't know that, Mum, I–"

"Well, can–"

"And, no – I'm not going to ask him. I barely know him. Look–"

"Oh, I bet he's from a good family. And a *doctor*. I knew you'd meet a nice doctor if you went to medical school." There went her mother, a staunch feminist, setting back the movement she'd supposedly supported fifty years with one old-fashioned statement. "Just you wait till I tell Eileen Martin about this. Always on about her daughter married to a pharmacist. Is he Catholic?"

"Mum," she snapped, "I've got to go."

"Oh! Of course, go, go. Sweets, I'm not sure that your pancakes are the best choice to make him for breakfast. Better maybe to ease him into your cooking skills. Some toast might be–"

"Love you, Mum," she said as she disconnected. Then she turned back to Jamie, who was still watching her. "Rosie, go to your room for a second please."

"But Mummy!" Rosie cried, stamping her foot in frustration. "I don't want–"

"*Go* to your room," Libby snapped, and Rosie blinked up at her, the smile she had been sporting since the flour-snow dying on her lips. Her bottom lip trembled for a moment before she turned on her heel and stomped away.

"Hey, look, you didn't have to–" Jamie started, but Libby was now boiling mad and not about to let him intimidate her.

"How *dare* you come into my home uninvited," she said, her voice shaking with rage. "How dare you offer something to my daughter, something you know I can't give her, something that if I refuse now she would never forgive me for."

"Okay, I'm sorry, I–"

"I don't know what this is and I've no idea why you're here, but I'll have you know that I'm a good mother, and *I* decide who I want my daughter to spend time with. To be frank, men who are happy to go to strip clubs but then sneer at the women they've come to see perform are not top of my list of people I would like Rosie to be around."

"Look, I said some bloody stupid things."

"You said what you thought, Dr Grantham," she told him, her voice devoid of expression, and he flinched at the use of his surname. "At least you were honest. I presume you're either here now out of guilt for your behaviour, or on some sort of "save the stripper" mission to convince me to make a respectable living whilst still attending medical school – which by the way is totally impossible. If it's the first option, then I'm not interested in pity, the second makes you a pious wanker and I've had enough of both of those."

"Crap," Jamie muttered, pulling his hand through his thick hair, leaving it standing up in short tufts. It was the messiest she'd ever seen him. Even when he'd been punched in the club he'd still looked immaculately turned out. "Look, I seem to be buggering this up royally but today was actually just my attempt at an apology. I shouldn't have said what I did to you that night and I shouldn't have said what I did to Pav in my office."

Libby's head jerked and her eyes widened in surprise. "Wh–"

"Dr Morrison saw you... er... communicating with my door." He risked a small grin but squashed it when it was met with another glare. "She was pretty pissed off with me. First bit of emotion I've ever seen her display, to be honest. Pav was convinced that she was a radiology cyborg sent from the government before that little outburst."

"I think it would be best if you just leave," Libby said, crossing her arms over her chest and unconsciously tilting her chin up to the exact same stubborn angle as her daughter had a moment ago.

Dr Grantham sighed and rubbed the back of his neck for a moment. "I didn't mean what I said to Pav... it was out of context. I–"

"I heard the context, you lying toad," she snapped, and blinked furiously to dispel the annoying sting of tears. "And don't worry – I have no intention of meeting your precious mother. I've no intention of having anything to do with you at all. So apology accepted; you can leave with a clear conscience."

"I DIDN'T MEAN..." JAMIE TRAILED OFF AS HE TOOK IN THE unshed tears which Libby was furiously trying to hide. He swallowed past a lump in his throat and squared his shoulders. He'd known this wouldn't be easy but he couldn't wait all weekend to apologise. He hadn't been able to sleep last night, thinking about what she must have overheard and with the other idiotic comments he'd made to her face running through his mind. Libby had let slip earlier in the week that she wasn't working this weekend, and he decided his best option was to just show up at her flat. He assumed the chances of her picking up the phone to him were slim so he thought it better that she wasn't forewarned.

"Look, let me do this. Let me take you guys out on the boat. I made a promise to Rosie and I don't want to break my word." They stared at each other for a moment before she looked away and surreptitiously wiped underneath her eye. When she looked back at him the tears were gone and a determined expression was in their place.

"I don't have the luxury of too many free weekends with Rosie. It might be distasteful to you but I do actually have to earn a living." She took a deep breath, further distorting the letters stretched across her chest. "I would prefer it if you left us in peace to get on with our day."

She was so sodding stubborn. For some reason he had the insane urge to reach out, swipe the flour and egg off her nose and kiss her until she stopped being so bloody difficult. Luckily, before he could do anything quite so stupid, the door to Rosie's bedroom flew open and the four-year-old emerged dressed in a pirate outfit complete with foam scabbard and eye patch.

"I'm ready," she shouted, moving into the room and swatting her mother on the bottom with her sword before poking Jamie in the stomach. "Take me to my ship."

"Rosie – I..." Libby started, dropping down to her daughter's level and turning the little girl to face her.

"Alan's ready too," Rosie said in a small voice, lifting the spider up between them to show that it was sporting a similar eye patch and was covered in skull-and-crossbone stickers. Libby closed her eyes slowly and Jamie watched as her shoulders slumped in defeat.

"Okay," she said through a forced smile, grabbing Rosie in for a tight hug. "Okay, honey, let's go pirating." Once she'd disentangled from Rosie's arms and stood up, she gave Jamie another glare.

"Right," she told him. "You can come back and get us in an hour."

"I'll wait," he said, and her eyes flashed.

"I'm in the middle of making pancakes."

"I can make pancakes," he told her, sauntering through to the kitchen and ignoring her huff of frustration. Yes, he could come back and pick them up in an hour, but even with Libby's overt hostility, he found he liked being in their small, chaotic environment. Not usually a fan of clutter or mess, he felt strangely at home in the haphazard space. Rosie's pictures covered the walls and cabinets in the kitchen area (which was also covered with a thick layer of flour and generous splodges of raw egg), the hooks on the back of the door were bursting with small, brightly-coloured coats in Rosie's size, and below that were rows of shoes, all for a little girl, with only one ratty pair of women's trainers and the battered black leather shoes he recognised as the ones Libby wore to work. The purple sofa in the middle of the space was strewn with children's books and the coffee table in front of it had a huge, half-completed Lego Millennium Falcon on top. There were more *Star Wars* toys on shelves at the back of the room, and a large globe taking up much of the corner by the window.

"Do you make it snow inside like Mummy?" Rosie asked hopefully, as she clambered onto the stool next to the kitchen counter so she could watch Jamie clean up the mess from the previous pancake attempt.

"Er..." He smiled and caught Libby's eye as she stared at him in annoyance, risking life and limb to give her a wink. An actual wink. Jamie didn't think he'd winked since he was a teenager. He just wasn't a playful winking type of guy. "No, gorgeous, that's a very special talent. I'm afraid I just make standard pancakes."

"Oh." Rosie's face fell.

"You can crack the eggs though," he told her, and she beamed at him. "Why don't you go and get ready?" he asked Libby, ignoring the fact that she was literally shaking with suppressed rage, her small hands balled into fists at her sides. She glanced at Rosie, who was bouncing in her seat with excitement, and her face softened.

He felt a flash of regret and annoyance as Libby's shoulders slumped slightly again and she sighed in defeat. He preferred her anger to this reluctant acceptance of the situation. As she shuffled out of the room he cleared his throat and started picking out the broken pieces of egg that were now in the bowl as a result of Rosie's rather overenthusiastic cracking.

He would make it up to Libby today. They would have a good time... no, a fantastic time... and she would forgive him. Maybe then he could get on with his life without this woman invading his thoughts twenty-four-seven.

Chapter 14

misogynistic, hypocritical caveman

"Rosie, I'm not sure Beauty wants your face buried in her fur the entire day," Libby said.

"She likes it," was Rosie's muffled reply, and Beauty gave the side of her face a lick as if to confirm. "Watch out for the pirate scar, Booty," Rosie giggled as the dog continued her assault with her tongue while her tail wagged furiously. Before they could leave the flat Rosie had insisted that she have what could only be described as a Chelsea Smile painted on her face – red lines extended from both corners of her mouth to her cheeks, punctuated with black "stitches". The effect was pretty gruesome but Rosie had refused to go anywhere without it.

"Don't worry," Jamie said, grabbing more and more food from his huge fridge and dumping it into a cool bag, "Beauty loves the attention." Libby was sitting on a stool at his vast kitchen island, still taking in the huge, sterile space with bewilderment. The massive mountain of smelly fur was totally incongruous to Jamie's house, which was all clean lines, order and absence of clutter – or in fact any life at all.

"Is it...?" Libby paused, then dropped her voice to a whisper, "Is it *really* a dog?" Jamie smiled, glanced over at Libby, and then started laughing when he took in her serious expression.

"I promise you she's a dog."

"She looks... part bear, well, to be honest she looks at least seventy-five per cent bear."

"And the other twenty-five?"

"Er... The Beast of Bodmin?"

Jamie laughed harder, causing Rosie to raise her head from the thick black fur it was buried in.

"Whatcha laughing at?" she asked.

"Your mummy thinks that Beauty looks like a beast."

"Mummy!" Rosie shouted, taking Beauty's large, ugly head between her hands and letting the dog lick the entire length of her face. "She is not a beast; she's bootiful. You'll break her feelings and hurt her heart." She went back to burying her head in the fur and Libby shuddered. Dogs had always made her nervous and this thing was not even a dog.

When Jamie had driven them back to his home in an expensive area of Wimbledon (Libby *knew* he'd been lying when he told her she was on his way to work), she had only had a few moments to appreciate the house (a beautiful Victorian semi-detached) before the biggest and most terrifying animal she'd ever seen in real life came bounding out of the perfect doorway and down the imposing stone steps, straight towards her. She'd frozen with fear but the monster kept coming. At the last minute it had jumped up so that its paws were on her shoulders and barked once in her face, revealing an impressive and terrifying set of teeth.

"Beauty, down," Jamie had clipped, and the dog-slash-terrifying horror-film werewolf had pushed away from Libby, causing her to stumble back into the car. "Sorry, she's a bit enthusiastic with strangers," he said. Libby gripped onto Rosie's arm to keep her by her side and away from those teeth. But Rosie, being Rosie, managed to wriggle her way free. She ran over to the beast and threw herself at the huge mound of fur. Her face had rarely emerged since; both dog and girl seemed to be utterly besotted with each other.

"She's an... um... interesting choice of pet."

Jamie laughed again.

"Well, when I brought her home she was actually pretty cute. Picked her up at a rescue centre – so she may be part beast for all I know." He shrugged. "Only went there with my nephew to choose a kitten, but couldn't resist that face." Libby glanced over at Beauty's massive, ugly, squashed-looking face and suppressed a grimace. "It wasn't the smartest move to be honest. I have to pay a dog sitter on my on-call days, and I don't think my sister-in-law will ever forgive me for having to walk her and check on her every lunchtime. She agreed when Beauty was a puppy, without quite realizing how much more of her there would eventually be to love, or how resistant she would be to any training... Right, let's go." Jamie swung the cool bag up and grabbed the other massive rucksack stuffed with equipment from the floor, his upper arms bulging in his T-shirt and causing Libby's mouth to run dry.

"Can I carry anything?" she asked once she'd swallowed a couple of times.

"Nope, you and Rosie just keep Beauty under control." He handed her a lead and Libby looked over at the Beast of Bodmin with trepidation. Beauty was eyeing the lead, the closest thing Libby had ever seen to a doggy scowl on her ugly face.

It was only when they were all loaded up into his car and Jamie had started driving that Libby finally thought to ask where his boat actually was. She'd had a vague idea that it would be on the Thames somewhere in London, but they seemed to be heading out to the M25.

"Uh..." Jamie paused, flashing her a wary look before clearing his throat. "Actually it's a *little* way outside London."

"How far?" Libby asked slowly.

"Well," Jamie drew out the word. "Have you ever been to The Solent?"

"The what?"

"You know, the stretch of water between England and the Isle of Wight."

"The Isle of *Wight*?" Libby's voice rose.

"The boat's not *at* the Isle of Wight," Jamie told her quickly. "It's near Southampton."

"Southampton?" Libby's mouth dropped open and she stared at him. What she had thought would be a couple of hours to humour Rosie was turning out to be a full-on day trip.

"It's a family boat. My parents keep it at the club there."

Of course they do, Libby thought. Of course Jamie's family are members of a Yacht club. She spent the next twenty minutes staring out of the window in furious silence. Rosie, however, didn't seem to notice the atmosphere in the car and chattered happily for the next hour about everything under the sun.

It was Jamie's patience with her daughter that finally broke through Libby's anger. Even Rosie's beloved Bumpa could only tolerate ten minutes of her nonsensical eye-spy games (the letter Rosie chose never corresponded to what she had chosen to spy, and the spied item was never something Rosie could have possibly seen on the journey – unless the embankments of the M3 were littered with flying ponies, ballerinas and aliens), but Jamie seemed to love it. By the time they arrived at the marina, Libby had started smiling as Jamie began spotting his own impossible items – dragons, the Loch Ness Monster,

The Queen – making Rosie squeal in protest, the little hypocrite.

Her good humour fled, however, during the short walk from the car to the harbourside. Libby was given Beauty's lead as Jamie carried the mountain of stuff they would need for the boat, and she soon understood that there were no short walks with that dog in the mix. Beauty seemed to take great delight in dragging Libby down the pavement at speed, then stopping abruptly to sit on her massive behind and smell something that urgently needed an olfactory once-over. On one occasion she'd spent a good five minutes on her own downstairs region – what possible interest her own genitalia could hold for even one minute of intense inspection was unclear, but Beast Dog was not going to give up however hard Libby yanked on her collar.

Dr Grantham, the bastard, had found her lack of ability to control the vast animal hilarious.

"She might be a wee bit stubborn but I've never seen her be quite such an arse."

To her further annoyance, when Rosie took the lead, Beauty seemed to snap out of her bad behaviour and trotted happily along at Rosie's side, looking up at the little girl in adoration.

When they arrived at the pontoon and Beauty sat on Rosie's command, Libby could have sworn the bloody animal actually smirked at her. The yacht club was just as intimidating as Libby had imagined: a large building sitting over the water and looking out on a harbour that was packed with hundreds of boats of all shapes and sizes. Jamie's BMW looked positively common compared to the other sleek, low-rise super-machines and SUVs packed onto the concrete of the car park.

Libby was just shoving yet another elastic band in her hair to contain the clumps that had managed to free themselves while Beauty was yanking her through the posh cars, when she locked eyes with someone she recognised. The blood slowly drained from her face as her hands dropped down from her head. The tall man standing in front of her was a lighter-haired, leaner version of Jamie. His face was now devoid of the red drunken tinge, and he was wearing shorts, with a baby strapped to his chest in a carrier – bit of a change from the pin-striped Saville Row number he'd had on that night, but there was no mistaking him.

"Dan, Amy, what the fu – I mean what are you doing here?" Dr Grantham's annoyed voice cut through Libby's shock and she looked over to see him striding up to Blonde Dr Grantham purposefully.

"I..." Blonde Dr Grantham, a.k.a. Dan, broke off, his eyes flicking between Dr Grantham and Libby and then widening as he took in Rosie snuggled next to Beauty. "You... er... well, we..."

"Hey, favourite brother-in-law." A short red-haired, pretty woman popped her head above the side of the harbour and then emerged up after climbing the ladder from below. "Don't be cross, but when you rang to see if we'd left any kiddie life-jackets in the hull we were a *bit* curious, and you know it's ages since you've taken us all out on the boat, so..." She trailed off as she caught sight of Libby and Rosie. A huge smile formed on her pretty, freckle-covered face and she started toward them.

"Uncle Jamie!" a child's voice shouted from over where the ladder was. Libby tore her eyes away from the redhead to see a little boy scrambling up onto the concrete. Like a small, red-haired torpedo he ran full pelt at Dr Grantham, slamming into his legs.

"Hey, Squidget," Dr Grantham chuckled, one of his hands going to the boy's red hair and giving it a rub, the other going under his armpit and starting to tickle.

"Jesus, Seb," a low voice rumbled from the side of the decking, and Libby watched in confusion as a teenage version of Dr Grantham pulled himself up the ladder and onto the concrete. "Don't jump off the bloody boat like that. Who do you think gets the blame when your bony little arse ends up in the water?" His brown hair was a little longer than Dr Grantham's and his physique more lanky, but the bone structure, eyes and hair were almost identical.

"Will," Blonde Dr Grantham snapped, tearing his eyes away from Libby to frown across at the teenager, "enough with the swearing."

"But Mum sai–"

"I don't care what your mother says or doesn't say. When you're with me, Amy and the boys you keep it PG, mate. Your *mum* doesn't have small kids to worry about." Will rolled his eyes but they froze as they came to rest on Libby and Rosie. With everyone on the harbourside now fixated on her, Libby started shifting uncomfortably on her feet, pushing her hands into the pockets of her long, cut-off shorts.

Dr Grantham cleared his throat and they all shifted their attention to him. "Guys, this is Libby and her daughter, Rosie." Libby forced a smile and gave a small wave. Rosie burrowed further into Beauty's fur, not saying a word. (To be honest Libby was a little relieved; Shy Rosie was better than Kicking Random People in the Shins Rosie.) "Libby's one of my medical students and Rosie is a pirate in the making, so I'm taking them out on the boat today."

Blonde Dr Grantham narrowed his eyes at Libby. His mouth dropped open to say something, before he snapped it shut and pressed his lips together in a tight line. "Libby, this is my brother, Dan, his wife, Amy, and my nephews: Will, Seb and Baby Rufus."

"Fantastic!" Amy practically shouted, shooting forward to engulf Libby in a very unexpected hug and then squatting down in front of Rosie. "Hey there, Pirate Rosie," she said, pushing back some of Rosie's curls to reveal her blue eyes. "You ready for the high seas?" Rosie gave a very small smile and little nod of her head.

Seb had disengaged from his uncle to come and stand next to Rosie and Beauty. Beauty gave a soft snort and licked the entirety of Seb's face. "Beauty is kind of *my* dog," he informed Rosie.

"Seb," his mother said in a warning tone.

"But you can play with him, I guess."

"Do you like woodlice?" Rosie asked, lifting her head from Beauty's fur.

"Yeah, course," Seb told her.

"Then you can be my friend... if you like," she said.

"'Kay," Seb muttered, looking down as he pushed a stone around with his shoe.

Will and his father were still watching Libby. Dr Grantham cleared his throat again and Libby caught him shooting Dan an annoyed look, which got him moving across to Libby with his arm extended around the baby on his chest. "Hi," he muttered, shaking her hand quickly before stepping back and flicking a nervous glance over to his wife.

"Yeah... um... hi," Will said, copying his father to move forward and shake her hand, his eyes moving to her chest. "Cool," he muttered, eyeing the wolf's head on her loose-fitting black T-shirt. "House of Stark."

Libby smiled. "Winter is coming," they said in unison, and then both smiled. He looked back up at her face and his eyes dropped to her mouth.

"Yeah," he breathed, keeping hold of her hand as his pupils dilated. Libby could practically smell the teenage hormones pouring off him.

"Will," Dan snapped. "Go get the tarp off the front of the boat will you?"

Will blinked a moment, then flushed bright red before letting go of Libby and moving back, next to his father. Libby looked over at Dan to see that his jaw was tight and a muscle next to his eye was twitching. She looked down at her scruffy Converse and bit her lip; it might be okay for *Dan* to visit a strip club, but he certainly didn't seem to want his teenage son anywhere near an actual real-life stripper. Libby wasn't entirely sure what he expected her to do that would lead Will astray out here in broad daylight surrounded by children and boats, but she suspected he'd rather not find out. She watched as Will climbed down the ladder and walked along the pontoon. He stopped in front of a large speedboat with the name *Bunty* written on the side and started pulling the cover off its nose. Feeling very much out of her depth, she sidled up to Dr Grantham and gave his sleeve a light tug.

"I think maybe it's best that Rosie and I stay behind," she said quietly. "Your family's here and–"

"Don't be crazy," Amy said, standing from her crouch next to the children and putting her hands on her hips. "We're the ones gate-crashing, and the more on the boat to crew the better. That way you can have a go at wakeboarding – it's super fun!" She clapped her hands and bounced on the spot to emphasise its *super-funness*, much like an adorable, overenthusiastic little pixie. Despite how awkward Libby was feeling, she couldn't help but smile over at her. That died, however, when she noticed the stony look on Dan's face: no chance of any over-friendly behaviour there.

"No, really," Libby started to protest, shooting Dan a nervous glance and letting go of Jamie's sleeve. "We'll be fine. Let's do it another day." She reached down to Rosie and tried to extract her from Beauty's huge body. "Come on now, Little

Louse. We'd better go." Rosie stood and Libby breathed a sigh of relief until she noticed the little girl's stance: feet planted wide apart, hands on hips and fierce expression on her small face.

"Jamie *said* we could go on his boat," she shouted, her whole body shaking with rage. "You pwomised!" The dropping of the rs was a bad sign. Libby squatted down in front of her.

"I know, baby, but we'll go and do something fun, just you and me, okay? We can go to the park or the beach, we can get ice creams." She leaned her forehead against Rosie's and put her hands on either side of her face, dropping her voice to a whisper. "Please, Rosie-Pose. Please. We can come back another day."

Rosie must have sensed the desperation in her mother's voice because instead of the all-out tantrum Libby was expecting she just sniffed and nodded her head, two tears coursing down her cheeks. "Good girl," Libby muttered, brushing the tears away with her thumbs and then kissing Rosie on the forehead.

"Right," she said, allowing Rosie to give Beauty one final cuddle before picking her up and securing her on her hip. "We'll leave you to it." They'd have to get the train back to London which would be a stretch, but there was no way she was hanging around here. When she looked over at Dr Grantham she took a small step back. He was staring at his brother; his face was dark with anger.

"Rosie," he said in a tight voice. "Play with Seb a minute, gorgeous. I thought I saw a couple of woodlice and maybe a worm over by the lifejackets. Amy, Libby, would you stay with the children a moment. Dan, I'd like a word." With that he spun on his heel and stormed off to the far edge of the pontoon.

Rosie scrambled down from her position on Libby's hip as soon as she heard the possibility of fresh woodlice-acquisition opportunities. Libby made a grab for her but she was too fast and ran off to where Seb was crouched down by the lifejackets.

Dan sighed but followed after him, and Libby watched with Amy as the men formed a tight huddle and started talking.

"What on earth?" Amy muttered, moving forward to go over there; but Libby caught her arm.

"Could you keep an eye on Rosie? I'll be back in a second," she said to Amy, and rushed forward before Amy had time to reply.

"What is wrong with you?" she heard Dan whisper-shout at his brother as she drew near. "You spend your entire thirty three years with the most boring, perfectly-put-together birds on the planet and then decide to... hook up with a stripper? Are you insane? And you time this rebellion just when it will get me in the shit?"

"I'll point out that you weren't even fucking invited on the boat today, you prick," Jamie retorted.

"Fine, we'll bugger off then," Dan said, crossing his arms over his chest and scowling at Jamie. "Last thing I need is for Amy or Will to find out she's a–"

"It's okay," Libby said. "I'm the one who should... bugger off."

Both men started and looked over at her as she drew alongside them. Dan had the good grace to flush with embarrassment. "Look, I'm really sorry. No judgement here. Each to their own and all that. I'm just worried about confusing Will, and I–"

"Confusing Will about what?" Amy asked from a foot away. Libby glanced back over to the harbourside to see that Will was with the children.

"Nothing, hun. Get the kids packed up; we're going home," Dan told her, his expression now more than a little panicked. Baby Rufus chose that moment to start waking up, emitting some snuffling sounds and wriggling on Dan's chest. Amy reached forward and efficiently unhooked the straps of the baby carrier to extract the now grumpy-looking Rufus and cuddle him to her. She raised her eyebrows and narrowed her eyes at her husband.

"What has crawled up your arse today? You're acting like a total git," she said, pressing one of Baby Rufus's ears to her chest and covering the other with her hand when she said the word "git". "Why are you being so weird?"

"Amy, baby. Please just get the kids and our stuff together. I'll be two seconds." Amy's face flushed red and her small mouth set in a firm line.

"Don't you *baby* me. *You* can go where you like," she told him. "The children and I are staying and we're all going to have a nice day on the boat together. You're going to remove whatever stick you've shoved where the sun don't shine and we're going to have a good time."

"Mum!" Seb shouted from across the habour. "Can we take home a dead frog?"

"Seb," Amy cried as she looked over at the now dirt-covered little boy. "Don't touch that! You don't know how long its been there." She trotted over towards the kids and Dan turned back to Jamie and Libby.

"Look, I'm sorry," said Dan. "We'll go. I didn't know that... I just can't ..." He trailed off and looked down at his shoes. "Amy would go crazy if she knew I went to one of those clubs again. I–"

"What?" Amy asked in a low dangerous voice. All three pairs of eyes flashed to her.

"Argh!" Dan squealed, his voice just that little bit too high to fall into the manly category, and his hand clasped to his chest in an almost comical display of fear. "You're like an assassin with your small silent ninja feet." She raised her eyebrows.

"Why are you talking about *those clubs*?" Amy looked between the three of them as she spoke in a low, dangerous voice and Libby started backing away; she had no interest in other people's marital disputes.

"Look, honey, it was for Jonty's stag. I wasn't drunk, I swear. It was all in fun – nothing like when..." He trailed off again and visibly swallowed as he eyed his wife, who was a small volcano of simmering rage.

"I think we can discuss this later," Amy said in a tightly controlled voice, shooting Libby an embarrassed look. "Let's not air our dirty laundry in front of Jamie's new girlfr–"

"Aims, she's a *stripper*," Dan blurted out, and Amy blinked.

"What?" she asked in confusion. "Who's a stripper?"

Dan turned his attention back to Libby, who was flushed with humiliation, and he softened his tone. "I'm sorry, it's just that I promised Amy I wouldn't go to another strip club after... well ..." He shook his head to clear it, his eyes desperate and clearly keen for a subject change, "and Will is at a really impressionable stage and I don't want him to think that–"

"Oh for fuck's sake," snapped Amy, and all of them started in surprise. "You misogynistic hypocritical caveman."

"Aims, look–"

A growl cut him off.

An actual growl.

And Amy did not growl in a cute adorable girly way; no, she growled like a furious six-foot cage fighter gearing up for an arse-kicking. How her small body could produce such a low, menacing sound was a mystery. She looked over at Libby, saw her flushed cheeks and mortified expression, and moved to wrap her arm around her shoulders.

"I expect there's a reason you know about Libby's other career?" Amy raised her eyebrows and Dan shifted uncomfortably on his feet. "Right, so it's okay for you perverts to go to a strip club and leer over women, just as long as they stay in their proper place and don't encroach on your real life. Well, I've got news for you lot; women like Libby don't just exist on a stage, wrapped around a pole. They have lives and responsibilities, just like the rest of us, and I'm sure Libby is making the best of a tricky situation.

"God knows if you had had the option of stupid women paying crazy money to see *you* shake *your* arse when you were Libby's age you would have gone for it. Are you telling me Will wouldn't have suffered without your family's support in the early years when you were starting out in the city? What would you have done if you'd had full custody and no super-rich family behind you?"

"Okay, okay," Dan held his hands up in surrender. He rubbed the back of his neck and looked over at Libby. "I'm sorry, really. I didn't mean anyth–"

"It's fine," Libby said, forcing a strained smile and holding up a hand to silence him. "Honestly, I totally understand, and I think it'd be better if I take Rosie and–"

"Dan, Amy, would you both please just get lost for a minute?" Dr Grantham cut in. Amy gave Libby's shoulders another squeeze before narrowing her eyes at her husband and dragging him off towards the children.

"Okay," Dr Grantham said, stepping forward into Libby's personal space and putting his hands on her shoulders. "Please give us another chance. This was supposed to be me making things up to you, and now... ugh, Dan is *such* a tosser."

"He's just being honest. I can respect that." When Dr Grantham went to speak Libby held up a hand to silence him. "But I don't want to be around it."

"Bugger," he muttered, his eyes dropping down to their feet, only inches apart. "We were only there for a stupid stag, we don't–"

"That's fine. Totally fine if it's all in fun, but not when it leaks into my life. Not when it makes me feel like crap."

"I swear I'll make it up to you."

Libby turned away and slowly shook her head.

"Rosie will be so sad," he went on. "She's so excited. Just a couple of hours. I'll send them away if you want. Hell, if you don't come with us I'll send them away anyway. There's another boat they can go on."

"Another boat?" Libby's voice rose. Of course this family had another bloody boat. They probably had a whole fleet of them, the posh bastards.

"Uh..." Jamie shifted uncomfortably. "Yeah, a sailing boat though, so dickhead Dan will make a fuss cause it's a bit of a faff with the baby. But he can just suck it up."

Libby saw Seb and Rosie crouching down next to each other, squealing, as something, either woodlouse or spider, scuttled from one of their hands to the other. She sighed.

"Okay, just for a couple of hours," she said eventually. Dr Grantham's face split into a wide grin and he pulled her forward into an unexpected tight hug. Her face was pressed into the soft fabric of his T-shirt and her head suddenly started feeling light. He smelt of washing powder and sandalwood, and she could feel the broad planes of muscle against her cheek. She felt him nuzzle her hair and take a deep breath in for a moment. A throat cleared from across the harbour and he jerked in surprise before setting her gently away from him. He gave a nervous cough and shoved his hands into the pockets of his shorts. The expression on his face suggested he was almost more shocked than her.

"Great," he said, his voice slightly strangled and the tips of his ears going a bright shade of red. "We should get going then. You good?" He glanced at Libby briefly and she gave a quick nod, after which he patted her arm awkwardly. "Great, great. That's... um... great."

His pink ears, sudden affinity for the word "great", and clear discomfort made Libby, for some insane reason, want to reach forward, pull his face down to hers and kiss the life out of him.

She shook her head to clear it. Two hours, she said to herself. She could do this for two hours. Beg, borrow or steal, she'd do whatever she had to for her daughter.

Chapter 15

Babies' cry

"That is the best thing I've done *ever*," cried Libby as she hauled herself up the ladder and onto the back of the boat.

Jamie had seen her smile before but not like this. Now she was beaming, her beautiful face animated with excitement as she shook out her long hair, which had fought its confines and was now plastered down her back. Jamie swallowed as she stood up and her figure – in the slightly-too-tight-around-chest wetsuit she had borrowed from Amy – was revealed in all its glory.

With annoyance he registered that he wasn't the only one to notice: Will was staring at her with a dreamy expression and his mouth hanging open; and Dan had turned fully around from his position in the driver's seat to watch her. Jamie deliberately stepped on Will's foot and pushed the side of Dan's head so that he was looking in the goddamn direction they were going, before he clambered over to Libby and grabbed her the largest towel he could find. He knew he should have sent those idiots home when he had the chance, but Libby made him promise to let them stay.

The day had started badly but over the course of the morning things had gradually improved. It helped that Rosie was so excited about the speedboat, about Beauty being on the speedboat, about their speed as they flew across the water, even about the soggy sandwiches Amy produced from the picnic cooler. It was hard to stay angry around that kind of absolute happiness and genuine joy.

Libby took the towel from Jamie and used it to wipe off her face and hair. Droplets of water still clung to her long eyelashes despite these efforts, and Jamie couldn't help watching in fascination as they dripped onto her high cheekbones. Once they'd powered over to Osbourne Bay off the Isle of Wight, it had taken a fair amount of convincing to get Libby out on the wakeboard. She'd watched Dan and Jamie first and eventually agreed to try it. After a couple of epic wipeouts she'd managed to stand up, and this was the third long run she'd managed. Her coordination was outstanding and Jamie was reminded of her flips from table to table and bench to bench at the club, and her gravity-defying chair antics. That kind of natural ability had to come from some sort of high-level sport requiring a lot of balance work. Seeing her enjoy something so much was incredible. But despite this he was now somewhat regretting the offer.

As he pulled another towel from the hull and wrapped Libby firmly inside it, making her more burrito than person, Baby Rufus started crying again. It had become clear over the last two hours that Baby Rufus was not a sea-faring baby. He seemed to regard the boat as some sort of terrifying, unnatural, and definitely hostile entity. Most of his time had been spent either in wide-eyed terror or yelling at the top of his lungs. Every so often he shot his parents looks of heartbreaking betrayal that they would be cruel enough to put him through this kind of torture. By now he had gone way past his normal nap time, but the adrenaline of the experience was keeping him awake.

"I don't understand," Amy said, trying to be heard above the screams as she held Baby Rufus to her chest. "He loved it last time."

"He was six weeks old last time Aimes, and strapped to your chest the whole journey," Jamie told her. "The only thing he'd have registered was the motion of the boat and the fact that he spent a good few hours communing with your boobs – which at that age is about the best place a boy can be."

Amy scowled at him. "I'll have you know Rufus is a *very* advanced baby. He knew exactly what was going on last time. Something must have spooked him." She sighed and Rufus let out another scream. "Maybe we'd better go back."

"Can I..." Libby hesitated as she glanced at Dan and then back to Amy. "Can I try something?" she held out her arms. Amy stared at Rufus's angry little face and shrugged.

"Go for it," she said, passing the baby over to Libby, who to Jamie's annoyance allowed the towel burrito to fall to her lap so she could take him. Baby Rufus and Libby stared at each other for a long moment as she held him up in front of her. He took a deep breath in, no doubt preparing another blood-curdling scream, when Libby blew on his face. Rufus blinked and then frowned at the stranger in front of him capable of such magic. She blew again and the blink she elicited this time was even longer. Whilst Baby Rufus was distracted, she rearranged him so that he was lying along her legs on the towel, and picked up Amy's filmy scarf from the floor. Baby Rufus looked left and right, his face screwing up in anger, but then froze as the scarf was fanned out and pulled gently over his face. He blinked again and frowned but before he had time to scream the manoeuvre was repeated. After about ten face swipes his eyes were mostly closed and after twenty his whole body had relaxed into sleep.

"That is some trick," Dan said into the stunned silence of the boat.

Libby shrugged. "I used to do some child-minding when I was saving up money for medical school. It was a great way of being with Rosie but still earning during the day. That technique helped me out a few times."

"Nothing I do seems to work when he gets like that," Amy said, and for the first time Libby could detect a trace of sadness in her words. Amy's shoulders were hunched defensively and she was looking down into the bottom of the boat. She sniffed and cleared her throat, forcing a fake smile. "Not much of a mother, am I? If I can't even comfort my own child."

Libby frowned. "But... babies cry," she said matter-of-factly. "They cry all the time. It's the only way they get any exercise in their little lives. As long as you've fed them, they're clean and they have cuddles there's not much more you can do. Rosie cried non-stop. Admittedly some babies cry less than others, and you might have gotten lucky with Seb, but most of them spend a large amount of their day screaming bloody murder. Believe me I've looked after enough of them to know."

Amy's mouth had dropped open and she was staring at Libby as if she'd imparted some vitally important, mysterious piece of knowledge, rather than just a simple fact. "Babies cry," Amy muttered under her breath, a slow smile spreading across her face.

"Yes," Libby told her slowly, obviously still confused as to why this was such a surprise to Amy. "Yes, they do. *All* the time."

"Do you want me to take him?" Amy asked, reaching over to the sleeping Baby Rufus.

"No way," Libby told her, leaning back in the boat, arranging a dry towel over her and splaying Baby Rufus across her chest. "They're yummy when they're all sleepy and floppy like this. You go wakeboard or something. I'll get my baby cuddles in."

"Mummy *loves* babies," Rosie said from the bottom of the boat, where she and Seb were draped over Beauty. "She wants to make them better and look after them all day. She's gonna be a paedi-electrician."

"Paediatrician, Little Louse," Libby said gently, and Rosie scowled up at her.

"Ugh, Mummy, that's what I said – paedi-a-giction."

"Well, I think your mummy will make a fab paedi-a-giction, sweetpea," Amy told her, and winked at Libby whilst she hurried to get changed to go on the water.

In the end they spent the whole day out on the boat. Libby didn't push to be taken back after the two hours was up. She was still very wary around Dan, but then again he didn't seem to be anyone's favourite person that day; his wife barely looked at him, and Will (who Jamie realized after the first hour and a couple of *Game of Thrones*-slash-*Star Wars* conversations with Libby, was totally besotted with her) had noticed something amiss and was, it seemed, very much on Libby's side.

Jamie was beginning to realize that Rosie didn't miss a trick, and halfway through the day she had gone to stand next to Dan who was still in the driver's seat and tapped him on the shoulder.

"Why have you got your grumpy knickers on?" she asked, tilting her head to the side, then putting her small hands on either side of his mouth and pulling his lips up into a smile. "There, much better."

"Yes, darling," called Amy, "why *have* you got your grumpy knickers on?"

"Boys don't wear knickers, Mummy," shouted Seb.

"Your daddy does," said Rosie, who had moved on to kneading Dan's cheeks like she did with Jamie. "Grumpy ones. All my crew have got to be wearing their happy knickers – isn't that right Mummy?"

"Uh... Rosie," Libby said in a warning tone, "why don't you leave Mr Grantham alone."

"Please, Libby, please call me Dan – and it's fine," said Dan through smushed-together lips courtesy of Rosie. "I'm happy to be your crew, Captain Rosie. In fact, why don't you steer for a while?" Rosie released his face and squealed so loud that Jamie was surprised the windshield didn't shatter.

"Hurrah!" she shouted, her hands straight up in the air and her head tilting back dramatically. Dan's face broke into his first real smile of the day. He sat her on his lap and they experienced speedboat-driving Rosie-style, which consisted of multiple jerky turns and at one point a rather too-close encounter with a small ferry.

The kids both wanted to wear wetsuits like the adults and luckily Amy had a spare one in four-year-old size. Once Rosie was in her wetsuit and her life jacket was put back on over the top, she shocked everyone by jumping off the side of the boat into the water. Jamie was about to leap in after her when she bobbed back up to the surface, splashed and laughed for a minute, then swam to the back of the boat in a surprisingly competent front crawl.

"Bloody hell," Dan whispered, his eyebrows in his hairline. "She's like a fish."

"She has lessons," Libby told them. "Every week."

Swimming lessons in London were not cheap. An image of Libby's worn-out shoes flashed into Jamie's mind and he felt his chest constrict.

Once back at the quay, and after Libby had changed back into her clothes under the cover of a strategic towel (this process was watched with avid fascination by Will until Jamie kicked the little shit in the shin again), Dan surprised Jamie by asking Libby to help him with the tarp whilst the others clambered up the ladder. Jamie was about to object but Dan held up his hand and shook his head slightly, mouthing "It's okay" to stop him, so he helped the kids up the ladder instead, but that didn't stop him watching from over the side.

Dan moved closer to Libby after they had covered the boat and she stiffened in response, but whatever he said made her relax her shoulders, and eventually she smiled. Before they parted she even chuckled and held out her hand for him to shake. She was still grinning when they eventually made it up the ladder.

"Jamie's gonna take us to Pizza Express!" yelled Rosie, bouncing on the spot with excitement. Libby smiled at her little girl and stroked her hair.

"That sounds great, honey," she said, pulling her in for a hug but shooting Jamie a venomous look, which made it clear this development was anything but "great".

"Right, well, we'd best be off," Amy said as Baby Rufus grizzled from his carrier. "Got to get this one home where he can scream his little head off for a few more hours. Not sure the good people of Pizza Express are up for that torture." She leaned forward and hugged Libby, then crouched in front of Rosie, putting a hand up to the side of her head to smooth her curls. "Good to meet you, gorgeous. We'll see you again soon, okay?" As Amy straightened up, her eyes came back to Libby.

"Hey – you guys around next month? You coming to the barbeque?"

"Yes."

"No," Jamie and Libby answered together. Amy grinned and gave Libby a wink.

"Okay then. If I know my brother-in-law, I'll expect you there."

"We'll see you then," Jamie said to Amy, giving her and Will quick hugs, Baby Rufus a kiss on the forehead, Seb a hair rub, and Dan an overly forceful slap on the shoulder.

"But I–"

"Let's get going," he muttered, picking Rosie up and settling her on his hip, then tugging Libby along by the hand.

Pizza Express was one of Rosie's very favourite places. Libby was quite sure her daughter had informed Dr Grantham of this fact at some point on the boat in order to secure an invite. (She was diabolical in her plotting capabilities.) Dr Grantham seemed bizarrely pleased to be in a kid-heavy environment early on a Saturday night, making Rosie giggle so much over the meal that she actually snorted some of her apple juice onto her dough balls, which was disgusting, but only seemed to make Dr Grantham even happier. When Rosie was totally engrossed in her ice cream at the end of the meal, Dr Grantham leaned forward and lowered his voice.

"Thanks for what you did with Amy."

"Uh... what do you mean?" Libby asked, lowering her coffee and frowning across at him in confusion.

"She's been struggling for the last few weeks with postnatal depression. Dan's been out of his mind with worry. I know he can come across as a bit of an idiot but he does love her."

"Depression? But she's... she's so ..." Libby shrugged helplessly, "so bouncy."

"You should see her when she's not depressed," he muttered darkly. "She was so happy on her wedding day Will could barely get her up the aisle without causing somebody permanent injury – lot of responsibility for an eleven-year-old."

"Will took her up the aisle? What about her dad?"

"Amy's parents didn't approve of her marrying a single dad who'd had a son when he was a teenager and some other... problems. Dan used to have a pretty bad drug habit before he cleaned up his act after Will. They weren't keen on an ex-addict no matter how many years he'd been sober for, so they refused to go to the wedding."

"Oh no," Libby whispered, horrified that gorgeous, bouncy Amy's parents could do that to her.

"So Will doubled as bride giver-away and joint best man with me – it was pretty funny."

"Poor Amy."

"Anyway, like I said, thanks for today. I think this colic business has got her all wound up. Seb never had any problems like that when he was a baby and she's been thinking she's a terrible mother. Her friends are all NCT-brigade know-it-alls and she's not close to her mum for obvious reasons. Dan's tried to get her to talk to our mother but she's embarrassed, and our mum is a bit... well, you'll see for yourself." Libby thought that was a weird thing to say – she had no intention of meeting his mother. "I think you gave her a real boost today."

"I just said what I thought," Libby told him. "I mean, Rosie was a colicky baby but I didn't have another child to juggle or–"

"Oh no," Dr Grantham cut her off. "No, *you* only had two jobs to work, medical school to apply for, then lectures and exams to contend with."

"I–"

"Look, Libby," he interrupted, his jaw clenching for a moment before his hand shot forward to grab hers on the table. "I've already apologized, but I know that doesn't make up for the way I treated you. I want you to know that I *do* respect how difficult things must have been for you. I *do* think you are amazing to achieve what you have, and I'm sorry if my reaction made you think otherwise." Libby's eyes slid to the side, but before she pulled away she allowed him to stroke across the top of her hand with his thumb, and suppressed a shiver in response.

"Don't worry about it," she muttered to the balsamic dressing as she fiddled with the corner of her napkin. She felt light pressure on her chin and lifted her head when she realized it was his fingers exerting it. When her wide eyes caught his, he let his hand fall away. His eyes were narrowed.

"You don't believe me do you?" he asked, but continued on before she could reply. "That's fine," he said bizarrely. "You don't have to believe me yet. I can wait."

"Why do you keep touching Mummy?" a loud, high-pitched voice cut through not only their conversation but every other conversation in the packed restaurant.

"I think it's time for the bill," Dr Grantham muttered, ruffling Rosie's hair. The tips of his ears had turned pink again as the majority of the patrons turned in their direction, and, God help her, despite what a grumpy bastard he'd been in the past, Libby couldn't help herself: she smiled.

Chapter 16

Rhabdomyolysis

Jamie was winning. He could taste victory. But, over the course of the day, the game he'd set out to win had changed. He'd gone from wanting to make it up to Libby for being an insufferable self-righteous prick, to simply wanting Libby. If he were honest with himself that was the real reason he wouldn't let her get the bus after the death of Brian, her car, a month ago. It had been the real reason he checked on her in A&E, and definitely the real reason behind wanting her on his boat today.

Yes, he was a selfish bastard.

Yes, she was too young for him.

Yes, she was a student.

The familiar weight of responsibility settled over him. As the younger brother to a man who went off the rails spectacularly in puberty, and having seen all the worry and upset it caused their parents, Jamie had always felt huge pressure to be perfect. To somehow make up for Dan's behaviour; to make it so his mum would stop bursting into tears over the dinner table and his dad would stop shutting himself away in his office. By the time Dan had pulled his head out of his arse after having

Will and the drugs behind him, Jamie's drive for perfection had become ingrained. The last thing he needed was to take any risks, and Libby was a risk.

But after watching her with Rosie and his family all day, listening to her infectious giggle, seeing how easily she took everything that was thrown at her in her stride, witnessing her forgive his total dickhead of a brother, and last but not least, seeing her body in Amy's slightly-too-small-in-certain-areas wetsuit, he no longer gave a monkey's. He'd never been this besotted with a woman before in his life. Even his overwrought feelings for his first girlfriend as a desperate teenager paled in comparison.

"Come on, Beauty," Rosie commanded once they arrived back at the small flat. She tugged on Beauty's collar and the dog practically bowled Libby out of the way of the door to bound in after Rosie. Both dog and little girl had slept the entire hour and a half in the car on the way back and now seemed to have a fresh wave of energy. Libby sighed and Jamie gave her a sheepish grin. Yes, he could have stopped Beauty if he'd wanted to, but if it meant that he wasn't turned away at the door, then he was prepared to play the untrained-dog card. It was even worth the fact that Beauty had chewed the upholstery of his car to shit whilst they'd been in the restaurant. Something that would normally have made Jamie go apoplectic.

"I guess... I guess you'd better come in," Libby said, her eyes flicking nervously to Rosie's bedroom door, which had slammed shut behind her and Beauty. "Tea?"

"Thanks," Jamie said, flopping down on her small sofa. He looked across the room and something on one of the shelves made him do a double take. "Woah!" he said, powering up to his feet to cover the short distance across the room. He lifted the Millennium Falcon from the shelf with the reverence it deserved, and turned to Libby. "This is insane. You've got the whole gang in here as well."

"Well, nearly. I had to sell the limited-edition Boba Fett. You know, the one that shoots actual rockets? They only made a few because it was considered too dangerous for kids. Once I found out how much he was worth I couldn't really justify keeping him," Libby said from his side, and he carefully put the ship back up on the shelf. "I should probably sell the rest. They wouldn't go for as much as Boba but it wouldn't be anything to be sniffed at. But... well ..." She shrugged and grinned up at him.

"You can't sell this," Jamie said.

"Yeah," Libby said, stroking the side of the first edition and highly sought after *Star Wars* toy lovingly. "I don't think I could bring myself to anyway." It was only then that Jamie realized how close they were standing. She smelt of the boat and her shampoo. Her hair had worked its way free of its confinement after her wake boarding efforts and was hanging around her face in wild waves.

Jamie had never encountered such a beautiful woman who seemed not to give a toss about her appearance. The only time he'd ever seen Libby wear make-up was when she was on stage, and her hair seemed a constant source of annoyance to her, rather than the plumage he knew other women would regard it as. He'd overheard her tell Amy that she would hack it off if she could, describing the stunning tresses as "a pain in my arse I could do without".

When his eyes caught hers he sucked in a breath at the intense blue colour that close up. Without any conscious thought, and totally at odds with the gradually-winning-her-over-and-convincing-her-I'm-not-a-total-dick plan he'd come up with on the drive over, his hand came up to her jaw and swept up into her hair at the side of her head. He leaned in until his mouth was a hair's breadth away from hers and searched her expression. Her pupils dilated and she took a sharp breath in, but she didn't pull away. He touched his mouth to hers and her eyes slid closed, shredding the last of his control.

The kiss started out soft, but as her hand came up to his waist and a small moan sounded in her throat he deepened it, backing her up until her calves hit the sofa, then pushing her down to lie across it. He hovered over her for a second before his mouth closed over hers again and her hands moved into his T-shirt to feel the muscles of his back. All his restraint was shot to pieces with the feel of her hands on his skin. His mouth left hers to kiss down her face into her neck, inhaling deeply from her hair as he stroked one hand down her arm to entwine her fingers with his. He brought their entwined hands above her head whilst his other hand traced a path down her side until he reached the hem of her T-shirt. But when he was finally touching the soft skin of her stomach a small giggle and a soft woof sounded from the room next door.

Jamie froze before lifting his head from Libby's neck abruptly. Her glazed eyes looked up at him in confusion and he felt like the biggest kind of lecherous arsehole alive. What the hell happened to asking her respectfully if she would consider dinner with him again? (This time without Rosie, and preferably tomorrow night.) Instead he'd practically jumped her, shoved his tongue down her throat in an all-out snogging session, and tried to cop a feel into the bargain.

He pulled back, lifting her with him, and gently steered her into a sitting position, before he shuffled away from her to the other end of the sofa (which, granted, was not very far, considering the minute size of the bloody thing).

Libby blinked and shook her head to clear it. That was her first kiss since she was seventeen years old and it was a blinder. Not that the sperm donor was a hard act to follow – if she remembered correctly there was a fair amount of saliva involved in those teenage kisses, to the extent that she'd taken to having a hand towel at the ready for the aftermath. But this kiss... this kiss was in a different universe. This kiss with soft, dry lips, the slight graze of stubble against her mouth, combined with the feel of the corded muscles of his back moving under the skin against her hand, had sent her a little insane.

Dr Grantham was without doubt the only *man* she had ever kissed. Sperm Donor may have ruled the school she was at and been a king in that small, closed environment, but he was only ever a boy. However, Dr Grantham was rubbing both his hands down his face now and sitting as far away from her as possible. Clearly the kiss hadn't been up to his high standards. He was probably used to women who'd had more than a few teenage fumbles of experience to draw on. She felt heat rise to her face and stood abruptly from the sofa.

"I'm going to check on Rosie," Libby announced, turning away from him to close the short distance to Rosie's room. Silence was never a good sign with her daughter. But when she opened the door it was to find a sound-asleep Beauty taking up most of Rosie's bed, with the little girl snoring into her fur. She closed it gently behind her, turned back to Dr Grantham and cleared her throat.

"They're asleep. I think–" She broke off when she realised how shaky her voice sounded, and took a deep breath to steady it. "I think you should go."

Dr Grantham pushed up from the sofa and took a step towards her. When she took one back he stopped and lifted a hand to rub the back of his neck. "Look, I'm sorry," he said. "I don't know what happened there."

Libby blinked back the stinging behind her eyes; he would not see her cry.

"Just leave," she muttered, crossing her arms over her chest.

"I... look... Libby, would you mind if...?" He trailed off and tipped his head back to look at the ceiling for a moment, as if searching for the right words. Libby's frown smoothed out and she put her head to one side as she watched the tips of his ears turn pink again. "Would you have dinner with me tomorrow night? I mean... without Rosie... not that Rosie's not great, but I... I... well ..." She had never heard him sound so unsure of himself; it was almost endearing. Almost.

"You want to take me out... on a date?" Libby asked in confusion.

"Well, yes," he told her. "Yes. If you want to..."

Libby glanced over at the tousled sofa. She hadn't been expecting that. An attempt to get into her knickers, yes, but not some sort of formal date invitation.

"Dr Grantham, I–"

"Libby," Dr Grantham groaned, a pained expression on his face. "Please, baby. Turn me down for a date. Kick me in the nuts – God knows I deserve it. Tell me to bugger off. But *please* don't call me Dr Grantham ever again." He moved into her personal space and took her face in his hands, resting his forehead on hers for a moment. "Please, Libby," he whispered against her mouth.

"Please what?" she whispered back, feeling like she was going to pass out as a rush of adrenaline shot through her system.

"What's my name?"

"I –"

"Baby, what's my name?" His voice had dropped to a whisper-growl and Libby felt her ovaries jump in response.

"Jamie," she whispered, and a slow smile spread across his face.

"Good girl," he muttered in the whisper-growl again but this time against her lips. Libby thought she would pass out from the wave of pure lust shooting through her system as he pressed his mouth to hers to deepen the kiss. Then it was back to the loss of control from before. She reached up into his thick hair and his arms came around her to hold her to him, her softness against the hard planes of his chest and stomach.

He backed her up against the wall and reached under her top again to the skin of her stomach, then up to enclose one of her breasts in his hands. She sucked in a shocked breath at the contact and started to move against him, suddenly desperate for some sort of release. All the tension between them had been building over weeks and now felt like something needed to snap or she'd die. She made a desperate noise at the back of her throat. "Okay, baby," Jamie whispered against her neck, his hand at her breast gently tugging at her nipple through her bra as his other hand went down into the waistband of her jeans and then down inside her pants, parting her and finding just the right place. He entered her with one finger and then pressed his thumb exactly where it needed to be. She writhed against him as he worked a slow rhythm, quickening his pace as she grew tighter and tighter. A low ringing sounded in her ears as the tension built and then she was shot over the edge, contracting against him as wave after wave of bliss overtook her. If he hadn't been holding her up after that she would have fallen to the floor in a boneless heap, but his arms came around her and held her to him as he kissed her lightly on her lips and the corner of her mouth.

"Okay," she muttered, her ears still ringing and the lightheaded feeling still persistent. "Wow, okay. That was... er... I don't usually..." She felt her cheeks flood with heat as the reality of the situation started to seep into her consciousness and she started to try to pull away.

"I'm sorry, love," Jamie said softly. "I didn't mean to push you. I wasn't actually planning to..." he trailed off and two slashes of colour appeared on his cheekbones. "Believe it or not, I'm trying to take things slow here. I want to try to convince you to trust me. To give me a chance. I wanted to start with a date."

"I guess I could get Kira to babysit," she told him, clearing her throat when her voice came out hoarse.

The corners of Jamie's gorgeous eyes crinkled as his smile cranked up another notch. He leaned forward and kissed her again, lightly this time before pulling back slightly to give her some space. Libby straightened her top and then tucked her hair behind her ears, her face still burning.

"Great," he told her, shoving his hands in his pockets. The tips of his ears were bright pink again and the sight managed to make the corners of Libby's mouth turn up almost involuntarily. They stood there smiling at each other like a couple of weirdos for a full minute before Libby's eyes flicked over to Rosie's door.

"I'd better get Beauty then, and head off."

Libby nodded and they both moved to Rosie's bedroom together, that current shooting up her arm again as she brushed against him.

"Crap," groaned Jamie as he looked at the sleeping girl and dog. "She's a bugger to move when she's like this." He went over to the side of the bed and gently prised Rosie away from the huge mound of fur, before slipping his arms under Beauty's front legs and attempting to lift her. When he staggered back slightly, Libby shot forward to grab Beauty's back end and they both hobbled out with the massive dog between them into the living room.

"Can't you wake her up?" Libby puffed, stumbling as she lost her grip on the mountain of fur.

"Not a good idea," Jamie muttered darkly.

"Jesus, she smells like socks and arse."

Jamie huffed out a laugh. "She's not too partial to water; goes ballistic when I try to shower her."

"Who's the boss out of the two of you?"

"Oh, her, definitely her."

Libby giggled and got another mouthful of arse-smelling hair as they started moving towards the door. "Aren't you supposed to be leader of the pack or something?" It was strange how incongruous this dog was with Jamie's perfectly controlled life. Libby remembered Jamie's story about the rescue centre again and it dispelled some of the regret she had for accepting the dinner invitation. Maybe he was a bit stuck-up but he was kind. His attitude to Rosie had proved that already.

Jamie snorted. "This dog is a sociopath. In her world she reigns supreme. Look, if you give her butt a shove up here I can..." He hefted Beauty up more securely into his arms with an impressive bulging of his biceps against his T-shirt, which, despite the smell in her nostrils, still managed to give Libby a punch in the ovaries. "You can let go now," he told her, and she took a cautious step back. Luckily Beauty stayed suspended up against his chest. "I'll see you tomorrow?"

"Oh... uh..." Libby swallowed and tucked her hair behind her ears again. To say she was rusty with the whole dating thing was a massive understatement, seeing as she'd never actually *done* the whole dating thing (unless a few fumbles behind the back of the local Co-op and a very unsatisfactory introduction to sex in the damp basement of her teenage sperm donor's parents' house counted). Somehow going out to dinner with a grown man seemed almost ludicrous. She'd spent most of her adult life fending off male attention, either at the club or at uni, with the small percentage of guys who thought that *single teenage mum* was code for *rampant slut*. "Uh..."

"Libby," Jamie's voice was now strained and she could see a slight tremor running through his arms as he continued to hold up the dead weight of Beauty between them, "I don't want to sound wet, but if I don't run this dog down to the car in the next ten seconds I think I'll be getting renal failure from rhabdomyolysis."

Libby blinked. Somehow a lame medical joke from an actual real doctor (rhabdomyolysis is when you strain your muscles so much that they breakdown and leach protein into the blood stream, which can clog up the kidneys) made him seem even older, even more out of her league than before. She bit her lip.

"Libby... I–"

"*Yes*," she blurted out. Fuck it; she was tired of playing it safe. Tired of controlling every aspect of her life so that it didn't fall apart. She was going to do something for *her* for once. Take a break from begging, borrowing and stealing for an evening.

He smiled over the top of his dog and then turned to stagger away. "Seven okay?" he shouted over his shoulder, his voice breaking slightly with effort as he started down the stairs.

"Okay," she whispered, unable to make her voice any stronger as she heard the bang of the downstairs fire door behind him.

When she turned the lock and leaned back against the door she looked down at her feet and smiled. A minute later she jumped away from the thin wood, clutching her chest in shock at the banging which had vibrated her body. She spun around and wrenched it open to be confronted by Jamie's unhappy face.

"You didn't check to see who it was," he said accusingly, and she rolled her eyes.

"I knew it was you. You only left a second ago."

He ignored her and pulled her door open wide, giving it a visual once-over. "You don't *have* a peephole," he announced something she already knew. "And you don't have a keychain."

"Well, I don't really need a–"

"Please don't finish that sentence," Jamie cut her off, his eyebrows now lowered in a frown. "This block of flats must be the least secure in London. The downstairs door isn't locked and there's no intercom; any old bastard could wander up to your flat, knock on your door, and then, when you open it, without checking the goddamn peephole, he could shove you inside: game over."

Libby narrowed her eyes and put her hands on her hips. She'd been looking after herself for a long time now, and she had never taken kindly to be told what to do.

"I don't think this is really any of your–"

"Look, I'm sorry baby, but if you say one more time that you aren't any of my business my head will explode." Libby started in surprise at the endearment, but he wasn't nearly finished. "It wound me up before, but now, after... well... your sofa ..." He trailed off and his ears went bright red before he cleared his throat to finish. "Well, now it is nothing short of infuriating."

Libby felt her cheeks heat. "Jamie, listen–"

"Right, so forget seven tomorrow night," he told her, and she blinked, disappointment flooding through her with surprising intensity. "I'll be here at *five*; I'm going to put on a key chain and install a peephole."

Her mouth dropped open. "You can't do that. I'd have to check with the landlord and–"

"*I'll* be talking to your landlord," Jamie said, his voice low with anger, and Libby instantly decided to keep Mr Tully's contact details to herself. Before she could say anything Jamie leaned forward to give her a brief hard kiss on the lips, and turned to leave. She considered shouting out after him but thought better of it when she saw Mrs Stricklen's door crack open; not that Mrs Stricklen would have minded a shouting match in the corridor – it would probably make her day – but Libby had no intention of giving her any more fodder to bring up at the next residents' meeting. No, she would set him straight tomorrow. She closed the door and wandered back into the kitchen to put the kettle on. A few moments later she jumped about a mile in the air when there was another burst of knocking.

"What?" she shouted.

"At least," Jamie said through the door with what sounded like a great deal of patience, "please, at least lock the locks you *do* have." Libby blew out a breath and stormed over to turn the lock.

"Happy now?" she asked.

"No, but I will be."

Chapter 17

Thundercats are cool

"Ah, it's Big Syringe, Little Syringe and his sidekick Dick Doc," Kira said as she strolled past the two men working on Libby's door, carrying a strangely large bag for just one night's babysitting. "How's it going, boys? Looks like you two are regular *DIY SOS* heroes."

"I can still go back and mark that report down you know," muttered Pav as he continued to screw in the last of the screws to the key chain. Jamie had arrived at Libby's at four, having ransacked Homebase for what he hoped were the appropriate tools. When confronted with the door, however, he realised that he had no earthly idea how to install either a key chain or a peephole, and that perhaps simply relying on his masculine instincts was not the most stellar plan. So he interrupted Pav's Sunday, as he knew the lazy bastard would have nothing better to do, making him bring over his drill and hopefully a bit of expertise. The drill was luckily working; the expertise... sadly lacking. But after a painful couple of hours the finish line was at last in sight, with male pride thankfully salvaged.

"Auntie Ki Ki!" Rosie shouted, dropping the screwdriver she had been holding on Jamie's bare foot.

"Sh–" he started, but managed to hold the rest in by biting his lip.

"He's always on about ships, Auntie Ki Ki," Rosie told her, and Kira barked out a laugh.

"I bet he is, babygirl." She bent down to pick Rosie up and gave her a squeeze. "So you're helping out Tweedle Dee and Tweedle Dumber here are you?"

"They kind of *need* helping," Rosie replied in a stage whisper. "Jamie hit his fingie with the hammer, and the other one made the sheep-mole too high." Kira looked over at the peephole set at the perfect height for a man of six-foot-two, then across to her five-foot-five friend, and burst out laughing again. "It's okay "cause Mummy's going to stand on my step to see out of the sheep-mole, aren't you, Mummy?"

Jamie glanced over at Libby to see that her lips were pressed together and her eyes were dancing. He sighed; maybe masculine pride hadn't been altogether salvaged.

"Thanks for coming, Kir," Libby said, her voice shaking with suppressed laughter as she hugged her friend. "You're a lifesaver."

"Of course I'd come. *You* on an actual real *date*? It's some kind of miracle. I was only going to mooch about the hospital accommodation anyway."

Jamie caught Libby's headshake as she mouthed "*Shut up*" to Kira, and he cocked his head to the side with curiosity.

"What was that?" he asked, abandoning his attempts to replace all Pav's drill bits into the case and straightening up to look over at the girls.

"Libby here is renowned for her skills in the art of rejection. I swear she's so accomplished at it now she could probably reject a bloke in her sleep and let him down gently in the process. I've never known her even accept a cheeky glass of cheap Pinot from a man before; so you, my friend, are off into unchartered territory... Ow!" Kira broke off to rub her ribs, which had been on the receiving end of a vicious poke from Libby. "She's violent too," she added before Libby managed to close a hand over her mouth and back her towards Rosie's bedroom. Jamie glanced at his watch.

"Libby, it's nearly seven-thirty," he said at the now closed bedroom door. "Er... if it's okay with you, we'd better go soon."

The door swung open and a determined-looking Kira strutted in, grabbed her bag off the floor, then turned to Jamie.

"Give me five minutes, Big Syringe, okay? I swear you won't regret it." She went to go back to the bedroom but paused and turned to Jamie again instead. "I'm giving you a pass for tonight," she told him as she got closer, her voice now lowered and a determined expression on her face. "The only reason I'm letting you off the hook for the shit you've said to Libby is because of the way you've been looking after them over the last few weeks. But I *swear* you say one more thing to make her feel like crap and I will cut your dick off and feed it to the badgers. Get me?"

Jamie rubbed the back of his neck. "I'm trying–"

"Try harder," she snapped, cutting him off. "I haven't seen Libby interested in a man since she was seventeen and that did not end well. The last thing I want now is my best friend asking me if I think she's a slut over a dodgy lunch in the canteen."

Jamie felt the blood drain out of his face and a tight band around his chest. "I... I never meant to..." He clenched his jaw and shoved his hands into his pockets. "I promise I'll make it up to her. I swear I will."

Kira watched him for a moment through narrowed eyes then gave a short nod. "Okay," she told him as she stalked back to the bedroom. "But, if you feel the urge to be a dick again, just remember the badgers and think again."

"What's wrong with what I'm wearing?" Libby asked. Kira flashed her an irate look as she dug through her huge bag. She then dumped her make-up case on the bed, before spinning to face Libby with her hands on her hips.

"Tell me you were *not* going out like this," Kira asked, exasperation lacing her tone. Libby threw up her hands.

"I'm not going to meet the Queen, Kira, you nutter. I'm just going to eat somewhere with an ordinary bloke."

"He's not going to be taking you to Pizza bloody Express, Libby. Trust me, you should wear something nice."

"What I'm wearing is nice." Libby looked down at her T-shirt; yes, it was a little faded and there may be a small rip in the seam, but still ...

"Is that... ?" Kira leaned in further and then snorted as she pulled away. "You have a Thundercat above your right breast."

Libby shrugged, feeling defensive all of a sudden. "Thundercats are cool, okay?"

"No Libby. Thundercats were cool in the nineteen eighties. If you were seven. Now, and at your age: not so much. All I'm suggesting is that for a date with a man like the one currently buggering up your front door – who in my opinion, and I suspect yours, is not an ordinary bloke by any stretch – you might want to make a bit more of an effort." She stepped forward and grabbed Libby's hand. "The ripped jeans and faded Thundercats T-shirt – it looks rude, sweetheart."

Libby yanked her hand away and stepped back. "Well, I'm sorry but I don't *have* anything else. You can check if you like. Ugh! Why am I even bothering? Why did I even agree to this?"

She sat down heavily on Rosie's bed and put her head in her hands. "I'm just going to embarrass him," she whispered at the floor.

"Hey," Kira said, sitting down beside her and pulling her in for a tight hug. "You could go out with that man wearing a bin liner and still be the hottest piece of arse in the room and he would be damn lucky to be with you." Libby snorted into her hands and Kira hugged her even tighter. "Look, I know you haven't got anything to wear. That's why I brought all this crap over for you."

"I can't borrow your stuff, Ki-Ki. My boobs won't fit into any of it."

"Well, Miss Negativity, I assure you they will fit into this." With a flourish Kira pulled out a suit bag and then from within it a beautiful pale-cream floaty dress with a high neck and short capped sleeves adorned with a row of nude-coloured beading, which ran into the low back. Libby's mouth dropped open as a pair of nude high heels followed.

"Did you *buy* these for me?" she asked, smoothing a hand over the gauzy material of the dress. Kira nodded and hastily removed the price part of the tags before Libby could make a grab for it. Libby pulled her hand away.

"I can't accept th–"

"Stop right there," Kira snapped, shocking her with the amount of anger in her tone. "Who helped me get through every exam, including my bloody A-levels when you were the size of a small planet? Who pushed Robbie Gates over when he was bullying me in Year 2? Who told me I wasn't thick like the teachers always assured me I was? Who encouraged me to apply for medicine? Who made me do my Duke of Edinburgh award so my CV wasn't complete rubbish when I applied?"

"Ki- Ki, I–"

"I'm giving you this *fucking* dress and these *fucking* heels and you are going to *fucking* well accept them." Repeated use of the f-word was a danger sign that Kira was reaching her limit of patience. Libby pressed her lips together for a moment as she gazed down at the dress.

"Thank you, Ki-Ki," she whispered, aiming a tremulous smile at Kira.

"Oh, you daft bugger," Kira said; but her own voice broke and her eyes were suspiciously wet as she pulled Libby in for another hug. "Right," she muttered as she pulled away and surreptitiously wiped under her eyes. "Get changed, then let me work my magic."

Ten minutes later a new and improved Libby stepped out of the bedroom.

"Fu–" Pav started to say, as his grip on Rosie's woodlice box slipped and it nearly fell to the floor before he could grab it again. His wide eyes flicked from Libby to Rosie. "I mean, clucking bell. You look–"

"Incredible," Jamie cut in, standing up from the sofa and staring at her with his mouth slightly open. The dress was perfect: it skimmed her figure in a way Libby was comfortable with (unless she was working she was not into showing much skin or making too much of her "assets"), and she had allowed Kira to use just a hint of nude, slightly shimmery eye-shadow and mascara with very light pink tinted lip-gloss. Kira had insisted she wear her hair down but did at least pull back the front portion to secure it in a clip.

Libby hadn't been sure about all the fuss and bother, and she was definitely feeling bad about taking the dress and shoes, but when she saw Jamie swallow and the tips of his ears go red she knew she'd done the right thing.

"You look like a pwincess, Mummy," Rosie said, her voice full of wonder, having never seen her mother in anything like what she was wearing. Libby smiled at her and then her gaze went back to Jamie. For a long moment they were both frozen, just staring at each other across the room. Kira's clapping cut through the tension and they turned to her.

"Right, kids, time to go," Kira said, ushering them to the door. "You too, Cock Doc. Take those power tools of yours and get."

"Aunty Ki-Ki," Rosie said, her little face now red with anger, "I am showing Mr Pavie my woodlice. He can't leave yet."

"Rosie, I–" Pav said, starting to hand back the box to her.

"Sit. Down," she told him, her voice surprisingly low and menacing for a four-year-old, and he let her push him over to the squashy sofa, where he sank down amongst the copious mismatched throw cushions.

"Be safe, you two," Pav called as he tried to hide his grimace when Rosie opened up the woodlouse box, which she'd plonked on his lap. Jamie ushered Libby out of the flat before she could change her mind.

Chapter 18

I don't have a choice

"So, what do you fancy?" Jamie asked. Libby bit her lip and read the menu.

"I ..." she cleared her throat, "I like everything, so... you choose." She closed the menu with visible relief and smiled across at him.

"Uh... okay," he said slowly, returning her smile with a slightly bemused one of his own. Libby sat back in her chair and pushed her hair behind her ears. She started twisting her fingers on the table in front of her, but when she noticed him focusing on them she quickly tucked them out of sight in her lap.

"Libby, what's wrong?" Jamie asked softly. He had closed the menu and laid it down next to his place setting, all his attention on her.

"What? I'm fine." She forced the brightest fake smile she could manage but it only made Jamie's frown deepen.

"You've been tense since we got here. Is it something I've done or–"

"No, no, of course not. Just... just ignore me."

Jamie's eyes went to the ceiling for a moment before he started chuckling and rubbing the back of his neck. "Libby, not sure how your dates normally go, but in general I try to avoid ignoring the other person. Look, if you don't like Thai we don't have to–"

"I've never eaten Thai food," Libby blurted out, her eyes on her spoon, which she had started fiddling with. "I've never eaten anywhere like this, okay? The closest I've ever been to a proper restaurant is Pizza Express and that's only when I've got all the vouchers that mean you pay about a fiver. I've eaten Chinese takeaway and curries at Mum and Dad's but ..." she threw her hands up "... well, you don't order Thai food in. At least not in my family. So... I ..." Her cheeks flushed pink, and she face-planted into her hands on the table. "Ugh, this is embarrassing." Her voice was muffled but she knew Jamie had still heard when he reached across the table and prised one of her hands away to take it firmly in his.

"Life interrupted," he muttered as he searched the beet-root-red side of her face that was now visible. She frowned as she slowly lowered her other hand.

"What?"

"Pregnant at seventeen, A-levels, then baby, then medical school. All you've done is work or look after Rosie since you were a child yourself." Libby looked to the side and shrugged one shoulder. "Listen, I'll talk you through the menu. Order what you think you might like. If you hate it we'll leave, go to my place and order pizza with Beauty." When she pressed her lips together and gave a short nod he sighed. "Honestly, it's fine, even if you hate it. Pav can't stand Thai food – something about a bad Pad Thai, a lady-boy he mistook for the real thing, and a drug-fuelled full-moon party on Ko Pha Ngan."

Libby's eyes widened for a moment before she burst out laughing, and just like that she didn't feel stupid anymore.

Jamie understood why she'd never eaten somewhere like this, he understood that it wasn't a life choice she'd made. Life choices were a luxury a single mother studying medicine did not have.

This was not the attitude of the majority of her fellow students. She'd seen them roll their eyes when she declined even a seemingly innocuous trip to the pub – but drinks cost money, childcare costs money (it's not like she could ask Kira to babysit when Kira herself would be the life and soul of the party at said pub; and, despite Kira's efforts, she had to keep her parents reserved for when she worked – that was enough of an imposition). When you wear scrubs to bed instead of buying pajamas, when you buy value ketchup instead of Heinz, when you wear your shoes until they have holes in the soles – then you could judge someone in her position.

Jamie watched Libby laugh, and felt his stomach hollow out at how beautiful her face was when it was lit with humour, and a surge of pride that he had managed to make it happen. Every male in that restaurant, and more than likely a few females, had noticed Libby. Her incredible blue eyes highlighted by subtle make-up, combined with that dress, made her look so beautiful it was almost otherworldly. Jamie had never felt such fierce resentment at having the woman he was with be openly admired by so many people. He was not by nature a very possessive man, but he found himself wishing as they moved through the tables that he'd just taken them back to his place and cooked her a shepherd's pie. (His shepherd's pie was bloody good – even if Pav did tell him he cooked like an elderly northerner during the Blitz.) And when she was so obviously uncomfortable sitting across from him, he was definitely regretting his decision to bring her out. But after what she'd told him...

He understood it; he did, given her situation. But for a woman as charismatic and beautiful as her – to have never been taken out for a meal, never eaten in a restaurant, never been on a date was insane.

"So, were you with Pav on Ko Pha Ngan?" Libby asked through her smile. "Any class-A drugs or lady-boy run-ins for you?"

"No, no way. I would never take any ..." Jamie cleared his throat and lightened his tone, hoping she hadn't noticed how touchy he was about drugs. "I was busy poncing around Central America in sarong trousers, trying to find myself." Libby's smile widened and she leaned forward into her hands on the table.

"Central America? Like Mexico, Honduras, Belize, Guatamala? What was it like? Rosie and I look at our globe at home and then we Google the countries – I think she reckons it's to prep for her work on the high seas. Central America looks amazing."

And so he told her about diving in Honduras, about the Mayan ruins in Belize, about the old American school buses they rode around in on their backpacker budget, stuffed with chickens and Mexicans. Even after their food had arrived she kept teasing out everything about his travels, everything he'd done in those long summers at medical school. Unlike his friends, Jamie had never had to work to earn the money to go away, so the entirety of his summers could be spent swanning around the globe, learning to dive, learning to windsurf, learning to ski, learning to sail: he'd done it all. And it was the only time he didn't have to succumb to the unrelenting pressure of perfection.

After some pushing it came to light that Libby had never

actually been on a plane. Her parents had taken her to Spain and France in their camper van as a child, but since Rosie she had just taken little trips in this country – the last one was last summer (possibly the wettest in recent memory). She'd borrowed a tent from a friend to take with her and Rosie to Cornwall. Brian had broken down twice. The tent had leaked and Rosie had ended up in Libby's sleeping bag once she'd started shivering with cold. It made Jamie feel like a horse's arse for banging on about his world travels for so long, but Libby had been so totally enraptured by his stories and asked so many questions that she was impossible to resist.

"That was the best bloody stuff I've ever eaten," she declared after putting away an impressive amount of pad Thai and red curry. "I feel like Mr Creosote."

"One wafer-thin mint?" Jamie asked in a bad French accent.

"Bring me a bucket," Libby growled, puffing her cheeks out and then collapsing into another fit of giggles. And watching her laugh, noticing the people nearest to them stop to watch her too (some with forks suspended in mid air) Jamie blurted out something he should probably have thought through first.

"Spend the weekend with me."

Libby's giggles turned into a coughing fit at his statement. He'd noticed her cough off and on before now and had been meaning to ask her about it, but decided it could wait for now, too keen to hear her response.

"Uh... what?" she managed to get out after the coughing subsided.

"Next weekend. Spend it with me. You and Rosie can stay in my house."

She smiled. "Wow, that's... well, that's an amazing offer but I don't know if I should confuse Rosie when it's so early on and we don't really know each other. So–"

"I know you. I know Rosie. This might be our first dinner alone but we've spent a ton of time together already. Say yes."

"I..." She trailed off and bit her lip. He could sense her wavering.

"Mum and Dad are having their monthly family barbeque on the Saturday. Seb will be there for Rosie to play with." He wanted her to meet his parents. He wanted her and Rosie surrounded by his family; somehow it felt like that would stake a claim on her – make this all more real. He had the sudden desire to pull her into his life, into his family's life, like she was his, like she belonged there. But as soon as he said the word "Mum" he saw her stiffen in his seat and watched as her smile died and her beautiful face drained of colour.

"Varping heck, what time is it?" she asked, looking down at her watch. Jamie smiled; he'd noticed Libby only ever used swear words from a galaxy far, far away, and guessed that having a four-year-old would probably do that to you. "We'd better be going – Kira's got a bit of a trek back to her place and we've an early tutorial with–"

"I mean it, Libby," he said, "I really would like you to come."

Libby's mouth tightened and she looked down at the table. "No... no you don't," she whispered.

"I don't understand. Of course I –"

"I heard you, Jamie, remember? I heard what you said."

Jamie's heart sank to his stomach and his faced flushed at the memory.

"Can you please forget about that? I was being a total knob, trying to save face. If I could go back I'd–"

"I'm working this weekend anyway," she told him, leaning back into her chair. He could see the shields coming back up around her to shut him out. His mind flashed to the image of her in her Victoria's Secret number in the club and a violent flash of rage went through his body. With a supreme effort of will he suppressed the anger, balling his hands into tight fists under the table and breathing slowly to control his voice.

"Why don't you skip it this weekend?" he asked, forcing what he hoped would pass for a casual smile but likely came out more like a grimace. "If you don't want to go to Mum and Dad's, I could take you guys out on the boat again and we could–"

"I can't *"skip it","* Libby told him carefully. "I don't have that luxury."

"Surely just one weekend wouldn't–"

"I have the final payment for Brian's repairs –" she held up her hands and started counting off on her fingers "–a term of swimming lessons to pay for, another month of nursery fees to find, an electricity bill to pay, and do you know how much I have in my current account, Jamie? Do you?"

"Libby, I–"

"I have exactly eighty-eight pounds and seventy-five pence in my current account. And I have to pay for these things *next week*. I have to sort it out *now*. Not in two weeks' time or whenever I can be bothered. This shit is relentless. My *life* is relentless. You have no bloody idea what it's–"

"I could give you the money," Jamie threw out in desperation, and then swore under his breath as Libby's jaw clenched tight and her face flushed red.

"If you *ever* make that type of suggestion again," she hissed. "I will punch you right in your arrogant face."

Jamie groaned. "I didn't mean it like that. I just can't stand the thought of you..." He broke off. What he really couldn't stand was her working there, wearing her underwear and being ogled by hundreds of men. But he knew that any objections along those lines would be met with hostility. "It's too much for you. You need to concentrate on your degree and have more time for Rosie."

"I don't have a choice," she said, her voice breaking before she cleared her throat to carry on. "I do what I have to do to look after my daughter, to get her a brighter future. You can tell your mother exactly why I'm not at the family barbeque. I'm sure that would make for a relaxed lunch convo – how you're dating a single mum-slash-stripper, and how the lady in question can't make it because she's got to shake her tits and arse for some random blokes so she can afford her kid's nursery fees. I'm sure Mummy Dearest will be *clamouring* to meet me."

Any reply Jamie could have made was luckily interrupted by the arrival of the bill. He received another glare from Libby as he paid on his credit card without letting her see the amount, despite her protests. After he was done he stood up, walked to her side of the table, reached for her hand and pulled her to standing, then prowled out of the restaurant with her in tow.

Once outside she stumbled in her heels and he caught her before she went down. "Can we maybe make it home without me breaking an ankle?" She shook off his hold and took a step back, eyeing him warily, and if he was honest he wasn't surprised. He was acting like a lunatic – but the whole stripping thing, coupled with the fact he had so obviously lost control of the way the date was supposed to go, had made him a little crazy.

"Right," he said, one hand going to the back of his neck, the other to rest on his hip. He looked down at the pavement for a moment, then back up at her wary eyes. "Can we rewind twenty minutes? Could you forget what I said about the family barbeque and your work and... well... the thing is... I'm sorry. And if you don't forgive me, again, then my penis is going to end up as badger food."

Chapter 19

Women have needs

"Hey girls," Jamie called as he let himself into the flat. Once inside and after a brief kiss and hug for Rosie (who was too busy for a longer greeting due to some sort of woodlouse emergency), he dumped the latest bunch of flowers on the side, crossed his arms over his chest and glared over at Libby in the kitchen. "The door was open."

Libby rolled her eyes. "Yes, I got one of your bossy little texts; I knew you were on your way over, so I left it ajar. You're lucky I didn't lock my new deadbolt."

Jamie smiled and moved to her, leaving the flowers where they were. Over the last three weeks since date night he had brought her something nearly every day; either leaving it in her pigeonhole at the hospital or ferrying it over to her flat. Sometimes it was bits of geeky memorabilia he knew she'd like, sometimes flowers. And yes, he was gradually wearing her down. His private parts were safe from the badgers for now, and he'd promised faithfully to keep his opinions about her work to himself.

That didn't stop him from being his normal dictatorial self, especially about her and Rosie's safety. He wouldn't let them take the bus after dark, didn't trust Brian "the death trap on wheels", and was always on at Libby about the flat's security.

He raised his eyebrows and Libby bit her lip to suppress a smile, before she wiped her hands dry on a dishcloth and walked across to him. "Don't be cross," she said as she slipped her arms around his middle, kissed the underside of his jaw and then laid her head against his chest.

It was the first bit of spontaneous affection Libby had ever initiated with him. She felt him stiffen in shock before he engulfed her in his big arms, pressing her body to his almost fiercely.

"Lock the door when you're here alone," he said into her hair. "Or at least bloody well *close* the door. You've not used the keychain or the peephole once."

"Mm-hm," Libby muttered against his chest, breathing in the delicious smell of washing powder and Jamie combined.

Of course he was a fantastic cuddler.

That much she knew already.

After the awkward end of what could have been a fantastic first date (had he not put his foot in it and Libby not lost her formidable temper), Jamie had not been deterred. He'd come round the next night with Beauty and a peace offering (this being a Mother of Dragons *Game of Thrones* mug) and stayed for macaroni cheese.

Rosie had watched them during the meal and seen Jamie kiss Libby on the temple when he thanked her. Libby wasn't sure how Rosie was going to react but when they were settling on the sofa after supper, Rosie told Jamie that "Mummy likes kisses and cuddles *all the time*." This was accompanied by a way-too-advanced-for-her-age eye-roll before she went on to say: "It's good you can help. Sometimes *I'm* too busy."

Libby had laughed at the implication that Rosie's schedule,

which, other than nursery and her swimming and ballet lessons, mostly involved dancing attendance on her woodlice, did not allow for copious cuddles – but her laughter had died at Jamie's reply.

"Well that's okay," he'd told Rosie, pulling Libby down onto the sofa next to him and tucking her into his side, "because I'm *very* good at cuddles and kisses, so we're all set." He'd smiled at Rosie and then given Libby a smaller but vastly different kind of smile accompanied by a wink, which for some reason she felt shoot through her body down to her toes.

Rosie and Beauty both fell asleep on Rosie's bed again, and Jamie prised out of Libby her entire life story – acting as if various holidays her family had been on to Skegness were just as interesting as his adventures around the world.

After the Thai Restaurant Argument, he'd avoided the subject of her work and simply planned on seeing her and Rosie around her schedule, but she knew he was still bothered by it. The way his jaw would get tight when he saw her bags packed ready to go, or the way he'd scowl at her phone whenever someone connected from the club rang (she had Lady Marmalade as her ringtone for work which he'd figured early on), would suggest that he hadn't changed his opinion of the way she earned her money, but was smart enough not to bring it up again.

To be honest, Libby was glad. She enjoyed being with this more relaxed Jamie who made her laugh, was kind to her daughter, and was so handsome that he still sometimes made her catch her breath when he smiled, and she didn't want to have to fight him the whole time about the unfortunate hard facts of her life: that she had to earn money and still have time for Rosie, her study, and survival.

In fact, she liked Jamie so much it had started to scare her a little. He drove her home, all the way home, from work most days. The unreliable Brian had been semi-retired. All four of them (including Beauty) spent the majority of their evenings together at her flat (Rosie's bedtime was seven and Libby didn't want to confuse her by putting her to bed at Jamie's house), and after Rosie was in bed Jamie would set out to prove his "cuddling" abilities. Libby had revision to do but he seemed content to read whilst she studied, both of them curled up on the sofa together.

He would even test her on the most boring stuff imaginable when she was done with a subject, claiming he enjoyed revision and exams (given the number of letters after his name this might even be true). Libby knew her life was dull. She might be content, ecstatic even, to be spending every evening with him, but she couldn't imagine why a gorgeous single man would want to spend his spare time ferrying around a mother and a four-year-old and be stuck in their dingy flat with them every evening.

Maybe – *maybe* – she'd understand if they were doing anything other than what could only be described as non-sexual hugging. At least, for him it seemed to be non-sexual. Libby's mind was so far in the gutter whilst in close quarters with Jamie that one evening, after half an hour of supposedly taking notes on renal failure, all she'd managed to do was a badly drawn Storm Trooper mask, an Ewok, and *Star Trek* logo. Her frustration was gradually ramping up but Jamie seemed completely oblivious, and seeing as her experience with men was limited to a couple of teenage fumbles she did not feel qualified to push the subject.

He'd even cooked for them twice; unfortunately, one of those times he put some chilli in the pasta sauce. Rosie had taken one bite, her eyes had gone wide and she spat it out before jumping down from the table and running to her stool so she could reach the kitchen tap and wash her tongue for a good ten minutes. It took no less than three rocket lollies before she would calm down, and the next time Jamie presented her with food he'd prepared (a guaranteed favourite of sausages) she'd sniffed them, poked them for an inordinate amount of time and then fully dissected them before risking a bite.

Other than the "Volcano Mouth" incident, as Rosie had dubbed it, there was no question that if the elder Penny female wasn't in love with him now, the younger one was a goner. Rosie let him read to her at bedtime; in fact she *demanded* it if he was there, declaring that he did "a better Gruffulo voice than you, Mummy".

They went out on his boat again on the weekend that Libby wasn't working, this time with Pavlos and Kira instead of his family. Within ten minutes Kira had pushed Pav into the Solent fully clothed after he'd asked her how she'd managed to get into medical school when she was clearly a psychopath: "Don't they have some sort of psychological testing to keep the nutters out nowadays?"

It was safe to say that Jamie and Libby's best friends were fairly volatile in each other's company – but for Libby, whose only real friend was Kira, the banter, the chaos and the attention they all gave her daughter was heaven.

Okay, so, yes, she was falling for Jamie in more ways than one...

"Hello my little cutie-pies!" Kira's sing-song voice made Libby jump in Jamie's arms. Before she could even turn to look at the door an over-excited Kira had shot over to them and wiggled her way under Jamie's arm.

"Auntie Ki-Ki!" Rosie shouted, abandoning her woodlice and squeezing her own way into the group hug.

"Isn't this cosy," said Kira, kissing the tip of Rosie's nose and snaking her arms around both Jamie and Libby to give them a firm squeeze. She then rested her head on Jamie's shoulder and blinked up at him. "You smell yummy, Big Syringe," she said in a dreamy voice. Libby rolled her eyes, pulled her arms free and pushed everyone apart, keeping hold of Rosie and setting her on her hip.

"Kira, what are you doing here?" she asked.

"Well, that's not much of a welcome. Not when I've come for a sleepover with my favourite Little Louse."

"Hurrah!" Rosie's arms shot up into the air and she started bouncing up and down on the spot. "Sleepover with Auntie Ki-Ki! Did you bring the popcorn?"

"Keep quiet about that, kid," Kira said out of the side of her mouth, tucking her handbag into her side with a suspicious rustle of packaging.

"But... but I didn't ask you to–" Libby started, but Kira cut her off.

"Listen, I think you and the big man need a bit of... alone time. Comprende?" Kira's voice dipped low for "alone time" and she gave Libby a big exaggerated wink. Blood rushed to Libby's face and her mouth dropped open. She *knew* she should not have confided in Kira about her frustration where Jamie was concerned. About how he'd given her the most amazing orgasm then backed off in an attempt to take things slow and win her trust. He was going to think Libby was a raging nympho if Kira kept on like this. The man in question's eyes were dancing as he pressed his lips together until he lost his battle and smiled.

"Now, off you go, kids." Kira shuffled them both out towards the door and thrust a small overnight bag into Libby's hands. "You're going to have your own sleepover, right?"

"Can Beauty stay here with us?" asked Rosie, clearly more concerned about being separated from the dog than her own mother. Kira sighed.

"The beast can stay," she said in a long-suffering tone. "But *no drool.*" She turned and pointed at Beauty. The dog's big head tipped to the side and a huge globule of clear spittle fell from the side of her mouth onto the purple rug. Kira's face scrunched in disgust. "Get out before I change my mind," she said, hustling Libby and Jamie towards the door. "I'll see you both tomorrow." She whispered something in Jamie's ear, which Libby couldn't quite catch, and his eyebrows shot up into his hairline before he stepped out into the hallway, pulling Libby with him.

"I... Ki-Ki–"

Whatever Libby was about to say was cut off as the door slammed in her face. Burning with humiliation, she turned towards Jamie, whose shoulders were shaking with suppressed laughter. Libby narrowed her eyes at him.

"What did she say to you?"

Jamie reached across and grabbed her overnight bag, slinging it over one shoulder. Libby dreaded to think what kind of nightwear Kira had thought to pack for her. She wasn't even sure Kira owned pajamas. The last time she'd stayed over she'd slept completely naked, saying she felt constricted by clothes in her sleep and that her vagina and breasts needed complete freedom at night. Libby wasn't so sure that Kira's vagina and breasts needed to be totally free whilst lying on *her* sofabed, but as Kira had been doing her a favour she hadn't wanted to argue.

"Nothing," Jamie said, a little too quickly and with a disconcerting smirk on his face as he reached for Libby's hand, engulfing it in his own.

"Okay... right." Jamie stood facing Libby across his kitchen island. The last three weeks with Libby had been wonderful and excruciatingly painful at the same time. But he was being careful: making sure Libby knew how serious he was; not pushing her too fast.

Women have needs, Big Syringe. Kira's whispered words floated through his brain again. The thought that Libby might have been feeling even a fraction of the frustration he was suffering twenty-four seven had galvanised him into action. As he'd ushered Libby to his car and then into his house, his only aim had been to get her alone and start working on fulfilling her "needs".

The drive over had been torture. But now that she was here, doubt started creeping in. What if Libby hadn't confided in Kira? What if she was happy with how things were going, intimacy-wise?

"So..." he trailed off, then yanked open a kitchen drawer, grabbing a few takeaway menus. "Let's get a curry shall we, seeing as we don't have to worry about Rosie and Volcano Mouth?" Libby's cheeks were still pink and she still looked a little bewildered, but she dropped her bag on the floor and moved around the island to him.

"Uh... I guess I quite like this one," she said, her voice slightly hoarse as she leaned over the menu and pointed out the Lamb Rogan Josh. Her arm was touching his and he could smell her shampoo along with the faint floral scent of her skin. Instead of looking down to where she was pointing, he turned his head and looked at her instead. She blinked up at him with a sharp intake of breath before her eyes dropped to his mouth. A few wavy strands of her hair fell forward and his hand came up of its own accord to brush them behind her ear. Her eyes came back to his, pupils fully dilated now, and her lips parted.

That was it for Jamie. Weeks of frustration gave his body a mind of its own and he launched forward to kiss her. Not a gentle kiss, not at all the kind of kiss that he really should have given at this stage. No, his mouth was hard on hers, his hand in her hair tilting her head to exactly the angle he wanted, and his other hand pressed her body into his.

A small moan from her was all the encouragement he needed after that. He lifted her up so that her legs were wrapped around his hips. Without breaking the kiss he walked them both to his bedroom, kicking open the door and then falling onto the king-size bed so that she was lying beneath him as he balanced most of his weight on his elbows. Her eyes were wide and there was a hint of apprehension on her face that jolted him back to reality, making him feel like a total Neanderthal.

"Shit," he muttered as he swiped a thumb across the soft skin of her high cheekbone. "I'm sorry. I don't know what happened. I don't want to push you into anyth–"

He was cut off as her hands came up to frame his face and her mouth covered his. Her kiss was just as demanding as the one he'd given her. He hesitated for a moment before he gave in to it, letting her take a little more of his weight and pressing his hips to hers. What shocked him more than the kiss was her hands pushing up under his T-shirt; that was when the last thread of his control snapped. They grappled with each other's clothes until they were down to their underwear. He might have seen her in as little before – and the black lace she wore on stage may have been more revealing than the one she had on now – but somehow the white cotton embossed with tiny blue flowers was so much more sexy and intimate. The shock of her perfect body up close was enough to make him feel slightly dizzy. His hand actually shook as it swept up her side to touch her breast, and when she arched off the bed into him he thought he might pass out with the rush of blood from his head.

It was obvious that her experience was limited. Nothing about the way she kissed him or touched him was practiced or premeditated, and everything he did seemed to be a huge revelation. When he'd finally unhooked her bra and pulled it off, he took in a sharp breath before lowering his mouth to her nipple. She let out a low moan and arched off the bed into him again as his hand slipped into the waistband of her knickers. He pressed into her soft folds and found her centre, moving his hand until she started panting and her eyes glazed over. The wonder in her expression as he brought her over the edge was the most incredible feeling he'd ever experienced in his life.

After that everything moved more quickly. Jamie ripped off his boxers whilst Libby was still slightly dazed on the bed. But once he came back to her naked and peeled her knickers down her legs she jerked into action, smoothing her hands over his arms, his back, his stomach and further down where he was harder than he'd ever been in his life. He groaned before grabbing her hands and pushing them up above her head, not wanting this to be over before it had begun, and feeling like an overexcited teenager.

"Fuck!" he swore as he shifted away and made a grab for his trousers, coming back with a condom and putting it on with superhuman speed, then covering her body with his again and pushing against her. Her breath hitched as her slick tightness only just allowed him to slide all the way inside her and he actually felt a bit overwhelmed. He paused for a moment and searched her beautiful face, feeling a wave of fierce possessiveness and all-consuming tenderness. Then she shifted her hips against his and he let out a growl before he started to move.

When he was finally thrusting inside her, with her breasts pressed against his chest, her legs wrapped around his back, and her small noises of awe filling the room, he felt a huge rush but also the most acute sense of relief; as if holding back from doing this had been an unacknowledged physical pain that was finally at an end. He kissed from the corner of her mouth down to her ear, then down her neck, lightly biting the skin there as he moved with her, his rhythm almost out of control as he felt her tighten underneath him. When he could feel she was close he lifted his head to watch her. She was so beautiful. Her hair spread out over his bed, her glorious breasts bouncing with every thrust, her lips parted and an expression of complete ecstasy on her face. He leant up onto one hand and used the other to reach in between them to put pressure on her centre. Her eyes rolled back then, and she let out a half-moan, half-scream as she came, pulsing around him and sending him over the edge as well. He collapsed on top of her, letting her take all his weight just for a moment before he shifted to the side, taking her with him.

Afterwards, as she lay on his chest and he held her close, he smiled up at the ceiling. Somehow he knew that this changed the whole game. As the almost overwhelming possessiveness swept through him again, he gave her another squeeze and she sighed, her arms closing around him in response.

Yes, he thought, this right now changes things. Now she was his.

Chapter 20

You're barred

Libby swung around the pole in unison with Tara and Claire, spinning from the top right down the to bottom with the world whirling around her. As the water started to fall and they began the next section, something caught her eye on the far side of the room. She tried to concentrate but couldn't put the face she'd glimpsed out of her mind. As they moved towards the finale she allowed herself to glance down at the audience, and there he was. The smug, self-satisfied prick was sitting right up in front of the stage, his arms crossed over his chest and a smirk on his arrogant face. Libby nearly stumbled, which would have been a first seeing as the choreography was hers (all the dances they performed were planned and coached by her. The rehearsals took up nearly as much time as the performing itself, especially when she had to get not only Tara and Claire, but the other ten girls up to speed). When the lights finally went down and they could escape to the dressing room, Tara grabbed her hand and gave it a squeeze.

"Hey, you okay?" she asked, turning to face Libby in front

of the mirrors the girls shared. "You were a bit off out there – problems with lover-boy?"

Libby blushed bright red, wishing fervently that she could control the blood flow to her face as Tara and Claire's eyes grew wider.

"You!" Tara shouted, bouncing on her toes and pointing at Libby, "You've had sex!" This drew the attention of most of the dressing room and Libby buried her face in her hands.

"Tara. Shut. Up."

No way was she talking about "Lover Boy" in front of this lot. Unfortunately, though, her face had other ideas – the involuntary smile she wore whenever anything to do with Jamie popped into her head was there and her pink cheeks were inevitable.

She'd been furious with Kira. When her brain had started functioning again after that mind-blowing first time, she'd demanded to know what that little traitor had whispered in Jamie's ear. He'd just grinned and pushed her back again, proceeding to kiss down her neck and addle her mind anew.

Libby was now wise to this distraction technique of Jamie's after the inordinate number of times he'd employed it over the space of one night and even a couple of times the next morning. Given Libby's very sad previous introduction to sex, that night and the week since had been a complete and wonderful shock.

No wonder people made such a big deal of this stuff. No wonder the other students were at it all the time. She had *no idea* it was this fantastic. After that first night all Libby had wanted was to lock herself and Jamie up for the next month, alone. Of course, that was not possible given that he had work and she had a degree to get *and* a child to raise. But he was creative. He showed her there were ways around lack of time and opportunity, including a large amount of time spent in the shower together (they were without doubt the cleanest but least environmentally friendly people in London). Last night she'd decided to redress the unfair balance of orgasms (Jamie having given her a good fifty per cent more than her fair share) and she dropped to her knees in front of him.

"Christ," he'd said in a chocked voice as she took him in her hands. "Libs, you don't have to..." he stopped talking when she drew him into her mouth. Libby had never actually given a blow job before, but she reckoned that what she lacked in experience she made up for in enthusiasm. Jamie certainly hadn't had any complaints. But the stubborn sod clearly wasn't ready to give up the title of Main Orgasm Giver. After he'd recovered, he'd taken a still soaking wet Libby, chucked a pile of towels on the floor and laid her on them, then proceeded to kiss his way down her neck, breasts then stomach before going down on her with such skill and precision that she almost blacked out.

So, when she'd finally gotten out of him Kira's whispered, "*Women have needs, Big Syringe*," she couldn't even hold a grudge against her friend. To be honest anyone who assisted in her discovering the wonder of sex with Jamie was to be thanked, profusely.

With the sex came a new sort of intimacy. In the post-coital glow late at night, snuggled up to him on her tiny sofa bed, she'd told him about the Sperm Donor. Not a bad kid. Quite the big man around her school – the best looking sixth former; football star, Head Boy. She'd been the envy of all her friends when he'd noticed Libby, who was two years younger. None of them were quite so envious, though, when she found out she was pregnant. Sperm Donor had begged her to have an abortion. Libby was a sensible girl and she was pro-choice. But when it came down to it, and with her parents' Catholic faith instilled into her from such a young age, she just couldn't do it. When she refused, Sperm Donor and his family cut all contact with her. She last saw him when she was three months pregnant and he was headed off to university, having successfully spread rumours around the school of Libby's supposed promiscuity during their relationship. Everyone but Kira believed him; so Libby being very obviously up the duff the next term came as no surprise.

The experience had hardened Libby. She had decided to tackle her life pragmatically. Up until that point her looks had not achieved a damn thing for her. All they'd done was attract a total loser and earn her an unsavoury reputation. Equally annoying was the gymnastics and modern dance she'd dedicated every spare moment to. Medals and trophies had lined her childhood bedroom walls, but what practical use were they now?

She'd always wanted to be a doctor, but she needed money to make it through medical school. Her parents had been bitterly disappointed by her pregnancy, but they remained supportive. Had they been better off, had her dad not injured his back and lost his business, maybe Libby wouldn't have had to make the choices she did. But since her dad's bankruptcy her parents had to downsize even their own home. They now lived in a tiny terraced house, relying on her mum's small income from working part-time in a local café whilst her dad battled his way out of depression.

Libby lived on their sofa for Rosie's first year, but it became clear that they needed their own space once Rosie was more mobile. In the last few years Martin Penny had started to recover. He found some work with local building companies, but nothing permanent, and things were still a struggle. They didn't bring in enough to pay Libby's fees and living expenses, especially with a baby in the mix. So she researched and researched, always coming back to the same conclusion: it was either stripping or prostitution.

When she'd first approached Steve she'd been just eighteen. The Main Attraction was renowned as one of the best strip clubs in London, and she'd been lucky that he'd agreed to meet her. He asked her to work the pole as an audition, and she'd been a disaster. Just as he was about to ask her to leave she'd kicked off the stripper heels he'd given her to work the pole, and performed a perfect front handspring into an aerial with double back-flip across the stage.

He hired her on the spot. Tara and Claire had taught her the pole, but Libby had started to choreograph the dancing. As profits increased, Steve allowed Libby more freedom. The gymnastics portion of the routine got bigger and bigger as the crowds grew. Eventually the focus had shifted, and Libby, Tara and Claire at least stopped taking off their bras. It morphed into a sort of burlesque show-meets-gymnastics display, and it worked. The Main Attraction had tripled its profits over the last four years.

"Knock, knock ladies." Steve's low voice came through the door, saving Libby from the embarrassment of further interrogation. "Can I come in? You decent?"

This was part of the reason she loved Steve. He had seen them all naked thousands of times before, but treated their changing room as if they were all Mother Superiors – a show of respect that he instilled into the bouncers as well.

"Come in, you big idiot," Claire called, grabbing her white wings from the chair.

"Got a bit of a problem," Steve said as he stepped into the room. "There's a bloke out there insisting on the "extra" from you Libby. High roller, willing to pay over the odds – but ..." Steve trailed off and scratched the side of his face, "can't put my finger on it but the guy seems off. *Real* specific that it had to be you. His table's been pretty rowdy all night."

The "extra" was the kind of thing Libby had done for the groom on the stag party Jamie had been with. Not a lap dance or anything; just a minute or two of attention for a specific man, and it came at a steep price.

She sat down heavily and her face paled, her embarrassed smile from before a thing of the past. "Blonde guy?" she asked. "Heavy set?"

"Yeah – how did you...?"

"I know him, Steve." She turned towards the mirror and stared at her reflection. Of course tonight would have to be the night they trialled their new angel theme. Libby was the dark angel with black underwear, smoky makeup and black wings. She would be exposed from the beginning of the routine to the end. Her chest felt almost too tight to breathe. Somehow this part of her life had been kept separate from university. It looked like that was about to change. She blinked once and her mouth set into a thin stubborn line.

Fuck him.

Fuck all of them.

"I'll do it," she said in a hollow voice.

"Libby, if this guy is–"

"He's harmless, Steve. It's not a problem. I'll do it. Don't worry about it."

She brushed off Tara and Claire's questions until it was time to go out again. It was like she was on some sort of automatic pilot. She noticed Tara and Claire muttering to each other but ignored the concerned looks they were shooting her way as she made it from the corner of the dressing room. Strapping her black wings into place, she took a deep breath as the girls formed a circle. They each put a hand into the centre and muttered their mantra: "*We* control the crowd, *we* are the ones in charge." It was something Claire had come up with two years ago and it was now a ritual.

The throngs of men could seem intimidating and it was impossible not to feel vulnerable wearing so little; control was important. Remembering that the men could not touch them and that essentially the women controlled the interaction helped them all face the performance.

They broke apart and walked to their separate entrances. Libby waited for her cue, taking deep breaths and muttering the mantra under her breath. When the doors opened she burst through, performing her first handspring of the evening and leaping up onto the table in front of her. Steve had given her the table number for the "high roller" but she didn't need it; she knew where he was, it was burned into her brain.

She flipped from table to bench to table until finally she was in front of him. Steve was right: the men on his table were rowdy. Her heart sank that little bit more when she realised that most of them were guys from her year at medical school. Catcalls and wolf whistles sounded all around her. Boys who had worked with her on physiology projects, discussed problems with her in tutorials, sat next to her in the library, suddenly saw her only as a sex object. Fair game to be jeered at. Yes, okay, they all looked nearly too drunk to stay on their seats, but she could still feel the respect she'd had from them previously slipping away.

Well, fuck them.

She crouched in front of Toby and pulled his shirt collar so that he was standing. Using his shoulders as a lever, she flipped over his head to land on the bench behind him, then fell backwards so that her hair brushed his shoulder as her body arched over his left shoulder. He reached up, but before he could touch her or the bouncers could move to stop him, she flipped her legs so that she was once again crouching in front of him and could drag him back to sitting. The full pint of beer on the edge of the table was just too tempting. She leaned in until her face was inches from his, her tongue came out to lick her bottom lip and his eyes went wide. His pupils dilated as he held his breath. The smallest movement of her little finger pushed the beer off the edge of the table and right into his lap. She heard "Bitch!" and "Fucking whore!" shouted in Toby's ugly voice as she back-flipped off the table and onto the stage, then caught sight of Barry's shocked face, but still managed to execute another perfect handspring. In fact she gritted her teeth and put in the performance of her life.

"Get that fucking guy out of here," Barry heard Steve's voice sound through his earpiece. He tore his eyes away from Libby on stage, whose face was unnaturally pale and whose jaw was clenched tight, and focused on the arsehole she'd covered in beer.

"That bitch!" the guy yelled as he grabbed napkins from the table to wipe at his crotch. His buddies were all laughing at him now rather than concentrating on Libby. Barry had seen the recognition on Libby's face when she'd reached this table full of little snots; she knew those men and they'd come here to humiliate her. He marched forward and laid his big meaty paw on Wet Crotch Guy's shoulder.

"You – out," Barry barked as he turned the guy to face him. The outrage on this idiot's face was priceless.

"What?" Wet Crotch Guy shrieked, a full octave above what a normal self-respecting dude would go for. "I'm the injured goddamn party. One of your sluts poured beer on me. I demand ..."

Barry felt his jaw clench as the anger shot through him, but he controlled himself... just. Killing this little piece of shit would not be easy to explain. "You're leaving." Barry pulled him away from his seat by the scruff of his neck and hauled him away from the table.

"Bloody hell," Wet Crotch Shithead screamed, way too close to Barry's ear – even Barry's missus couldn't screech as high as that. "You, listen to me you bloody–"

"No," Barry said, drawing to a halt by the exit and pulling Little Shit up so that his eyes were nearly level with his. "*You* listen to *me*, you spineless twat. This place is nice and fancy for a strip club, expensive – yeah? That does not change the fact that I am a *bouncer* at a fucking *strip club*. You get me? We're not in one of your wine bars now, you little snot. I could crush you like a fly in that alley right out there with no fucking CCTV, and have a dozen witnesses swear I was right here in the club the whole time. Now," he opened the doors and re-established his hold on the back of the guy's neck, "get," he drew back with his arm, bringing the bastard with him, "the fuck," his arm flew forward, propelling the guy through the air, "out," he said as the guy landed heavily on the pavement. "You're barred."

Chapter 21

I'll do it all with a smile on my face

Libby knew something was wrong as soon as she walked into the mess. It was partly the tense expectation in the atmosphere, and partly the fact that most of the guys were smirking and avoiding eye contact with her. Kira had been like a Rottweiler on guard duty all day, which had initially confused Libby but then it occurred to her that *she knew*; somehow the grapevine had gone into overdrive and Kira knew those blokes had seen her at the club. By now it was likely that her entire year knew – if not the entire medical school, in fact probably the entire hospital. But there was only so long you could burn with humiliation, and after the first couple of hours of knowing looks, whispers and smirks Libby had felt herself go numb.

Beg, borrow or steal, she repeated over and over to herself in her head as she marched over to the kettle in the kitchenette area off the main lounge. But something caught her eye on the noticeboard as she passed, and she stumbled to a halt.

"You disgusting bastards!" Kira yelled, pushing past Libby to get to the A4-size picture tacked up to the board. It was a grainy image of Libby on stage, she was guessing taken by one of their camera phones on Saturday night. "Haven't you and your tiny dicks got anything better to do?" She reached up to yank down the paper, but Libby caught her hand to stop her.

"Leave it, Ki-Ki," she said to her friend, then turned to face the packed mess, which had fallen silent. It was obvious that most hadn't actually noticed the picture until then. One pathologist was so shocked he dropped his cheese sandwich. But there were a good few of them there that knew, and one in particular who looked very pleased with himself.

"Yeah," Toby said, lounging back on the sofa with a smug grin on his face. "Leave it up there, *Ki-Ki*. Let's all see what Little Miss Perfect does in her spare time." He pulled out his phone and tapped the screen, after which the large space filled with the sound of Christina Aguilera's "Dirty". "Why don't you give us all a demo, huh?" The bloody loser had synched his phone to the speakers in the mess to set this whole thing up; in that moment he struck Libby as more than a little sad.

"Fine," she told him. Her rage was so extreme it felt like a physical force inside her: hot and uncontrollable. Holding eye contact with him, she ditched her bag and kicked off her crocs. After shaking her hair out of its elastic band she took a few steps back. Toby, who obviously hadn't anticipated anything more than a tearful reaction from Libby, was starting to look a little unsure.

She sprang up onto her toes, and then launched into a front flip until she was standing on the back of the sofa. She proceeded to flip almost casually in a flight serial from hands to feet along the sofa, until she launched herself forwards and landed on her feet on the coffee table in front of Toby, in the centre of the mess. Toby noticed too late the exact replica of his position from two nights before, and didn't have time to react as she tipped his can of coke all over his crotch. He fumbled his phone as he jumped up from the sofa, but Libby snatched it up and dropped it into a conveniently placed pint glass full of water, which the pathologist had been having with his now trodden-in cheese sandwich. Toby leapt up and took a swipe at her, but she was too quick for him. She ducked down before stepping gracefully off the table and jumping back.

"Mummy and Daddy pay your fees, right? Am I right?" Libby asked. Toby's face was bright red and so furious that he was beyond speech. "Well, I have a child to support, exams to study for (which by the way I kick your pathetic arse in every time and you know it), and goddamn rent to pay. So, you can take your smirking and your judgement and go fuck yourself, because I'm pretty sure you're the only human up for the job.

"Yeah I dance to support my family, I'd dance buck-naked in front of a packed O2 stadium if it achieved my dreams for me and my daughter. I'll take money from stupid men like you who'll pay the ridiculous cover charge and then drink over-priced drinks just to see the likes of me shake my arse, and I'll do it all with a smile on my face if it gets me what I want."

When Libby had finished there was a shocked silence for a few moments before someone started clapping. Before long the entire mess was clapping and cheering her, even the friends of Toby's who'd been with him at the club.

Toby, however, did not clap. He focused on her with hate-filled eyes as the applause gradually died down. "You... you bi–" He made a lunge for her but a large body stepped in between them, and a big hand on Toby's chest stopped his progress so abruptly that his head snapped back.

"That's *enough*," Jamie said, his voice low and vibrating with anger. "You're done. You come within ten feet of her again and I'll have you thrown out of the student programme." Toby's nostrils flared and his face stayed so red it looked almost painful.

"Are you threatening me, Dr Grantham?" Toby asked.

"No," Jamie replied. Toby looked up at Jamie for a long moment before he grunted and stepped back, grabbing his bag off the sofa and stalking past all his mates, whose smirks had faded into looks of embarrassment.

"You okay?" Jamie asked as he turned to face Libby. She blinked at him.

"What are you doing here?" Generally the consultants didn't venture into the doctor's mess too often; they had their offices and their own coffee rooms.

"Libs, don't be mad, okay?" Kira said. "I may have sent him a *little* text when I saw that poster. I thought–"

"I can look after myself," Libby told them, taking a step back from them both. She felt the burning behind her eyes but she refused to cry. None of these people would see her break down. A low murmur of noise had returned to the mess. "I can look after us by myself," she whispered as she wrapped her arms around her middle. When she looked up, two sets of concerned eyes were fixed on hers. Jamie made a move towards her but she dodged around him.

Once out in the corridor she started jogging.

"Libby, wait," she heard him call out, and slowed to a walk as he caught up with her, resigning herself to this discussion.

"It's my half day," she told him as she carried on walking with him beside her. "I'm getting Rosie early and we're going home."

"Hey," he said gently, his warm hands reaching for her arms, which were still hugging her middle tightly. "Hey, slow down. Give yourself a minute before you see the squirt, okay?"

Her head was pounding, anger and humiliation still

burning through her. Maybe he was right. She took a deep breath and slowed her steps. He had a hand to her back now and was directing her forward. Before she knew what was happening they were both in his office and the door was shut behind them.

"Right, sit down and I'll make you a cup of tea." He put both hands on her shoulders and pushed her into his big comfy leather chair. Her throat felt tight but she swallowed down the emotion that threatened. This unfortunately provoked a coughing fit. By the time she'd recovered from it he was crouched in front of her, holding a steaming mug.

"That cough's been there a while now," he said, and Libby shrugged.

"Just the remnants of a cold I picked up from Rosie," she told him, reminding herself again to replace her inhaler. "It's fine." She took a sip of tea with hands that she realised were shaking slightly. "How much did you see?" she asked as he sat on the edge of his desk in front of her.

"I arrived to see you flip off the back of the sofa," he said. "Which, by the way, is about thirty years old and you didn't know if it was safe."

She shrugged again. "I had a point to make."

"I think you made your point, baby," he told her; and his voice, maybe because of how gentle it was or the still suppressed rage in it on her behalf, broke something in her. Her hands started to shake in earnest, tea sloshing over the sides of the mug until it was taken from her and she was lifted up. Suddenly it was Jamie sitting in the leather chair with her in his lap, his big arms holding her to him. Her face, which was tucked into his neck, crumpled and for the first time in what felt like a decade she allowed herself to dissolve into gut-wrenching tears. For a long time they just sat there, her soaking his shirt and him stroking her back and murmuring about how everything was going to be okay, telling her to hold onto him.

But she knew... she knew she couldn't hold onto him. She couldn't fall down. She had to rely on herself.

So after the sobs had died to silent tears, she pulled her face out of the comfort of his strong jaw and sat up, wiping the backs of her hands under her eyes.

"I'm okay now," she said, starting to pull away, but his arms tightened around her and drew her back in. "Seriously, Jamie, I don't want to waste any time I could be spending with Rosie. I've got to go."

"Rosie's a bright little girl, Libby," he told her – something she already knew.

"What's that got to do with anything?"

"She won't miss that you've been crying if you go and pick her up now. She doesn't miss *anything*. Just give yourself a minute, okay?"

Libby sighed but let the tension leave her body as she relaxed back into him.

"We need to talk about the club," Jamie said carefully, and Libby tensed again.

"I think it's better that you and I avoid that subject."

"I know, and I understand that," he told her, his arms giving her a squeeze. "But after what happened in the mess and with your exams coming up we've *got* to talk about it."

"I've said all I need to say."

Jamie kept his arms around her but his eyes slid away from hers for a moment as his jaw clenched. "Libby, today just proved my point. You can't carry on earning money that way and expect no backlash. More importantly you haven't the time to work at the moment. I could help. Please, please, let me help."

"The only thing that episode just now *proved* is that a lot of medics are privileged, judgemental arseholes." Libby looked straight at him and raised her eyebrows, then pushed out of his arms to stand up.

"Okay," Jamie said slowly. "I know I deserve that but please don't lump me together with those pricks." He rose up from the chair so he was standing in front of her. "I care about you and Rosie." He took a step back and rubbed his temples. "I can't help it that the thought of you in that club makes me crazy. I mean, apart from the whole half-naked thing," his fists clenched at his sides, "there's the fact that places like that just aren't safe. Look at what happened to me."

"I've told you before: I'm safer in that club than I am working in this hospital."

"Bu -"

"Nobody had *ever* been allowed to lay so much as a finger on me in the club, which is more that I can say for this hospital. Yes, it's not safe – for the punters who act like idiots. For the women who work there it's one of the safest places on earth."

"You can't tell me you *like* working there."

"Okay – no," she admitted. "I don't exactly enjoy working there but I do like paying my bills, I do like affording nice things for my daughter, and I do like *surviving*."

"Just let me help." Jamie's voice now carried a hint of desperation, his hands held up in front of him almost as if he was begging her. "It can be a loan. You can pay me back. Please, baby, please." He moved to her and framed her face with his hands before dropping his forehead to hers and whispering one final "please" against her lips. She closed her eyes. There was actual pain in his voice; she was causing him pain.

"I can't," she whispered, and felt his grip tighten for a moment before he pulled away and took a step back. And she really couldn't. It seemed there were limits to beg, borrow or steal for her, and one of those was taking money from a man she was falling in love with. The heels of both his hands went to his eyes until he pulled them both through his hair, leaving it sticking up in an uncharacteristic mess.

"Can you stop being so fucking stubborn," he snapped, clearly at the end of his patience with her. "You can't carry on working this hard. You need time to revise. You need time for your daughter. I'm offering you that." Libby looked away from his furious eyes and felt her chest constrict.

"I'm not taking your money," she replied, crossing her arms over her chest.

Jamie threw his head back and let out an actual growl of frustration, his hands at his sides once again bunching into fists before he suddenly turned and stalked to the door of his office.

"Libby please," he said, his voice now defeated. "I can't do this anymore with you, Libby. It's killing me to see you struggle."

"Jamie, I–"

"No," he snapped, cutting her off. But when she flinched his expression softened. "I'm sorry but I just can't do it. I can't carry on caring about you and watching you run yourself into the ground."

Libby took a deep breath and nodded her head slowly.

"I understand," she told him. "I really do. But I can't see a way forward for us if that is the case."

Jamie's chin dropped to his chest and he let out a deep sigh. When he looked back up his expression was blank. "I... if you won't change your mind then... I suppose you're right."

It was what she had expected, wasn't it? Why then did she feel swamped by the most crushing disappointment? As she moved past him to the door she saw what might have been regret, and definitely pain, in his expression, but he pressed his lips together and clenched his jaw.

"Yes, I suppose I am," she told him, straightening her shoulders and tucking her hair back behind her ears. He looked down at his feet as she slipped out of the door.

She should have remembered that she only had herself to rely on.

She needed to focus on that from now on.

Beg, borrow or steal, she would do what it takes to get by, just so long as she didn't take *this* man's money.

Chapter 22

I can't be sick

"Hey, loser," Pav said as he slammed Jamie's office door behind him. Jamie glanced up from the audit he was going through to jerk his chin at Pav before looking down again. Pav sighed. "So we're still going with the miserable-bastard routine, are we?" he asked, plonking himself down on the chair opposite Jamie's desk and lifting his feet up to rest on the meticulously organised papers in the inbox. Jamie scowled at Pav's feet but Pav just smirked and settled in more comfortably.

It had been two weeks since Jamie's stand-off with Libby, and yes, he was miserable. He missed her and Rosie so much it was like a physical ache, but he was still so angry that every time he lifted the phone to call her or went to say something to her on the wards he held himself back. That didn't stop him from thinking about her. He'd seen her at the bus stop a couple of times. Once it had been raining and it took all his willpower to drive past the damp woman and child (he had broken and phoned Pav though, offering to write up his Morbidity and Mortality meeting notes for presentation just so Pav would drive them home).

"Listen up, Misery Guts," Pav continued, his normal jovial tone now laced with irritation. "I know this is no longer "any of your business", but Libby was in my theatre today."

"Pavlos, that is not exactly big news. She *is* a medical student here."

"I had to send her home, you stubborn bastard."

Jamie frowned and looked up at Pav. "Why? Did she fall asleep again?"

"No, no, nothing like that. She was coughing, badly. I'd noticed it the other night when I drove her home."

"What do you expect me to do about it?" Jamie snapped, a wave of worry for Libby bringing that now familiar feeling of helpless frustration.

Silence stretched between them until Jamie was forced to look up at Pav, who was staring at him, his lips pressed together in a firm line of disapproval and his brows drawn down over his eyes.

"What?" Jamie asked, throwing his hands up. "She's not my problem, man. It's highly unlikely she'd listen to a bloody word I say anyway, so what exactly do you want me to do?"

"Okay then," Pav said, pulling his feet off the desk and causing an avalanche of paper – none of which the lazy bugger made any attempt to clear up. "I was under the impression that you cared about her, but I guess, since she's "not your problem", don't trouble yourself. Wouldn't want to put you out or anything."

"I *do* care about her," Jamie muttered, throwing his pen down on the desk. "But she won't listen to reason and I can't keep banging my head against a brick wall."

"Oh dear," Pav sing-songed, "did the big baby not get his own way with the pretty lady? Did she not accept your superior wisdom in all things and bow down to your wishes? Grow up, you daft article. She's been looking after herself and her kid for a long time. You can't expect her to give up her only source of income because it offends your delicate sensibilities."

"It wasn't like that. I–"

"It was exactly like that." Pav pushed up from the chair and stood, pointing his finger at Jamie, which in itself was slightly shocking – Pav was not a finger-pointer, he was more of a laid-back hand-wave kind of guy, gesture-wise. "You're problem is you've been too privileged your whole cushty life to understand what it's like to struggle. You can't understand the choices that girl makes, because you've never had to worry about how *you* were going to afford medical school, how *you* were going to pay *your* rent." Pav had a large Greek family. They supported him as far as they could but with three other siblings in the mix it wasn't that much help financially. He'd had to work the entire five years he was at medical school at the student bar during weeknights, and for a catering company on the weekends, despite the fact that he'd only had to pay minimal rent to Jamie. Jamie's dad owned a drug company. Before he became a doctor Jamie had never worked a day in his life.

"Pav, look–"

"Don't bother," Pav snapped as he stormed to the door, wrenching it open. "Just you go back to your boring privileged well-ordered life and find a nice horsey girl to introduce to Mummy. Forget about Libby."

The door slammed and Jamie sighed as he sat back in his chair. Maybe Pav was right... but he was not about to go down that rabbit hole again. He pushed away the concern and grabbed the mouse to fire up his screen. He'd finish this bloody audit, go home to his grumpy, sulking dog (Beauty was not on board with this sudden Libby-and-Rosie-sized gap in her life – her usual extremely over-exuberant, drool-filled welcome had been replaced by a brief doggy scowl and a snort of disgust) and try not to think about the look on Libby's face before she left his office.

~

"That is not the right test," Dr Morrison said, her eyes not moving from the screen in front of her. Libby felt the sweat trickle down her back and started to feel a little sick.

"Well, I think they just want to know ..." She grabbed the doorframe and took some shallow breaths, "the state of the chest and if it will ..." Willing the feeling of pressure in her chest to abate, she tried to get her breathing under control. The walk here from the ward seemed to have knocked the stuffing out of her again. When would she shake off this bloody cold? "... if it will cause a problem for the general anaesthetic."

"The history is consistent with fibrosis. The patient needs a high-resolution CT scan."

Libby had the crazy urge to rip Dr Morrison's monitor out of the wall and throw it at her head.

"That's fine. I'll go and change it ..." She broke off with a coughing fit and stepped out into the corridor to try and get her breath. The sweat was pouring off her in earnest now as she leaned against the door. When she'd recovered and could straighten up from her embarrassing position bent over double in the corridor, she looked up and straight into Dr Morrison's eyes. They were an unusual grey colour. Libby had never noticed them before, having never really been afforded full eye contact by the woman. Dr Morrison watched her for a good few seconds, her face giving nothing away.

"You are not well," she eventually said, no pity in her tone, just stating the fact.

"I'll be fine," Libby told her, but knew it wasn't overly convincing when her voice cracked at the end. Sweat was beading on her forehead and for a moment she thought she might actually vomit all over Dr Morrison's designer shoes.

"You are *not* fine," said Dr Morrison accusingly, standing up with a sudden movement that only served to make Libby feel more sick. "Sit down." Dr Morrison hesitated a moment before reaching up and putting her hands on Libby's shoulders to guide her into Dr Phillips' vacated chair. Libby was feeling so crappy by that stage, she wasn't up to making much of a protest.

"Listen, honestly I'm okay," she muttered, pushing her hair behind her ears; but she realised she was talking to an empty office. She sighed and dropped her head into her hands; the humanity she was exhibiting must have scared Miss Perfect away. She glanced at the clock over Dr Morrison's desk and groaned. It was nearly six and she had to pick up Rosie. She put her hands on the armrests and started trying to push herself up, only to be forced back into the chair by Dr Morrison's hands on her shoulders. Libby looked up to see that Dr Morrison had wheeled in an observation trolley. Before she knew what was happening a sats probe was attached to her finger, a blood pressure cuff to her arm, and a tympanic thermometer was shoved in her ear.

"Sit forward."

"Really, I'm okay. You don't have to–"

"Sit. Forward." Libby sighed and did as she was asked. Dr Morrison listened to her chest, then crouched down in front of her.

"You *are* sick," she told her, frowning up as though it was entirely her fault.

"I'm fine. It's nothing. I –"

"You have asthma, yes?"

Libby nodded.

"Where is your inhaler?"

Libby shook her head, concentrating on exhaling through what felt like a tight straw.

"There's wheeze all over your chest. You have a right lower lobe pneumonia. Your pulse rate is over one hundred. Your temperature is thirty-nine. You're septic."

Libby pulled off the sats probe and the blood pressure cuff and fought off the dizziness in order to stand up without swaying. "I've got to get Rosie. I'll sort it out after I get her. I can't–"

"You are septic. You are sick. You need to listen to me. You–"

"No," Libby shouted, her arm slashing through the air. "You listen to me. Don't you understand – I *can't* be sick. I can't ..." She trailed off as the edges of her vision started darkening and another cold sweat and wave of dizziness assaulted her. She swayed and Dr Morrison caught her before she went down, plonking her back on the chair.

"We'll get you to resus, and I need to call Dr Grantham," Dr Morrison muttered, causing Libby's head to come up and her hand to shoot out to land on Dr Morrison's forearm.

"No," she croaked, trying to put as much force behind the word as possible. "No. He's... we're not... just *no*."

Dr Morrison pressed her lips together and narrowed her eyes. "Okay. What about your loud scary friend? Can I call her?"

"You mean Kira? I–" Before Libby could say any more Dr Morrison had extracted her mobile from the pocket of her scrubs. Libby gave her the code when asked, now beyond arguing. In fact she was fast becoming beyond anything at all; her breathing had become more laboured and the sweat was pouring down her back. A few minutes later Kira came bursting into the office, swearing violently when she saw Libby hunched over in the chair.

"Badgering hell," she muttered as she put her arm around

Libby and a hand to her forehead. "What have you done to yourself, you daft sod? Come on let's get you to A&E."

"Ki-Ki, I can't," groaned Libby as she was forced upright and was shuffled towards the door. "What about Rosie?"

"Your mum and dad?"

"They're over an hour away. I need to–"

"I will go and get the child," Dr Morrison put in, and both women turned their shocked faces to her. "I can look after her. She knows me."

"She does?" asked Kira, her eyebrows in her hairline. Libby started another round of coughing and her vision darkened again, but this time, with Kira holding her up, she couldn't fight away the loss of consciousness, and everything faded to black.

"Jamie!" Rosie launched herself out of Dr Morrison's lap across the room, colliding with his legs and wrapping her arms around them. She proceeded to shimmy up his trousers and tug on his shirt until he bent down to pick her up and the standard face-smushing commenced.

"Hey, sweetheart," he said through his smushed lips, his confused eyes flicking between the little girl and the woman sitting in the office chair with half her hair down and the other half shoved into a bizarre pink scrunchy arrangement. He'd come down to find the on-call radiologist, and heard noises coming from Dr Morrison's office. "What are you doing here, Little Louse?"

"Mummy's sick so Millie's looking after me," Rosie told him before her voice dropped to a whisper and she leaned forward to cup his ear. "Millie says I've got to be very brave whilst they make Mummy all better and good as new. They gonna takes away her coughin'. I might have cwied... a bit. But Millie says that's okay, and she let me do her hair." Dr Morrison was frantically pulling out the scrunchy and trying to right her light brown hair into its usual order. "She won't let me smush her face though. And Granny and Bumpa is coming soon. Hurrah!"

"That's great, honey. Why don't you count up my money a sec whilst I talk to... Millie."

"'Kay," said Rosie, grabbing his wallet out of his pocket and sliding down him to sit happily on the floor. Dr Morrison stood up from the chair, still smoothing down rogue hairs.

"What the hell is going on?" he snapped in a low voice, immediately regretting it when she took a small step back.

"She's been admitted to–"

"Admitted?" he shouted, and Rosie's head popped up from her perusal of his wallet, her little face clouded with worry. He forced a reassuring smile at her, but she frowned.

"Be gentle to Millie," Rosie told him firmly before turning away. He took a deep breath to get himself under control.

"I'm sorry," he muttered, noting that Dr Morrison had now put a chair between them, and that the knuckles of her hands that were clutching the leather had turned white. "Please, would you mind telling me what happened?"

Dr Morrison was focusing on his shoulder, and the corner of one of her eyes was twitching. "I don't know if–"

"Please, Millie," he entreated, using Dr Morrison's Christian name for the first time in his recollection. "Please tell me what's going on. I *do* care about her."

She looked down at the floor for a moment before her eyes went back to his shoulder and she sighed.

Chapter 23

Not that self-sacrificing

"All I'm saying, love, is this wouldn't happen if you didn't run yourself into the ground."

Libby closed her eyes, feeling the deep dragging pain in her right side every time she took a breath – one of her coughing fits had torn an intercostal muscle. The pain of that, combined with the irritation of the lining of her lung from the pneumonia, was bearable when she was just breathing normally, but when she coughed it was horrific.

"Dad," she said, hating that her voice was so weak, wanting to be strong for her parents, but failing yet again. She pulled her oxygen mask down so they could hear what she needed to say. "I have to work. You know that. This is... just a setback."

"Setback?" Martin Penny's face was turning red and his fists had bunched at his sides. He towered over her bed, his greying hair standing on end from the number of times he'd run his hands through it with worry. "My baby girl lying in a hospital bed with pneumonia is not just a ruddy *setback*. You know you have to look after yourself with your asthma. That's what all that fitness was about when you were a youngster. All the dancing and the gym. I can't believe you didn't even have an inhaler with you."

"I'll be fine."

"Martin, calm down." Libby's mum glared at her husband across the bed. Her bright red lips pressed together in a thin line. There was no situation that Rita Penny was without her lipstick – visiting her sick daughter in hospital being no exception. She'd always been disappointed in Libby's lack of enthusiasm for cosmetics; she once said she'd rather go out without knickers on than miss her coating of Very Berry. Libby had no doubt that her dad would be on the receiving end of a swift kick in the shin had their incapacitated daughter not been separating them.

"Listen, woman," Martin snapped, and Libby rolled her eyes to look up at the ceiling: her mother was about to blow. Her husband calling her "woman" was Rita Penny's nuclear trigger. She might have been a good foot shorter than him but there was no doubt who wore the trousers in their marriage. It was an indication of how stressed her dad was that he would be willing to go head to head with his wife. "I'll calm down when *your daughter* agrees to stop this bloody cocktail-making business and start taking care of herself."

"Dad, I have to–"

"I can support you and Rosie. I'll get extra work. No problem." He wasn't as thin as he'd been at the worst of his depression but he still wasn't back to the dad she knew. Maybe he never would be. But over the last two years the shadows under his eyes had lightened, and he'd started smiling again. The last thing Libby wanted was to hinder his recovery.

"Daddy," she whispered, reaching out to enclose one of his fists with her hand. "We both know you can't do that." Martin flinched and looked away from her and Libby felt the all too familiar guilt. This situation made her dad, her strong, proud, hard as nails dad, feel weak. The fact that he couldn't support his daughter and granddaughter was tough for him to take. He had always provided for his family, but Libby, through her stupid mistake at seventeen, had taken that pride away from him.

"Right," said Rita, "enough of this nonsense. We can talk about Libby giving up the *bar-tending* when she's better." Her parents exchanged a significant look, which Libby didn't quite understand. "For now we need to go and get our grandchild and take her back to your flat, Libby."

Libby closed her eyes again and blew out a breath. The sofa bed in her flat had long since given up folding out. She had taken to dragging the cushions off it and sleeping on the floor. Rosie's room had a tiny single bed in it that definitely wouldn't accommodate her dad's large frame. Her parents' house was too far from the hospital and they'd rented it on Airbnb so they could afford to visit Libby's aunt in Cornwall for the week.

"Mummy?" Everyone turned towards Rosie's small voice across the side room. Libby's mouth fell open when she saw who was holding Rosie's hand.

"You!" Kira burst in behind Jamie and Rosie and poked Jamie in the chest. "What are you doing here? I've just run all the way from a Rosie-less x-ray department after *you* kidnapped her!"

Rosie, ignoring the adult drama, broke away from Jamie, ran to the side of the bed and scrambled up to snuggle into Libby's neck.

"Hey, Little Louse," Libby muttered into Rosie's soft curls, bringing her hand, complete with cannula and drip attachments, up to pull the little body into hers.

"Mummy?" Rosie's voice was smaller than Libby had ever heard it. "You look weird." Libby blinked back tears. Rosie's voice was shaking now. Libby could just imagine what she must look like hooked up to drips, an oxygen mask on her face. To her frustration, when she tried to answer her throat closed over and she couldn't get the words out.

"I told you, sweetheart," Jamie's voice came from her side and Libby looked over Rosie's head to see him leaning right over them both, pushing some curls away from her face, "they're making Mummy better. All these bits and bobs are giving her medicine." Rosie shifted across so she was facing Jamie, making Libby wince in pain as she pressed down on her ribs. When she looked up again Jamie was watching her closely.

"Come here, Little Louse," he said softly, slipping his arms underneath Rosie and trying to lift her up. Rosie clung on to her mum. "We've got to give her space to recharge now." Slowly Rosie let go of Libby's neck and let Jamie lift her up to hold her against him. The release of weight from Libby's chest enabled her to take a much-needed breath.

"Russell got sick and now he won't uncurl," Libby heard Rosie whisper, and felt her chest constrict. "Mummy had to bury him outside in Mrs. Stricklen's daffodils." The woodlouse turnover in their flat was, unfortunately, fairly high.

"Your mum's going to be fine. From now on you're both going to be just *fine*." Jamie's voice was firm. Libby saw his eyes flash and his jaw clench tight.

"You promise she won't curl up?" Rosie whispered, smushing his face with her little hands.

"The next time Mummy curls up it'll be around you and me on the sofa," Jamie told her, and Libby's mouth dropped open again. What was he playing at? Her parents were *right there*, taking in this exchange with open mouths; her father's expression was one of stunned awe, her mother's far more wary.

"Would you mind explaining exactly who the bloody hell you are?" Rita asked, her hands going to her hips.

"Of course, Mrs Penny," Jamie said, extending his free hand to her mother. "Jamie Grantham, I'm Libby's boyfriend. We spoke on the phone, remember?"

It had taken Libby a good few weeks to convince her mum that Jamie was just a friend after that phone call, and now he was blowing all that careful lying out of the water.

"Boyfriend," her dad breathed, and Libby nearly rolled her eyes. Clearly Jamie would not have to work too hard to win one of her parents' approval.

"Gwanny," Rosie interrupted, "you said "bloody"!"

"Yes, love," she said. "Yes – yes, I did. And when you're fifty-eight you can say bloody whenever you want too."

"Hurrah!" Rosie cried, all signs of small voice gone. Libby was pleased that Rosie wasn't scared anymore, but irrationally annoyed that Jamie was the one to take that worry away. "Can I say bum and poo and wee at the table as well?"

"No," Libby said before her mum could give Rosie any more ammunition for pre-school.

"Ah... the anaesthetist?" her mum asked.

"A doctor," her dad said, again with the awe-filled voice. Libby did roll her eyes at this. She could practically hear the cogs turning in her father's brain. Never mind that his daughter was well on *her* way to being a doctor, *no*, the fact that she had caught the eye of a medical professional was much more important in that man's warped brain.

"What are you – ?" Libby started.

"Don't worry, darling," Jamie cut her off smoothly, shifting Rosie more firmly onto his hip. "Your mum, dad and Rosie are going to come and stay with me whilst you're an inpatient. Then you're going to move in until you recover."

Libby's eyes flashed and she opened her mouth to speak;

but all that came out was a succession of hacking coughs. She struggled to sit up in the bed for a moment, before strong arms lifted her forward. She continued the coughing and wheezing fit with a warm familiar hand on her back, which stayed there as the hacking subsided and she tried to catch her breath. When she was finished she searched the room for Rosie and saw her tucked into her Bumpa's arms, her bottom lip trembling dangerously. Libby forced a smile.

"It's just a cough, Little Louse," she croaked. "I'm fine. Okay?"

"'Kay," Rosie whispered, sounding anything but.

"Rosie-Pose can stay with me," Kira put in, throwing Jamie a dirty look and then smiling at Libby's parents. "Then you guys don't have to put yourself out staying down here.

"Ki Ki, you can't do that," Libby said as she sank back down into the pillows and tried to steady her breathing. "You're in halls. They're not going to want a four-year-old around."

"Everyone loves Rosie. I'm sure they'll bend the rules for her," Kira said, her face set with stubbornness.

"And then there's your revision, honey," Libby said softly, and Kira's eyes slid away. Kira hadn't been doing nearly enough work this term and she knew it.

"You're sweet, love," Rita said, moving to Kira and squeezing her hand. "But we're not leaving for the moment. Not until Libby's back on her feet."

"Great," Jamie said, "it's settled then. I'll take you all over to Libby's. We can pack a bag for Rosie and then come back to mine for the night. Kira, you can stay with Libby."

"Bossy arse," Kira muttered.

"Kira!" Martin snapped. "Dr Grantham is being very kind. I think you should show a little more respect."

"Can I say "arse" when I'm fifty-eight?" asked Rosie, and all the women in the room replied "No!" together, whilst all the men chuckled.

"Good plan, mate," Martin said, slapping Jamie on the back, which in Martin Penny's world was as high a recommendation as you could get. "We'd be very grateful. Must say I wasn't keen to squeeze onto the dreaded sofa bed from hell."

"Good, that's settled then."

"Jamie," Libby tried to make her voice as firm as possible – tricky when it was emerging in a series of squeaks and croaks. "I don't think–" Her words stalled as Jamie bent down to her and brushed his lips against her temple, reaching up to push the hair that had fallen in front of her eyes back behind her ear on the other side.

"Just rest," he muttered into her hair. "Everything is going to be okay now." She wanted to tell him to bugger off. Wanted to say she could manage without him; didn't want to accept this help given out of pity; but the conviction threaded through his words was too much to resist. So just for tonight – just whilst she felt so weak – just for now, she let herself believe him.

"Did I tell you about the bathrooms?" Libby's mum asked, this breathy voice becoming the norm for her when discussing anything Jamie-related. And yes – yes, her mother *had* told her about the sodding bathrooms. Multiple times. Just as she had described in detail every kitchen appliance, every floor covering, every piece of furniture (although she had made sure, again *multiple times*, to mention that the house needed more soft furnishings–"a woman's touch", she had said pointedly, complete with raised eyebrows and pursed lips). Rita Penny's feminist principles seemed to have gone out the window when it came to Jamie.

The only thing her parents were slightly less keen on about perfect Jamie and his perfect house was Beauty, who had eaten a pair of her mum's knickers the first night they moved in and "smelt of a sewage works", as her dad put it.

After two days staying there her mum had wrestled the massive dog into Jamie's walk-in shower and shampooed her with an entire bottle of her Pantene. Her mother may be relatively tiny but she was surprisingly strong. Since then she had sprayed Beauty daily with Febreze. Three more pairs of her knickers had gone missing.

"Could you pass my washbag, Mum?" Libby asked, suppressing a much needed eye roll. She was finally getting out of hospital today. The pneumonia had been so severe that it had required two days of intravenous antibiotics, and only now were her oxygen saturations and peak flows improving.

She had also been measured, poked and prodded, declared "underweight", her lung function deemed "poor". Unfortunately, the need for her to eat properly, keep more regular hours and take better care of her asthma had been reiterated in front of her parents and Jamie many times over the last few days. Libby's mantra, that she could look after herself, was beginning to look a little far from the truth. Her parents wanted to stay down longer but she knew her dad couldn't afford to take any more time off. Work was scarce enough as it was; if he was thought to be unreliable it might dry up altogether.

"Your father's on his way over, then I'll pop off to pack up what you need from the flat and pick up Rosie before we head to Jamie's house."

"Mum, I've told you," Libby said, gritting her teeth to keep from losing her temper. "I'm not going to Jamie's house. It was kind of him to let you stay but I'm better now and I'm perfectly capable of–"

"Hello, ladies," Jamie called from the doorway.

"Dr Grantham," Libby's mum breathed.

"Please, Rita, I've told you, it's Jamie," he said, smiling at Libby's mother as he moved further into the room.

"Of course... Jamie." Rita had recovered somewhat but she still sounded like she'd jogged a good few miles. "It's just a reflex when you've got your *doctor clothes* on."

"They're scrubs, Mum," Libby said through her teeth, then looked over at Jamie and forced a smile. "I was just telling Mum that I'll go straight back to the flat and collect Rosie's stuff later after nursery pick-up." Jamie's smile dropped and he frowned as he moved further into the room.

"Oh, that's okay," he told her, taking her bag out of her hands and zipping it up with annoying ease; the buggering thing had been refusing to budge for the last ten minutes. "I can give you a lift. Henry's covering my list this morning, and I'll bring Rosie back later." Libby turned to him and crossed her arms over her chest.

"*My flat* will be out of your way, and I've got nothing else to do." She watched as Jamie's frown deepened and his jaw clenched tight.

"Seeing as you're coming home to *my house* today and after I take you there you're going to spend the day resting until *I* bring Rosie home, that shouldn't be a problem."

"It'd take a load off me and your dad's minds if you had someone with you, love," Libby's mum said. "I think you should listen to Dr... I mean Jamie. He knows what he's talking about."

"Rita?" Jamie turned to her mother and smiled. Rita Penny looked like she had stopped breathing altogether. "Would you mind awfully popping to see if Libby's medication is ready? The ward pharmacist should have sorted it by now. I just need a moment with Libby."

"Of course, Jamie," Rita said after finally taking a breath. Then she bustled out of the room.

"Look, I really appreciate everything you've done for my family over the last few days, but I'm fine now. I can take care of Rosie and myself. There's no need to –"

"No." Jamie grabbed her bag off the bed and dumped it behind him. "You are *not* fine. You will *not* go home to that bloody little flat alone."

"Listen," Libby said, softening her tone. "You don't have to feel guilty, okay? I'm a single mum and I got sick; that is not your responsibility. These are not your problems; they're mine. I know you feel you owe us something but you don't." All of a sudden her throat felt tight and she had to swallow to get her next words out in a whisper. "The time... the time we spent with you... well... it meant a lot to me... and to Rosie. You don't have to feel bad. You're free to do as you want."

"I'm not–"

"But Jamie," she hesitated, and then reached up to put her hand on his chest. "I can't go through it again. I can't live that dream and then have it taken from me, taken from Rosie. It's not fair to either of us. That's why I've got to go *home*."

"I see," Jamie said, his voice tightly controlled.

Libby blew out a breath in what she hoped was relief but suspected was more likely to be disappointment. Now that she had absolved Jamie of any lingering guilt he might feel, he would be free to go back to his nice, uncomplicated life again. She didn't blame him. "I knew you'd understand."

"So the past week has been about pity has it?" he asked her, and she blinked.

"Uh ..."

"I felt sorry for you and Rosie, so I invited your whole family to stay at my house. Allowed your mother to traumatise my dog. Have a family of woodlice living in one of my house-plants, because I felt bad?"

"Uh... yes?"

Jamie moved so quickly that it caught Libby off guard. Before she knew what was happening she was up, sitting on the side of the bed and he was standing over her, his forehead very nearly touching hers and his hands either side of her hips. "So then, nothing to do with the fact you are the most beautiful woman I have ever seen in my life?"

Libby's mouth fell open and her eyes went wide as she looked up at him.

"Nothing to do with how funny, kind and clever you are; what a wonderful mother to Rosie you are? Nothing to do with the thought of you and Rosie not being in my life making me feel like I can't breathe? That when I knew I was coming home to you at night I would be smiling all day, and when that stopped I was like a bear with a sore head? Nothing to do with the fact I would do *anything* to be with you. I would beg, borrow or steal. I would abandon *any* of my stupid pointless stuck-up "principles" just for one sodding day in your company?"

"I ..."

"You seem to think I'm a better man than I am. I promise you, Libby, I'm not that self-sacrificing."

"But... but you said ..."

"I think it's best if we forget what's been said." Libby opened her mouth to speak but snapped it shut when his hand came up and a finger settled over her lips.

"Now," he went on, his tone softer and his breath feathering across her face, "I can understand your concerns. I can see why you don't trust me at the moment, but I'm afraid that whilst you're unwell I'm not prepared for you to make any decisions that might hinder your recovery. You'll be coming home with me. All you will be doing over the next two weeks is revising for your exams, and you *will* let me take care of you and Rosie."

Libby's eyes flashed and she batted his hand away from her mouth. "You can't dictate to me what–"

"Look, I didn't want it to come to this, Libby, but it's pretty obvious your parents don't know exactly what it is you do at that club."

Libby blinked and her brows pleated in confusion. "What's that got to do with anything?"

Jamie huffed out a breath and pushed back from the bed to take a step away. She watched as his eyes went cold and his jaw firmed. "If you're prepared to put your health at risk *I will* tell them how you've been making your money."

"You wouldn't," she whispered, feeling all the blood drain from her face. Desperation clouded her thoughts. All her frantic mind could focus on was convincing him not to tell her parents.

She had already let them down so badly. She knew she wouldn't be able to bear it if they knew. It would kill her father. Fear meant that she wasn't even aware of her movements as she jumped down from the bed and walked towards him, before laying both her hands on his chest and looking up at him, her eyes wide with desperation.

"You can't tell them," she said, annoyed that she couldn't keep her voice steady. "Please, please... I couldn't stand it if they knew. I've already let them down so much. I ..." She broke off as her breathing became more laboured, the wheeze, always lurking in the background, became more pronounced.

"Shit," Jamie swore. Just as she started really struggling she was lifted off her feet and up onto the bed. Within seconds an oxygen mask was over her face and her inhaler was in her hand. One large hand supported her back to sit her forward and the other moved the mask and then closed over her shaking hands to bring the inhaler up to her mouth. She gave herself five puffs, then inhaled deeply, fighting the suffocating panic which always accompanied a bad attack.

~

As Jamie looked down at Libby's colourless face he felt like the worst kind of bastard. Bloody hell, he knew stress was a trigger for her asthma and he definitely knew how much anxiety threatening to tell her parents would induce, but, selfish prick that he was, he'd gone ahead and done it anyway. The funny thing was that Libby's parents had already confided in him that they knew all about Libby's job.

"You fell out, didn't you?" Libby's dad had asked the first night at Jamie's house. "That's why she's being a stubborn article, isn't it?"

"Uh–" Jamie hadn't been quite sure what to say or how to explain what had happened.

"Don't worry," Martin Penny had said, his mouth flattening into a grim line. "I can guess what it was about. Cocktails my arse: I know what Libby does and where she does it."

"Martin, love, don't," Rita had cut in, laying her hand on her husband's arm.

"He knows, Rita," Martin had gone on. "Same as we do. I'll admit it doesn't sit well with me. No father wants to hear that his daughter makes money like that. But who am I to tell her to stop? It's not like I can support her and Rosie. Anyway, I've spoken to the guy that owns the place a few times, decent chap. I know she's at least safe."

"Why haven't you ever talked to her about it?" Jamie had asked cautiously.

Martin shrugged. "She takes everything on herself. Thinks she's a disappointment to her mother and me. Thinks we're not proud of her when nothing could be further from the truth. I don't want to add this in as well."

So yes, Jamie knew he was making an empty threat, but he'd thought the means justified the ends. He hadn't considered the stress that a threat like that would put on Libby.

He watched as she finally relaxed back into the pillows, relieved that her cheeks were becoming flushed rather than the deathly pale with blue-tinged lips he'd witnessed mere minutes ago. He ran both hands through his hair and then scrubbed them down his face.

"Libby, I'm sorry," he said softly. She closed her eyes and turned her head away, but not before he saw the shimmer of tears across them. He reached up to touch her face but withdrew his hand before it could make contact. "I... I just can't let you go home alone. Not today. Not after the scare you've given me. Please under–"

"Could you check if Mum's found the poor nurse yet? Last time she talked their ears off for a good twenty minutes about whether they felt stereotyped in their traditionally female roles. She was only appeased once they managed to produce Jeff from the urology ward." Jeff was a large tattooed nurse who scared the crap out of most of the junior doctors.

"Right, yes, okay. I'll just–"

"I'll ask Kira to bring Brian over to your house later. She can pick up Rosie." Libby's defeated tone made Jamie feel even worse, but it didn't change the relief that swept through him at her capitulation. Whether she liked it or not she needed a break. She needed to heal. And, for his sanity, he needed to be the man who enabled her to.

"Good... that's good, Libby," he said, and she gave a jerky nod, still with her face turned away from his. He sighed and turned on his heel to leave the room.

When he'd made it out through the door he could hear Rita

Penny's voice carrying down the corridor. Some poor nurse was receiving a lecture on the dangers of female domestic abuse and how to guard against it with your male partner. When the nurse in question, obviously at the end of her tether, told Rita that she was a lesbian Rita was thrilled, telling the bewildered nurse how fantastic that was and how if more people went for that option men could be phased out entirely after a few generations. Jamie caught Libby's dad's patient expression as he waited by his wife's side, and despite his worry for Libby he almost laughed.

"Oh Dr... I mean Jamie," Rita said as she saw him walking towards them, her tone switching from militant feminist to soft and deferential in the blink of an eye. He looked to the nurse.

"Could you do a set of obs – Libby just had another bout of wheeze."

As the nurse went off to Libby's room Jamie turned back to her parents and took in the worry clouding their features.

"Maybe you should stay on a bit, love," Martin muttered to his wife.

"I can phone the café now," she said, digging out her mobile from her cavernous handbag. "With any luck they'll still keep me on."

Jamie laid a hand on her arm to stop her. "I promise I'll look after her," he told them both. Some of the fear faded from their expressions and they both looked up at him as though he was the answer to their prayers and not the bully he felt like.

Chapter 24

I'm on to you

"It's been over two weeks," Libby said through gritted teeth as she looked down at Jamie, Rosie and Beauty, all of whom were sprawled across his vast sofa, ignoring her in favour of the National Geographic channel. Since they'd moved in Rosie had commandeered the remote with ruthless efficiency. Her particular love was wildlife programmes, preferably with insects. She had even asked Jamie if he would buy her a tarantula – he'd gone a little pale, it was the only time Libby had seen him deny her daughter anything; he'd promised her a lizard instead. "We're going back to the flat today, remember?" That drew Rosie's attention and she turned her big blue eyes to Libby.

"Please, Mummy," she begged, untangling her hands from Beauty's fur and clasping them in front of her. "I want to stay with Jamie and Beauty." Rosie knew exactly how to work the adults around her: she added just the right amount of trembling sadness to her voice and allowed her lip to give the barest hint of a wobble.

"Little Louse," Libby said, sinking down onto her knees in

front of her daughter and gathering up her small hands. "We don't live here, baby. Jamie's been kind letting us stay but we've got to let him get on with his stuff now."

"We *are* his stuff!" Rosie protested, yanking her hands away and shoving them back into Beauty's fur. "He'd be bored without us around."

Libby rolled her eyes; she was pretty sure Jamie would not miss the drawing of a "family" Rosie had done on the side of his kitchen island: the pristine white surface was now marred with purple felt tip, the "mummy", "daddy" and "little girl" in the picture were just smiling heads with two legs that bizarrely met in the middle, giving them the appearance of happy sperm. The "dog" next to them was more like a squiggle with matchstick legs. So, to the untrained eye it was simply three sperm and a sort-of-sheep.

On the discovery of this artistic endeavour Libby had sent a tearful Rosie to her room whilst Jamie (unhelpfully) had been battling with his laughter. He'd refused to let her break out the industrial cleaning products to wipe it off, declaring it "a masterpiece", yet again making him Rosie's hero.

"You kind of *are* "my stuff"," Jamie told Libby, trying to move his leg out from under Beauty and earning a low growl for his efforts.

"Jamie, please, you're not helping," Libby told him in a low voice, shooting him a warning glance. Jamie smiled and managed to push a disgruntled Beauty fully off his legs so he could stand up. He grabbed Libby's hand, pulled her up from her squat on the floor in front of Rosie, and then drew her away from the sofa. Once they were next to the sperm/sheep picture on the kitchen island he turned to face her, keeping hold of her hand and giving her a wide smile. She opened her mouth to speak but before she could get any actual words out his lips were on hers. And just like that, her mind blanked.

In her defence Jamie had been gradually chipping away at her resolve since they moved in. When Libby first arrived from the hospital it had just been handholding and the like. Over the last few days, any chance he had he would kiss her, hug her, tuck her under his arm when they went out. Her revision had been conducted mostly on his sofa with her held between his legs whilst either she read or he tested her. Every question she got right he would kiss the side of her head or nuzzle her neck. She was on track to be the most well prepared student in the year at this rate – none of her friends had their own personal consultants helping them learn the curriculum and doling out affection for every correct answer. The whole thing was scrambling her mind. The feel of his big body against hers and his strong arms around her was like a drug.

So when his lips covered hers, his clean, masculine, citrusy scent surrounded her and his hands sunk into her hair, she lost her mind again and kissed him back.

"I'm on to you, you know," Libby breathed as Jamie pulled back and proceeded to kiss both her eyelids in turn.

"I don't know what you're talking about," he murmured, moving on to kiss the tip of her nose, then giving her a smug grin.

"Every time I talk about moving out you start with the... the... mind-scrambling stuff."

Jamie's smile turned up a few notches and his body started shaking with suppressed laughter. "How am I mind-scrambling?"

She rolled her eyes and pushed back slightly, gaining an inch or two of distance so that her brain could function again, but still in the circle of his arms. "You and your... lips and your stubble and... and... ugh!" Libby gave him one final shove against his hard chest and this time he let her move away.

Her hair was loose down her back and shoulders *again*

(Jamie had an annoying habit of pulling it down every time he had access to it), so she dug another elastic band out of her pocket and started shoving it all back into a messy arrangement at the back of her head. Jamie just stood there watching her jerky movements with a slight smile on his face and his arms crossed over his chest. When she was finished she put her hands on her hips and took a deep breath.

"Right, okay," she started, but her eyes wandered down to the muscles of his forearms and she lost her train of thought. When she looked back up at his face, his smile had gone from small to wide again and he took a step forward. She took a corresponding one back and held up her hand.

"Stay right there, Big Guy. I'm going to say my piece with *no* mind-scrambling nonsense this time." Jamie held both his hands up in a gesture of surrender and stayed where he was. "Now, I've packed up our things." At this pronouncement the smile on Jamie's face died and his brows drew together. "We *are* leaving today."

"Libby–"

"I appreciate everything. I really, really do. But Rosie and I, we have to get back to real life now. We–"

"Helloooo?" a very loud voice sing-songed down Jamie's hallway, and both of them turned in its direction. "Darling? Are you all ready? Daddy's got some lovely pork chops on the go, so ..." A tall middle-aged lady, immaculately dressed in wide-leg white trousers and a camel-coloured, sleeveless, cashmere jumper, came striding into the kitchen. Her short, ash-blonde hair was beautifully styled and her face flawlessly made up. And as if her appearance did not scream "Posh" loudly enough, the pearl earrings with matching necklace sealed the deal.

Libby felt instantly at a disadvantage in her torn jeans and *Star Wars* T-shirt. The woman froze for a moment in the doorway, her eyes on Libby, before her beautiful face broke into a wide smile. "You must be *her*," she said, moving across the kitchen to take both Libby's hands in hers and then kissing her cheek. "I've heard so much about you from my family. It's frightfully good to finally meet you."

"Uh... hi," Libby squeaked out, more than a little overwhelmed.

"Libby, this is my mum, Olivia."

"Oh don't be so ridiculous, darling," Olivia said, looking over at her son but still holding onto Libby's hands. "Nobody calls me Olivia." She turned back to Libby and softened her tone. "I'm Bunty."

"Hi Bunty," Libby said, smiling up at this perfect woman and wondering why all posh people had such weird nicknames. Bunty sucked in a breath as her eyes swept Libby's face. "My God, you really are beautiful," she whispered; then her eyes dropped down to Libby's chest. "Is that a Storm Trooper over your breasts darling?"

"Uh... yes," Libby replied, feeling her face heat.

"How fascinating."

"Mummy?" Rosie's voice sounded from across the room, where she was standing with Beauty. When the dog caught sight of Bunty her ears pricked forward and she came bounding up to her.

"Sit!" The command was belted out in a way that only incredibly posh, incredibly doggy people can master. Libby nearly fell into a squat herself. Beauty came to an abrupt halt and her backside sunk to the ground. It was the first time Libby had seen her obey a direct order. Bunty released Libby's hands to give Beauty a scratch behind the ears and then moved to Rosie, who was bravely standing her ground in the doorway, clutching Alan in front of her like a shield.

"Well, aren't you a scrummy thing," Bunty said as she crouched down to Rosie's level. Rosie frowned at her and pressed her lips together. "I hear Beauty has fallen head over heels in love with you. I think you and I are going to be the only ones who'll be able to train her – we'll have to work together." Rosie's frown melted away and she gave Bunty a tentative smile. "And who's this one?" Bunty asked, pointing at the dog-eared, fluffy spider.

"He's Alan," Rosie told her.

"Ah, I had a second cousin twice removed called Alan, terrible whiskey problem but an overall good egg – strong name. He must be very special." Rosie nodded and her smile widened a fraction.

"Do you think he'd like a friend?" Bunty asked, reaching inside her bag and pulling out another soft toy, this one brand-new, also fluffy and... a woodlouse. Rosie's eyes widened for a moment as Bunty held out the toy. She looked over to Libby, who gave her a nod, then she slowly reached out and reverently took the new toy from Bunty's outstretched hand.

"Thank you, lady," Rosie said, snuggling her face into the fluff.

"Seb calls me Nana Bunty. Would you like to call me that too?"

"'Kay," muttered Rosie as she gathered both toy mini-beasts up into one arm and took Bunty's hand in her free one.

"Right then," Bunty said, leading Rosie across the kitchen to Libby and Jamie. "Now, we really must get going. The Beeb have forecast a good half hour of sunshine this afternoon. If we're not careful we'll miss it and your father will have eaten all the pork, the old sod."

"What's a sod?" asked Rosie.

"Oh, don't worry, darling," Bunty said briskly, moving towards the hallway and pulling Rosie along with her. "You'll get to meet one this afternoon."

"I... er... Mrs Granth... I mean Bunty, I was just explaining to Jamie that we–"

"Ah, yes. Jamie went through all that. I'm sure it can wait. Jamie, darling, *please* tell me you're going to bring something for that animal. Last time he ate nearly a year's supply of Luther's food and you do know we have to have it specially imported."

"Right, Mum," Jamie muttered as he slung Beauty's huge sack of dog biscuits over his shoulder.

"But... I'm... I'm not really dressed to go anywhere. I..."

"Nonsense. You look absolutely fabulous. And it's just family. Nothing to worry about."

Chapter 25

Independent lady

Libby leant over the huge sink in the massive bathroom she'd managed to sneak off to, and splashed water on her face. Rosie was having the time of her life with Seb and the two dogs (Jamie's parents had a Shih Tzu called Luther – a tiny ball of fluff with an inordinately loud bark, which Rosie loved almost as much as Beauty) in the grounds – yes, *grounds* – of the goddamn mansion which was Jamie's family's London home in Richmond (it was only one of the family homes, the other being on the south coast – you know, near the *two* boats they also owned). Libby had known from Jamie's accent that he was posh and his house in Wimbledon suggested a certain amount of wealth, but that was nothing compared to this. However it wasn't just the shock of all this luxury that had pushed her to her bathroom retreat.

"Just family and nothing to worry about" – that was what Bunty had said. Well, it might just be family, but it was becoming clear that Libby was not considered a part of that, and the whole *nothing to worry about* assertion seemed to be very far from the truth. Giles, Jamie's father, was the polar

opposite of his wife. He seemed quiet and watchful, and viewed Libby with undisguised suspicion.

Although this was annoying, the truly upsetting aspect of the day was Jamie's older nephew's new reaction to her. Something had changed for the sixteen-year-old. He could no longer meet her eyes when he greeted her, he made no comment on her *Star Wars* T-shirt: all signs of open friendliness were a thing of the past. When she spoke to him he blushed and moved away. Libby was only in his company for ten minutes when she realised that *he knew*. He wasn't being deliberately rude to her, but it was obvious she terrified him and he didn't know what to make of her.

She wiped her face with the hand towel and took a deep breath. One more hour tops and she could leave. If Jamie wouldn't drive her she'd call a taxi. Any more silent disapproval from Jamie's dad or embarrassment from his nephew and she thought she would scream. A knock on the door made her jump and she clutched her chest before she turned to open it, revealing a concerned Amy just outside.

"You okay?" Amy asked, smiling as she walked into the bathroom. "I thought you might have fallen down the bog or something."

Libby forced a smile. "I'm fine," she said. "Got lost on the trek over here."

Amy laughed. "I know, right? This place is super intimidating at first but you'll soon get used to it. Come on, I'll walk you back so you can find the way." Amy linked her arm through Libby's to pull her along the corridor and back out to the garden, chattering happily about Seb and Rosie and how well they got on, and how Libby was a saint for putting up with "The Beast" for the last two weeks. Libby wasn't sure whether Amy meant her brother-in-law or the dog.

"When are you planning on moving out of Jamie's house,

Libby?" Giles's voice cut across Amy's chatter as they rejoined the group and Libby stopped in her tracks.

"I–" she started, but Jamie turned around from his position at the barbeque to glare at his father.

"Dad, when, or if, Libby moves out is between me and her."

Giles shrugged his broad shoulders as if he didn't care either way, but his shrewd gaze was fixed on Libby. He was slightly shorter than his sons, but still well over six foot, with a full head of grey hair. "It just seems to me that things have moved on awfully quickly. I mean, you haven't even been seeing each other that long, have you?"

"Libby was sick, Dad," Jamie said through gritted teeth. Libby noticed that his knuckles were white where he was gripping the barbeque tongs.

"Ah yes, you were taken ill at work I understand. Jamie was quite the knight in shining armour by all accounts."

"Yes," Libby said warily, "yes, Jamie's been really kind."

"No family or somebody more *appropriate* to take you in after this conveniently timed illness." There was a loud clatter as the tongs fell onto the tiles of the patio and Jamie took a step towards his father.

"Dad!"

"Giles!"

Jamie and his mother shouted out together, but Giles just grinned and held both his hands up in surrender.

"Okay, okay. Calm down you lot. Just saying things how I see them. I'm sure Libby here appreciates a little honesty."

Libby was staring down the immaculate lawn at her daughter and Seb taking turns down the slide from the huge climbing frame, to be showered with copious Shih Tzu and mutt-dog beast drool at the bottom. She straightened her spine. All this beauty and wealth didn't make you a better person. Maybe it made you lucky to be born into a rich family, maybe it made you shrewd and cutthroat in business. But the man in front of her implying that she was a gold-digger wasn't any better than her. She realised that she was done defending herself to men who were too pig ignorant and judgemental to get their facts straight. Giles Grantham could believe what he wanted about her.

"Thank you so much for the offer of lunch," Libby said to Bunty, who was staring furiously at her husband and looked ready to rip his head off. "I'm sorry but Rosie and I have got to go. A friend is coming to help us move back to my flat today and I told her I'd be ready by three." She took a step away and then stopped mid stride to turn back to Dan and Amy. "Your son knows I work as a stripper by the way," she told Dan, and wasn't surprised by all the shocked gasps around them. Will was out of earshot over the goddamn *stone balustrade* (the minute Libby had seen that around the patio she should have known she was out of her depth). "I don't know if you told him or he overheard but he knows. It might be a good idea to talk to him about it, but I'll leave that up to you."

"For fuck's sake, Dad," Jamie whisper-shouted once Libby moved off down the garden. To his frustration his dad was still staring after Libby in shock with his mouth slightly open.

"She's a *stripper*?" he asked, and Jamie stepped into his line of sight.

"No, Dad," he snapped. "She's a medical student and a single mother, and she had to fund her own degree. Stripping is a means to an end. And anyway, it's more like, I don't know, gymnastics meets burlesque meets modern dance in your underwear – and she's bloody fantastic at it." As Jamie said the words he realised that it was true. She *was* bloody fantastic up on that stage.

"I'll second that," muttered Dan, earning a scowl from Jamie.

"Dad! You've *seen* her dancing?" Will had rejoined the group and his wide eyes were fixed on his father. "Am I the *only* one who hasn't seen her dance? You know that's totally unfair, don't you?" He was all six foot of bristling teenage injustice.

"Stop being weird around her, Will," Jamie snapped. "She doesn't wear any less than she would to swim, and it's all gymnastics stuff with a few pole spins thrown in, all right?"

Will's eyes went slightly unfocused. "Poles," he muttered into the middle distance, lost in his own thoughts.

"And you." Jamie pointed at his brother. "Why did you tell him about it? Wasn't that a bit unneces–"

"I overheard *you*, Uncle Jamie," Will snapped out of his trance to interrupt. "When you and Dad were arguing, you weren't exactly subtle."

"Right... well..." Jamie trailed off and rubbed the back of his neck. "Can you just be normal around her, okay? Talk to her about *Games of Thrones* or *Star Trek* or something. She's still the same nerd she was before you found out what she does to earn money for university."

"Be glad that you won't have to strip to earn your uni fees, young man," Amy said, aiming a furious look at her stepson. "Bet there's plenty of male students out there doing a bit of the Full Monty for some cash."

"A stripper," Jamie's dad repeated, his wide eyes still fixed on Libby, who was trying to extract a resistant Rosie from the climbing frame.

"Dad," Jamie said in a warning tone. "Before you start–"

"I thought you were supporting her?"

"What? No. She makes her own money and she's in the middle of her medical degree so–"

"Medical degree?" His dad's wide eyes shot to Jamie's and the old bastard bit his lip. "Oh balls. I've made a right pillock of myself, haven't I?"

"Dad," Jamie growled. "I *told* you she was a medical student."

"Giles, you never listen, you stupid bugger," Jamie's mum put in, aiming a frustrated look at her husband. He shrugged and threw up his hands.

"I thought she was a bloody loafing sponger like the last dozen. My hearing aids have been playing me up. A lot of the time I just nod along when you lot are on about something."

Jamie's mum rolled her eyes and put her hands on his hips. "Giles, you can hear just fine, you just choose not to listen. For goodness sake, does she look anything like the others?"

"But ..." Jamie's brow wrinkled in confusion. "But I thought you approved of the others? I thought that's what you wanted for me?"

Bunty sighed. "All we've ever wanted for you is to be happy, darling."

"But I thought you wanted me to be with someone... er... someone who..."

"Oh God, please don't say someone from a *nice* family. Is that why you brought home all those vapid girls? Darling, we are not living in the eighteen hundreds." Bunty narrowed her eyes at him. "And we're not snobs, although I'm starting to think perhaps *you* are."

Giles looked over his son's shoulder to Libby and smiled. "By Jove, what is she wearing? Is that a Storm Trooper?"

Jamie sighed. "Yes, Dad, she's kind of into *Star Wars*."

"And *Game of Thrones*," Will put in helpfully. "Oh, and

Harry Potter, Star Trek, Lord of the Rings, Buffy the Vampire Slayer, Doctor Who..."

"Never seen a dolly bird dressed like that," Giles said through an amused smile. "Are those holes in her jeans? How eccentric."

"You like her now because she has holes in her jeans?" Jamie asked, his eyebrows going up in confusion.

"Jamie." Giles focused on his son and his voice became softer. "The last woman you brought home was stunningly beautiful, dressed top to toe in designer clothes, the very definition of high-maintenance, and she had not done one bloody proper day's work in her life. The girl before that wasn't much better. You, my boy, have a type."

"Dad–"

"I'm afraid that when I looked at this woman I didn't get past her face and I made assumptions. Add in the child and our experience with your bro–"

Giles broke off and glanced at Will. "It's all right, Grandpa. I know Mum was a total bi... not a nice person back then."

"Will, it's not that–"

"And I know she's never worked a day in her life either. I love her, but I'm old enough to understand those things about her."

"Well," Giles cleared his throat. "I didn't know that this Libby girl was an entrepreneur and an independent lady on her way to being a doctor. That changes things."

"Great," Jamie bit out as he watched Libby struggle up the steps towards them with a reluctant Rosie. "That's great, Dad but thanks to you I'm right back at square one. Again."

"Thank you so much for everything Mrs Grantham," Libby said as she lowered Rosie onto her feet and then grabbed her hand to stop her making a run for it back to the climbing frame. "But we really must be going."

"I'm afraid I've been the most terrible arse," Jamie's dad said, moving past his son to block her path.

Libby frowned and in her shock she made the mistake of letting go of Rosie's hand. The little girl shot off back down the steps towards an excitable Beauty, Luther and Seb.

"You... but I..." Libby stuttered to a halt and shook her head as if to clear it. After taking a deep breath she stepped closer to Giles and lowered her voice. "You don't need to apologise for wanting more for your son," she told him, her expression earnest. "I totally understand that most families would not want... well; I understand that. It's just, I can't be around it, and I can't allow my daughter to be around it either. You're protective of your children so you'll understand that I'm protective of mine."

She touched Giles's arm briefly, giving him a small smile, which did not reach her eyes, then stepped back to call Rosie. Luckily Rosie was already running towards her, holding a dead slug aloft for Libby's inspection. At that moment Kira came bursting onto the patio followed by a stunned-looking Will.

"Bugger me," she said as she spotted Libby. "This place is massive." She moved to Giles and Bunty and slapped them both on the back saying, "You must be Mr and Mrs G. Good going – fantastic pad. Have you thought about holding a mini festival in the garden?"

"Bunty, Giles, this is Kira," Libby said, her wide eyes fixed on her friend, who was steadfastly ignoring Libby's desperate head gestures towards the exit.

"Bunty and Giles?" Kira asked, her eyebrows lifting into her hairline and her lips smashed together to suppress laughter, which instead came out as a strangled snort. Jamie's parents were too busy taking in Kira's tie-dye-covered, pink-haired appearance to be offended by her amusement at their names. Kira had been threatening to go back to the full-on pink look for a while and Libby had assumed that working on the wards would be some sort of deterrent. Apparently not.

"I thought I told you to wait in the car," said Libby through her teeth.

"Goodness, what an interesting hair style," Bunty said, smiling over at Kira.

"Thanks, Bunty. I can give you the name of my hairdresser if you like – half-price dye job at the mo."

"I'll take it under consideration. Now, tell me more about this festival," Bunty encouraged.

"Oh, I help organise it every year. Just some local folk bands, a few bongos, big bonfire, that type of thing. No hard drugs or anything like that, maybe a couple of reefers but it's more about communing with nature than anything else. Naked fire-dancing, glitter blessings. We usually have to trek out to a field in Hampshire to do it." She nudged Giles with her elbow. "Be right up your street, eh, Giles?"

"What a capital idea, young lady," Giles said through a wide smile, and Libby's mouth dropped open. "We could get the parish council up here for it instead of the annual tea and cakes on the lawn. Shake those stuffy old buggers up a bit."

"Mummy, can I say bugger when I'm fifty-eight?" Rosie asked.

"Maybe best you forget that word for now, honey," Jamie put in as he lifted Rosie up from the ground and settled her on his hip.

"Is Mr Tully an old bugger?" Rosie asked, and Libby sighed. Mr Tully was their landlord and the very definition of "old bugger".

"Yes, of course he is, Squidget," Kira said, muzzing up Rosie's hair.

"Ki-Ki," Libby growled.

"What?" Kira shrugged her shoulders. "He is. You shouldn't lie to children."

"Come on you two," Libby ushered Kira towards the patio doors and reached for Rosie, who was still on Jamie's hip. Unfortunately neither Jamie nor Rosie were cooperating.

"Stay," Jamie whispered in her ear.

"I can't," she muttered back, putting a hand around Rosie's middle to tug her away.

"Will you excuse us for a moment," Bunty suddenly put in and strode over to Libby, steering her away from the group and into the house.

"Bunty I–" Libby started, as she turned to face her when they were away from the others, in the large living room, but Bunty raised a hand to cut her off.

"Let's start again, darling," she said. When Libby opened her mouth to speak Bunty shook her head. "Give us a chance. I've never seen Jamie this happy with a woman before. He's never talked about anyone like he talks about you. He's ..." Bunty's eyes misted over and she leaned further into her. "He puts so much pressure on himself. We had a lot of... trouble with Dan when he was a teenager: drugs, alcohol, expulsions from schools, missing persons' reports. It was very stressful. Eventually we had to send Dan away to a detox unit. When he came back he found out a girl he knew was pregnant. Will came along, which was probably the best thing for Dan, although Will's mother ..." Bunty grimaced. "She's an acquired taste; let's leave it at that. Anyway, Jamie was younger and he saw how worried we were, how much it affected us. I don't want to think about how many times he saw me crying when he came home from school. So he turned into Stepford Son.

Everything he did had to be perfect. He had to come top of the class. Never put a foot wrong. I think he was trying to make up for Dan. He's always been the type to take everything on himself.

"But life's not perfect, and he doesn't have to be perfect for us. We just want him to be happy – and the way he's talked about you and Rosie over the last few weeks, I *know* you make him happy."

"That is kind of you to say, and please believe me that it means a lot to me. But Giles–"

"Giles is just an idiot and I know Jamie won't speak to him for months if he's buggered this up for him. It'll damage their relationship *forever*. Just stay. Ask your... interesting friend to stay, and you'll see we're not a bunch of stuck-up old farts."

"Is Mr Tully an old fart?" Rosie said, peeking around Bunty's legs, and Libby closed her eyes in defeat.

Chapter 26

Stand down, Casanova

Libby looked around at the bedroom, strewn with their stuff, and forced herself to shut the door. She knew it was time to leave. It had been a week since they'd gone to Jamie's family home. After The Chat with Bunty, complete with the emotional blackmail, Libby had reluctantly rejoined the party. They had insisted on Kira staying as well and, after a couple of glasses of Pimms, Libby had actually started to relax. It became obvious once everyone got over the initial awkwardness that Jamie's family get-togethers were not staid perfunctory affairs from which people left as soon as possible.

The never-ending supply of food and alcohol stretched into the late afternoon and evening. By that stage everyone knew way too much information about Kira's exploits in India (she hadn't in fact got much further than Goa on her travels, as this was where she said she met "her kind of people" – from the photos it appeared that Kira's kind of people sported long beards, red rimmed eyes and had questionable hygiene, but that was not a huge surprise), including *Kira's Bowels Versus the Mumbai Surburban Railway Incident* in graphic detail.

After the kids had been tucked up in one of the many spare rooms and Bunty had moved onto the spirits, she'd toasted Libby's career choice, declaring that she wished she'd taken *her* clothes off more in her twenties before her body had waged its war with gravity and lost.

In the week since, Libby had spoken to Jamie's mother no less than *three* times, once being when Bunty and Giles both came to babysit so Jamie could take her out for their second ever official date. This was when Bunty had breezily informed a horror-struck Libby that she had taken it upon herself to phone her parents.

When Libby asked, with strained politeness, why on earth Bunty would consider that appropriate, Bunty had just shrugged and told her that "If my little boy was recovering from a very serious illness and had exams to contend with, I would want to know the lay of the land."

Libby had no words. She wasn't sure anyone except Bunty would refer to Jamie as a little boy, and she, being a mother of a four-year-old child herself, was certainly no little girl. She did however manage to let Bunty know that her mum had no idea about the stripping. Bunty reassured her that she had only referred to Libby's "work" in their discussion, not the nature of it.

"But of course we both agree that you'll have to be concentrating on your studies from now on," she'd told her, as if that was a totally obvious solution. The only thing that was obvious to Libby was that she had a total of seventy-two pounds and twenty-eight pence in her bank account and her rent was due in five days.

She turned and left the room. The next few days would be her last in his house and unbeknownst to Jamie this weekend would be her first back at work.

"We're not open, mate. Come back later. Much later." The large bouncer crossed his massive, tattooed arms over his chest and blocked the entrance to the club. Jamie gritted his teeth. He had been banging on those bloody doors for the last twenty minutes, with the pedestrians passing him by in a busy Covent Garden eyeing him like a lunatic – there was no way he was going anywhere.

"Look, *mate*, I know she's in there," he told Tattoo-Loving Bouncer.

"Who's in here or not is none of your fucking business until later, when we're open, and only then if you pay. A lot."

Jamie looked away and took a deep breath. The last time he lost his temper in this place he'd ended up unconscious. "I just want to talk to Libby for a moment. I'm her boyfriend, okay?" Tattoo-Loving Bouncer responded by planting his feet even wider and shaking his head once.

"Nobody disturbs the girls during practice."

Jamie ran his hands through his hair and paced away for a moment. An image of the same Tattoo-Loving Bouncer hovering around Libby with obvious concern the night of the disastrous stag party sprang into his mind. This man cared about her.

"She's not well," Jamie told him, and watched as Tattoo-Loving Bouncer's expression turned from hostile to carefully blank.

"What do you mean? I thought she–"

"She hasn't recovered fully and she has exams to study for. That's what she needs to be doing this weekend – not prancing around some pole so perverts can drool all over her."

"I think you know very well that none of the perverts get

close enough to those girls to even breathe on them, leave alone drool," Tattoo-Loving Bouncer said, his chest puffing up to even more ridiculous proportions so that his neck disappeared altogether. Jamie could practically smell the steroids.

"Okay, okay. Calm down. All I'm saying is that Libby shouldn't be here this weekend." Tattoo-Loving Bouncer's chest deflated slightly, his arms uncrossed and one of his hands went up to rub the back of his neck. "You know I'm right, don't you?" Jamie probed, sensing he was getting somewhere. Tattoo-Loving Bouncer sighed. "She looks tired, doesn't she?" Jamie went on.

"Look, the boss already told her not to dance," Tattoo Loving Bouncer said after a long pause. "She's one of the main attractions and Steve is normally all about pulling in the punters, but... well... she's Libby. We know this isn't really her gig. And, yes, she does look like shit at the moment."

"Barry?" The double doors were pushed open behind Tattoo-Loving Bouncer and a shorter, older but still well-built man stepped out onto the pavement. He looked closely at Jamie for a moment. "I know you. You're the bloody idiot that climbed on stage. What's going on out here?"

"Boss, I–"

"I'm Jamie, Libby's *partner*, and I'm here because she shouldn't be working at the moment. I've come to take her home." The shorter man's eyes widened for a moment before a slow smile spread over his face.

"Listen, boy," he started – it had been a long time since anyone but his mother had referred to Jamie as a boy. "If Barry here or I couldn't stop her dancing, what makes you think that you stand a snowball's chance in hell?"

Jamie puffed up his own chest, wishing just then that he too indulged in anabolic steroids. "She listens to me, okay?"

The shorter man started laughing. Jamie felt the last few threads of his temper fray.

"If she listens to you, fella, why the fuck is she currently shaking her gorgeous arse all over my club?"

The threads broke and Jamie made a sudden lunge forward to push past the two men, but Barry's large hand planted itself firmly in the middle of his chest and stopped him dead. He turned wild eyes to the shorter man and his fists clenched at his sides.

"Stand down, Casanova," the shorter man said, his amusement still evident in his voice. "They're practicing. No thongs in sight." He sighed. "Look, I know she shouldn't be dancing. I've offered to pay her for the weekend anyway if she'll go home. Even offered her a cut of the tips on top. But that woman in there is the most stubborn female I have ever come across in this business, and believe me that is saying something. She once told me she'd do anything to get ahead, "beg, borrow or steal", she said, which is total crap because she won't take charity. When I pushed it she threatened to go to another club."

Jamie felt his face drain of colour and he stepped back. "Shit."

"Shit is right, Romeo," the shorter man said. "You might not like *this* club much, but we keep our girls safe. Those other dives... private lap dances, back rooms ..." he trailed off and shook his head whilst Jamie gave a compulsive shudder. "Dragging her out now is not going to go down well, right?"

"Right," Jamie muttered, shoving his hands in his pockets and taking another step back.

"Hey," called the older man as Jamie turned to go. "I'll limit her to one set, okay?"

"Right," Jamie muttered again, ready to just get out of there. He heard the older man sigh and felt his hand on his arm.

"Look, I'm Steve, the owner." The man held his hand up for Jamie to shake. "I run the girls. She'll only be on stage for a few minutes later on, and you don't have to worry about what she's doing now."

"Right..." Jamie said, eyeing Steve's hand and making no move to shake it. "Whatever. I'll just leave you to "run your girls" then. Good luck with that."

"Ugh! You stubborn bastard. You're not getting it, are you?" Steve withdrew his hand and crossed his arms over his chest. "I'm not the enemy here. My girls are more safe within *my* club than they would be in *your* hospital from what I've seen." That statement had Jamie stopping in his tracks and his mouth falling open.

"What?"

"Took Claire an extra twenty minutes to cover up the bruises Libby was sporting a few weeks ago. That would not have happened in my gaff, mate."

Jamie felt his face heat and for once he was lost for words.

"Listen," Steve said, his tone softening as he registered Jamie's shock. "I care about Libby too, and not just because she's a great girl. I *owe* her."

"What do you mean?" Jamie asked, turning back to face the other two men and cocking his head to the side.

"Come in here and I'll tell you. Even better, I'll show you."

Jamie sighed; he had no desire to go back inside this place unless it was to extract Libby. Tattoo-Loving bouncer, a.k.a. Barry, did not look like he was going to allow an extraction to take place and Jamie did not want to see Libby dance on that stage again. But curiosity got the better of him and he followed the two men inside.

Once through the door they turned away from the entrance to the main club, down a dark corridor and up a small set of stairs, leaving Barry at the bottom. Steve pushed open a heavy oak door at the top and they both stepped into an office. There was a large desk with a desktop computer in the centre of the room, filing cabinets along one wall and a plush carpet underfoot. But the most striking thing about it was that the far wall was glass from ceiling to floor.

Jamie instinctively walked towards the glass, and froze at the view beneath. Three women were at the side of the stage, all of them using a waist-height bar to gracefully execute what appeared to be the type of stretching ballerinas performed. They were all wearing an assortment of leggings, T-shirts, the occasional leg-warmer, and they were definitely all covered head to foot.

The scruffiest woman, her hair restrained by multiple haphazardly applied elastic bands and her T-shirt declaring her allegiance to the Rebel Alliance, was the one Jamie's eyes immediately focused on. Libby was smiling at the woman next to her, who gave her shoulder a playful shove, causing her to hop a couple of steps, given that her other leg was suspended on the bar, and then retaliate with a slap to the other woman's arse. Steve had walked to his desk and Jamie heard him flip a switch. Feminine laughter filled the room.

"Don't make me punch you in the ovary," one of the two blondes with Libby was saying through her laughter.

"Punch me in the ovary and I will olive oil your pole later," Libby warned, smiling as she switched legs on the bar.

"Yes! Do it, Lib," the other blonde cried, abandoning her stretch to jump up and down with enthusiasm. "That was the funniest thing I'd seen in years."

"I nearly broke my arse, thank you both very much!" blonde number one retorted. "And then I had to just prance around you lot unscripted. You know I'm no good without choreography."

"I think at one stage you actually did the hula," Libby said. "It. Was. Awesome."

"Oh, bugger off, dancing sensei – we can't all have your talent."

Libby rolled her eyes. "Don't be a dick, Claire."

"Ah yes! Dicks!" blonde number one cried. "Back to the original subject. You were going to tell us if this guy has popped your cherry or not."

Libby straightened and put her hands on her hips. "Tara, you do know I have had an actual baby out of my vagina? My cherry is very much a thing of the past."

"Five years is a long time, Libby. I expect things have grown over again down there by now."

"I may not be a doctor yet but even I can tell you that what you've just said is a medical impossibility."

"Come on, Libby. Just–"

"Let's start," Libby cut them both off, and grinned. "If you're good girls I'll tell you what kind of kisser he is."

"Kissing? Ugh! You're such a Girl Guide. We want the juicy stuff."

Libby was facing away from the others now and fiddling with her phone. Jamie gave a start as the first beats of the Black Eyed Peas filled the office and the club below. After a moment the two blondes jogged off the stage and up the runways through the tables and chairs of the club. The music cut off as both girls got into position.

"From the top," Libby shouted, before starting the song again. The expressions on the women's faces faded from amusement to fierce concentration; they both flipped twice down the runways in time to the beat until they met in the middle and started a dance routine. Libby was shouting encouragement above the music throughout, and a couple of times she paused it to show them how one of their moves should be perfectly executed.

On the third pause one of the blondes interrupted her, asking her to change the song and give them a break. Libby shook her head. But after a few minutes of encouragement, and when it became clear she was facing a mutiny, she relented, moving to the centre of the stage as "Tears" by Clean Bandit filled the space. Jamie frowned; it was not a song he could imagine a stripper using to work a pole.

The blondes moved back to watch from the side of the stage as Libby fell into a deep crouch. What followed was one of the most beautiful things Jamie had ever seen. Libby danced the entire song as if the music was part of her body, her movements a combination of complex gymnastics and sweeping ballet. By the end he could actually feel a sting in the back of his eyes.

"My God," he whispered, stepping back from the glass. The blondes clapped and cheered as the song ended and were joined in their applause by Barry and two cleaners who had abandoned their duties to watch.

"So this teenager comes to me one day," Steve said, and Jamie jerked in surprise, so caught up in what he was watching he'd forgotten the bastard was even there, sitting behind his big desk. "Tells me she wants to dance for me. I thought no way was she eighteen. To be honest I would have guessed more like fifteen, what with Libby's aversion to make-up. I tell her to get lost. To come back when she's legal. She ignores me, walks up onto my stage and gives a performance that blows any dancer I've ever had out of the water.

"Selfish prick that I am, I hire her on the spot. I could tell you that I did it for altruistic reasons, seeing as she would have gone to another club had I not snapped her up, but I'm not that good of a bloke. I hired her because I knew immediately what she could do for my business.

"A month in, my take was up by a third. Two months on she'd started training the other dancers. Three months on I doubled my profits. That was when I splashed out on reinforcing the benches and tables. She showed me that insane Olympic gymnast shit on a bench one day – said she could work it into a performance as long as I let her ditch the stripper heels. Six months on, the heels were ditched and my business was the most successful of its kind in the UK. Now that she's teaching the girls all this other fancy shit, reckon profits will go up yet again. Believe me, I owe her. Every chance I get I slip extra money into her purse, her handbag. She's so disorganised that she's never even noticed. I pay her extra for coaching the girls, which she accepts, but she won't be paid more than them for dancing."

"Stubborn," Jamie muttered as he watched the girls on stage fall into a group hug.

"As fuck," Steve shot back. "'Fraid you're going to have to think outside the box if you want to sort this one out, sunshine." Jamie dragged his eyes away from the scene below him and focused on the man at his side.

"Are you serious about owing her? Would you help her even if it meant she didn't dance for you anymore?"

"She's trained the others up. One of the girls can even do the bench work. It wouldn't be the same, but it would still be totally unique." Steve paused and his eyes drifted to the women below before he hardened his expression. "I pay my debts and... she deserves to live the life she wants. Yes, I'd help with that."

Jamie's eyes followed Libby across the stage, an idea forming in his mind. All this time he'd been trying to restrict Libby, control her, box her in. He hadn't acknowledged the incredible talent involved in what she did here. He hadn't shown her the respect she deserved. It wasn't Libby who needed to change, it was him.

His eyes wandered to the rest of the club. The décor was plush, beautiful even, like an old ornate theatre; nothing like a typical strip club.

"How much would it cost to temporarily remove the poles?" Jamie asked.

Steve looked back at him for a moment, and then he smiled.

Chapter 27

Step down

"You've ..." Libby broke off as she stared down at the paper in her hand, then back up at Dr Morrison's averted face, "you've had a CRB check? I... I don't understand – why are you showing this to me?"

Dr Morrison had been waiting outside Libby's locker in the surgical department that morning when Libby arrived with Rosie and she'd asked if she could talk to Libby in her office. (The earliest Libby could drop Rosie off at the nursery was eight but the surgical team she was now placed with started much earlier. Libby had taken to bringing Rosie with her into the hospital before she dropped her at the nursery so she could print off the list and go through the patients in the secretaries' office; not an ideal activity with a four-year-old in tow, but it meant that although Libby was late for the ward round she was at least well prepared.) To be honest Libby had assumed it was about an inappropriate radiology request.

"I am approved for childcare purposes," Dr Morrison said to the desk, before affording Libby very brief eye contact. "I also hold a Paediatric Advanced Life Support certificate."

"Um... well. That's great. Good for you." Libby smiled awkwardly as she handed the papers back to Dr Morrison. Dr Morrison took a deep breath and squared her shoulders.

"I can look after Rosie for you in the mornings so you can start at seven-thirty with the surgical team. She would be safe with me and I know Dr Grantham starts work even earlier, as does the other student Kira."

Libby's mouth fell open. "I–"

"Hurrah!" shouted Rosie, jumping up and down at her side and jolting her hand. "I can stay with Millie!"

"I am always here at 0700 hours and I will provide a nutritionally balanced breakfast for Rosie every morning." Dr Morrision shoved another piece of paper under Libby's nose certifying her in dietetics for children. "The only referees I can provide are Dr and Mrs Phillips, but they are upstanding citizens and have four children and twelve grandchildren. Rosie would not be in any clinical area and would be under my observation the entire time."

Libby glanced at Dr Phillips, who was smiling up at Dr Morrison from his office chair. "Millie, love, I think you've given the girl enough evidence to be going on with." He turned his lined face toward Libby and winked. "The little lass will be fine with us and I can personally recommend Millie's "nutritionally balanced" breakfasts – she feeds me every day."

Libby frowned. "I... um ..." Rosie dropped her hand and moved over to Dr Morrison to pull on her skirt.

"Can we play the number game again?" Rosie asked.

"I can take her to the nursery for eight," Dr Morrison said to Libby.

"I can't ..." Libby cleared her throat and it was her turn to break eye contact. "I can't pay you or anything," she whispered, and Dr Morrison jerked in surprise.

"I do not need anything in return for taking care of Rosie."

"Millie's my friend, Mummy. Stop being so obtuse," Rosie said impatiently, and Libby's eyebrows travelled up into her hairline.

"Where on earth did you learn that word?" she muttered, but noticed Dr Morrison's face flushing as she cleared her throat. Libby sighed. "Okay, well, I guess if you don't mind. That would be great, Dr Morrison." To her shock the other woman's body visibly relaxed in relief and she smiled. It was the first real smile Libby had ever seen Dr Morrison give anyone. It transformed her face from cold, flawless perfection to a warm beauty that was almost breathtaking.

"Thank you," Dr Morrison whispered.

"You can call her Millie you know," Dr Phillips cut in. "And call me Donald."

"Yes, please. That would be... vastly preferable," Dr Morrison added.

"Okay... Millie," Libby said slowly, still feeling a little wrong-footed by this different side to Dr Morrison. Millie sat on her chair and Rosie climbed up into her lap.

"What bacteria do you want to look up today?" Millie asked Rosie as she clicked her computer on and brought up dozens of microbial images.

"Oh! What's that one?" Rosie asked, bouncing up and down and pointing at the central image.

"That is Chlamydia."

"Combidia?"

"No Cla – mid – ee – a."

"Maybe move on to the next set of slides, eh, Millie?" Donald put in, and Millie shrugged.

"This is one of the most important single-celled bacteria for her to–"

"I think the correct pronunciation of common STIs can wait a few years. You can revisit it with her when she's a teenager," Libby said gently. Millie blinked and when she looked up for a brief moment Libby could have sworn there were unshed tears in her eyes before she looked away.

"Are you..." Libby moved forward and touched Millie's shoulder, but withdrew her hand when Millie gave a tiny flinch.

"Yes," Millie said in a hoarse voice, then cleared her throat. "Yes, of course. I was just... well, I mean..." She closed her eyes for a moment, squared her shoulders, then gave Libby direct eye contact. "I would very much still like to know Rosie as a teenager. It was kind of you to... to say... to imply ..." She trailed off and looked back at the screen. "Thank you," she muttered, blinking as she took in the images.

"One of the girls in our flats is called Chlamydia," Rosie said, and Millie refocused on the little girl. Libby rolled her eyes to the ceiling. She really had to get enough money together to move out of that place.

"That is a strange, uninformed choice and highlights exactly why microbial knowledge is so important," Millie said as she glanced up at Libby again with a small smile. "Although maybe the correct pronunciation can wait until after you've left pre-school."

Libby hovered for a moment as Millie clicked through another set of slides and started to discuss the physical symptoms of Campylobacter (to a four-year-old, talk of bloody diarrhoea before nine in the morning was obviously quite acceptable). She caught Dr Phillips' eye as she turned to leave. He gave her an almost imperceptible nod of his head, then directed a warm look at Millie and Rosie.

"See you later then, Little Louse," Libby said.

"Mummy! This one can be flesh-eating!" Rosie cried, pointing at a picture of Streptococcus. "Can we get some to take home?"

Libby started backing away, wishing for the first time that Rosie were the kind of child to be appeased by a simple trip to Toys R' Us.

~

"We just think that you might want to step down from any educational role whilst we get this sorted out, Dr Grantham."

Jamie ground his teeth and forced himself to stay in his seat. He was separated from the Hospital Director by a huge expanse of desk – something that had long been abandoned as a way of intimidating patients, but was still used in the world of managing employees, which, it was being brought home to Jamie, was exactly what he was.

"I've *built* the educational programme in Anaesthetics from the ground up here, Nigel." Jamie refused to sink to Nigel's level and revert to the cold formality of "Mr Derwent". "All the simulation training across all the specialties is coordinated by me. You're saying I should just walk away from years of work over something so bloody ridiculous?"

"Are you or are you not in a relationship with Miss Penny?"

Jamie clenched his fists. "That's none of your goddamn business," he managed to get out through his gritted teeth.

Nigel sighed. "I'm afraid it is, when it affects the other students."

"How is it affecting the other students?"

"Right, well," Nigel looked down at a piece of paper in front of him, then back up at Jamie. "Apparently "favouritism", leading to prime learning opportunities being denied to other students. "Embarrassing situations and comments" in teaching sessions and lectures, which have proved at best a distraction and at worst very distressing for the students involved."

"Can I see that?" Jamie asked, holding out his hand.

"I'm afraid the complainant has asked to remain anonymous."

"*One* complaint? All this over *one* complaint? I can tell you exactly who "the complainant" is, and that snivelling little prick has had a more detrimental effect on his colleagues' educational experience than anything I've done this year."

"This may only be one complaint, Dr Grantham, but you are actually *living* with one of your students. You can't argue with that."

"She's not a schoolgirl, Nigel," Jamie retorted. "And I am not her direct supervisor."

"But you *are* in charge of the education programme. You've got to admit that makes the situation look a bit dodgy. Look, I'm sorry but the deanery has put its foot down with this. For the moment you're going to have to keep a low profile on the education front. In fact..." Nigel cleared his throat, looking uncomfortable for a moment, "I've had to ask Dr Maitland to take over your SIM training today."

"Terry? You asked Terry to do it? Nigel, Terry is an unmitigated twat. The last time he helped with SIM training he suggested that the students take a history from the dummy so that he could speak to them through the microphone from the other room. He couldn't even understand why that was weird. Believe me, it took a long time to explain why a seventy-thousand-pound piece of simulation equipment shouldn't be used for pointless role-play that could be done with an actual human face-to-face."

Nigel looked away from Jamie and shifted uncomfortably again before clearing his throat.

"Christ," Jamie swore, pushing up to standing so suddenly that Nigel jumped in his chair. "That is what he's doing, isn't it? He's using that state-of-the-art equipment to fucking *role play* without having to look the students in the eye."

"If there was any other way of sorting this out, Jamie, believe me I would have gone for it. But there's no getting around the fact that you are shacked up with a student, which is just not the done thing when you're Education Director."

"Fine," Jamie said, stalking to the door, "let Terry-Twat-Maitland use up valuable SIM time on pointless bullshit. Maybe you lot will realise how much bloody extra work I put in to keep the shit going week in, week out." He shut the door behind him before Nigel could respond, and looked at his watch. For a moment he panicked, thinking he was already five minutes late for teaching, but then he froze. He'd been complaining for three years about the amount of time the teaching took up, but now, faced with a free afternoon, he couldn't think of anything he wanted to do with it.

"Where's Jamie?" Libby whispered to Kira, as Daisy, the first of the students picked to take a history, went up to talk to SIM-man, who was propped up in the bed with his head turned toward the seat that Daisy was about to take. She looked back at the other students for a moment, a slightly bewildered expression on her face, and then jumped as SIM-man gave a dramatic groan.

"What is the point of interviewing a bloody dummy?" Paul, one of the other students in the row in front of Libby and Kira said. "This is mad. Where's that weirdo gone anyway? Is he seriously talking to Daisy through a mic from another room?" Paul turned to Libby. "Listen, where's your bloke? We need some proper teaching here, with the vivas coming up. Not this dickwad playing "let's pretend"."

"I don't know, honestly," Libby whispered back. She was starting to get a bad feeling about Jamie's absence, which only intensified when she saw Toby's barely suppressed smirk when he caught her eye. She turned fully to him and frowned.

"What did you do?" she hissed, feeling her face flush with anger and embarrassment.

"What? Me?" Toby asked. "I don't know what you're talking about."

"Argh!" Paul groaned and punched Toby on the arm. "What did you do now, you complete tosspot?"

Quite a few of the students were now directing angry glares at Toby.

"Hey!" he whisper-shouted. "I'm not the one banging the Educational Director, all right? If you want someone to blame for Dr Freak Show taking our teaching, maybe you should think about that."

Libby felt Kira's hand curve around hers and stared straight ahead, willing the tears she could feel building not to fall.

"*You're* not banging *anyone*, you pillock," Paul spat out to Toby in disgust. "Maybe you should concentrate on your own issues for a change."

Libby managed a tight smile for Paul and successfully blinked away the moisture in her eyes to get through the rest of the lecture. Okay, so Toby must have complained, and yes, he *was* a tosspot and a pillock. But she had to face facts: if it weren't for her relationship with Jamie he'd be teaching them right now. She paled as she considered the fact that she was directly affecting his livelihood. Okay, so she knew he didn't need the extra money, but his career was important to him. And she knew he loved it, he was good at it. All the students would be worse off because of her.

"Miss Penny." The sharp voice from the front of the room cut through her frantic thoughts and she jumped before looking up. "You may have been allowed to daydream through my predecessor's teaching sessions," Dr Maitland said, having finally emerged from the side room, "but *I* expect your full attention." Libby felt the heat creep up from her neck and flood her face. All eyes in the room turned to her and she wanted to melt into the chair with embarrassment. "Now, as I was saying: what did Daisy leave out of the history?"

There was a long pause and Dr Maitland's face began to look decidedly smug. Libby swallowed past her dry throat and forced herself to speak. "She forgot to ask about perineal sensation," she said, willing her voice not to break or waver. The smugness in Dr Maitland's expression morphed into annoyance and he gave her a sharp nod before dismissing the room.

If there was one thing the last four years had taught Libby to do, it was multi-task. She wasted no time in snatching up her bag and weaving through her curious colleagues to make it out of the door.

Chapter 28

Problem-solving

"One squillion times a kigillion?" Libby heard Rosie ask as she turned the corner to Millie's office.

"There's no such thing as a kigillion or a squillion," she heard Millie's quietly amused voice reply.

"Uh!" Rosie huffed out in a disgruntled sigh.

Dr Phillips piped up. "Okay then, ninety-five times one hundred and fifty-seven?"

"Fourteen thousand, nine-hundred and fifteen," Millie replied without missing a beat as Libby came to stand in the office doorway. Millie was sitting on the floor of her office in front of Rosie, who was perched on the leather chair, attempting a very weird plait at the side of Millie's head.

"Yowsers! That's cool!" Rosie shouted, pumping her little fist in the air. "You're a superhero."

"That she is," Dr Phillips put in. "A maths superhero."

"You'll be able to do that when you grow up," Millie said as turned to give Rosie a smile, and then started when she saw Libby in the doorway.

"Will I?" Rosie asked doubtfully.

"Yes, you're gifted," Millie told her as she pushed up to her feet. It was said as a statement, not an effusive compliment, as if it was a fact Rosie should be aware of already. For the second time that day Libby felt her eyes sting with tears.

"Mummy!" cried Rosie, jumping off the chair to shoot across the room and throw her arms around Libby's legs.

"Hey, Little Louse," Libby said, stroking Rosie's curls and smiling over at Millie, who was trying to get her hair back into some kind of order.

"Did you hear how super-cool Millie is? She can do any sum in the whole wowld."

"That *is* cool, darling," Libby muttered.

"If only all children felt like you, Rosie, I might have had friends at school," Millie said, smiling down at Rosie as she pulled her mass of brunette waves into the sleek knot she always wore, then carefully straightened a couple of items on her desk so they were back in perfect alignment.

"What d'you mean?" Rosie asked. "Didn't you have fwiends?"

"Oh... I ..." Millie froze, her eyes still focused on the desk. "Well, I am a bit... different, Rosie."

"I like your different," Rosie told her, and Millie glanced at her briefly, flashing a small smile.

"I'm glad. But at school they didn't really like different."

"That's stupid!" Rosie shouted in affronted disbelief.

Millie smiled and squatted down in front of the small tower of rage that was Libby's daughter. "Most of the time I wasn't even with children the same age as me, so friends... well, making friends was tricky. Not everyone has a gift for this. Now you – you are twice gifted: you can make friends *and* you can do maths."

Libby tilted her head to the side as she studied Millie. Could shy and awkward actually be mistaken for rude, arrogant and dismissive by an entire hospital? For a moment her mind flashed to an image of a small, serious little girl alone in a sea of older children, ignoring their laughter and banter as she bent over a maths book; just as the adult version tried to ignore other people now whilst bent over her scans.

"Thank you for picking her up today," Libby said, then hesitated a moment before she reached out to touch Millie's arm. Millie looked startled and stood from her crouch but didn't pull away as Libby had expected. She even managed some eye contact and the corners of her mouth pulled up for a second before she moved back. It was the closest thing to a smile Libby had ever seen from Millie at anyone other than Rosie.

"Bye," Rosie shouted, breaking from her mum to throw herself at Millie and hug her legs fiercely. Millie blinked and her eyebrows went up, giving her the slightly startled look she always seemed to wear whenever Rosie was affectionate. It took a moment, but Millie hugged her back just as fiercely.

"I can... I can look after her if you need to study this weekend," she offered after Rosie had moved away.

"Thanks, Millie, that's really kind but we're going to stay with her grandparents this weekend. I've got to work."

"But... but it's so close to the exams. It's not logical to work now. You must study."

"Well, it can't be helped I guess," Libby said, shrugging and backing out of the office.

"But... but you have to revise. I don't under–"

"Dr Morrison," Libby cut in, deliberately reverting to their previous formality. Millie's face went from concern back to the blank mask Libby was used to, and she felt a twinge of regret for shutting her down. "I *have* to work, and that I'm afraid is that."

Millie watched Libby and Rosie walk away down the corridor and wrung her hands together. Before she knew what she was doing, her fingers had travelled up her sleeve and were twisting the skin of her inner arm. She would have bruises later, but that was nothing new. Confrontation was not easy for her. She should have known not to overstep the mark with Libby.

The woman was not her friend. Luckily for Millie, it was convenient for Libby to let her look after Rosie. She was sure that if there were any other option Libby would have taken it. Who wanted an oddball like Millie in charge of their offspring?

Her quick mind flicked through the facts: Libby was a single mother who evidently supported herself; she only ever wore one pair of shoes; she used elastic bands to tie her hair back; she was incredibly proud and stubborn.

Millie glanced down at her own Louboutins, frowned, and then forced her hands apart. Reaching into her desk drawer she pulled out the arnicare cream to rub on her forearm; her years of practice made it possible for her to barely look as she applied it. She stared at her computer screen and cocked her head to the side, before hacking into the Dean and the Bursar's email accounts.

Problem-solving was one of her particular skills.

Chapter 29

Tell her we live here, with you

Libby's heart sank when she arrived home – wait, *not* home; Jamie's house was not supposed to be her home. She saw him as soon as she pushed through the front door. He was leaning over, both hands braced against the kitchen island, his head bent low between his arms and a deep frown marring his forehead. As soon as he was alerted to their arrival by an over-enthusiastic Beauty nearly bowling him over to get to Rosie, he cleared his expression and smiled. But Libby could see the strain around his eyes. Strain that *she* had put there. Strain he wouldn't be under if it weren't for their "inappropriate relationship".

"What happened?" Libby asked, moving toward him and away from the pile of little girl and dog beside her. "Why was Dr Maitland teaching us today?"

"Oh, we've been meaning to involve Terry more, to be honest," Jamie said, shrugging and trying to distract her by reaching down, putting both his large hands over her hips and lifting her up onto the kitchen island in front of him.

"Hey, Mr Big Bum," Rosie shouted as she ran past him,

slapping him on the arse, closely pursued by Beauty in one of the rare bursts of energy that she seemed to reserve only for four-year-old girls.

"Hey, Squirt," Jamie called after her as she continued out into the garden to throw sticks for a dog who had never retrieved anything in its life and was not going to start now, even for her favourite human. Exhausted after her uncharacteristic activity, Beauty collapsed onto her side on Rosie's feet and presented her large belly to be tickled.

"I know you were supposed to be giving the lecture," Libby said, determined not to be put off. "It's right up there on your terrifyingly anal colour-coded calendar."

Jamie shrugged again. "I must have got it wrong."

"You never get anything wrong on that bloody thing. Please tell me what happened."

Jamie sighed. "Libby–"

"They told you not to teach today, didn't they?"

"Don't blow this out of proportion. It's not a big deal. So I take a little break? Maybe it's time I took a step back anyway." His gaze fell to her lips and he leaned in slowly.

"Don't you dare try to–" He cut her off by pressing his lips to hers mid-sentence, the height of the counter putting her mouth exactly in line with his, "– distract me," she finished as he broke away to kiss down her neck. The breathy quality of her voice made her objection sound fairly weak, and her hands developed minds of their own, moving up from his wide shoulders into his thick hair and she felt a low rumble from deep in his chest vibrate against her body. But before she could lose herself completely, the image of a dejected Jamie leaning against the kitchen counter flew into her mind and she stiffened in his arms.

~

Jamie felt Libby's body go solid and he almost groaned in frustration. She was *so* stubborn. All he wanted to do was kiss her, have dinner with his favourite two females in the world, put the younger female to bed, and cuddle / fool around with the other one on the sofa. The last thing he needed was a post mortem of the day from hell, and the last thing *she* needed was another excuse to hold herself back from him. Her small hands fell from his hair to his chest and gave him a firm shove, which she'd obviously put a fair amount of effort behind. He didn't move an inch. She glared up at him, raising one of her eyebrows, and he sighed.

He gave her angry mouth another brief kiss before he moved back. Once she had enough room she jumped down from the counter, swearing as her glorious hair worked itself loose to come tumbling around her shoulders.

"Uh! I wish I could just cut the whole lot off," she grumbled as she scowled down at the now broken elastic band in her hand, threw it onto the counter and started tying some sort of knot at the top of her head. No sooner had she taken her hands away than it all came tumbling down again. She growled and blew out a puff of air to push up the strands covering her eyes.

"Why don't you?" Jamie asked, keeping his expression as innocent as possible.

She narrowed her eyes at him. "You know why, Jamie. Stop trying to–"

"No, actually I have no idea why you won't," he said, crossing his arms over his chest. "It gets in your way, it pulls on your scalp and gives you headaches, you have to wrestle with it on a daily basis and it pisses you off. So no, I can't imagine why you still keep it long."

"I have to have it like this for work," she said through gritted teeth, and Jamie threw up his hands in annoyance, stalking to the other end of the kitchen and back again. "Anyway, most men love long hair. I don't know why you're complaining."

"Of course I love your hair," he told her. "Christ, it's absolutely stunning. But I'd rather my woman had short hair, no headaches, less frustration and not ..." He stopped himself in time but he could see that the damage was already done. Her face had turned a shade paler and her mouth was trembling. He took a step towards her but she held out a hand to ward him off.

"I think I need to pack," she said, her voice hoarse. She cleared her throat, then continued. "For real this time."

"Bugger," Jamie muttered, his chest suddenly feeling tight. "Look, Libby, I don't mean–"

"I know exactly what you meant, and I know exactly what you think of me."

"No, I–"

"It's okay to be ashamed of someone like me you know. I can just imagine the gyp you've been getting from your mates."

"Nobody has said anything to me about you. Nobody even thinks–"

Libby laughed but it was so hollow it made the steel band around Jamie's chest tighten further. "I know what people think," she said, a lone tear escaping, which she brushed away before it could run over her high cheekbone. "And now ..." she broke off as two more tears were viciously scrubbed away, "now, not only am I a sponging gold-digger, but I'm someone who's put your career in jeopardy."

"Baby," he muttered, moving towards, her but she backed away and held up her hand again to stall his progress. "Don't be ridic–"

"Did you or did you not lose your position as Educational Director because of me?" she asked, her voice high-pitched and her eyes filling with fresh tears.

"That's not–"

"Just answer the *fucking* question." He'd never heard her swear before in a non-*Star Wars* manner. It made him feel a little panicked.

"Look, I don't care about the sodding teaching. They can stuff it up their sanctimonious arses. It's none of their goddamn business who I see in my own time."

"It was because of me," she whispered, and Jamie clenched his jaw before making a sudden lunge forward and catching her in his arms.

"I don't care about any of this shit," he muttered against her apple shampoo-smelling hair. "All I care about is right here in my arms and outside attempting to play catch with a morbidly obese dog." He felt her burrow her face into his shirt front and her arms come up to hug him for a few seconds before she started pushing him away.

"I know you think you feel that now," she told him as she backed away again, this time towards the spare bedroom, where he knew she thought her cases were (in reality her cases were hidden under a tarpaulin in his cluttered garage as one of his many strategies to prevent her moving out). "But you'll resent me for it eventually. You'll resent me for a lot of things. If I carried on dancing you wouldn't be happy, and if I sponged off you for the next three years you would eventually resent that too. I can't stay. Not when it's affecting your work. Not when I feel so bad about it." She moved into the room and pulled open the cupboard door then huffed out a sigh.

"Enough now," she told him, meeting his frustrated gaze with her own. "Enough."

"Mummy?" Rosie's voice came from outside the door, sounding uncharacteristically tentative. "Why are you cwoss?" Dropping her Rs was the first sign of stress with Rosie, who had now sidled up to Jamie and had both arms around one of his legs as he stroked her head. Libby forced herself to smile.

"I'm not cross, darling – just busy. We're going back to the flat today, so we've got to pack up all our stuff. Will you help Mummy?"

"But..." Rosie's big eyes went from Libby and then up to Jamie, "but we live *here*."

"No, Little Louse, we don't live here. We live at *our* home. Remember?"

"But this *is* our home," Rosie said, her voice now a little shaky. She turned around so she was facing Jamie and tugged on his trousers. "Tell her," she said, stamping her foot as the tears streaked down her cheeks. "Tell her we live *here*, with you." Jamie looked over at Libby, his expression begging her to change her mind. She gave a slight shake of her head and wiped away another two stray tears. He knew he could throw another spanner in the works to stop them leaving. He could tell Rosie that yes, they lived here, with him. But he also knew that would be wrong and it would confuse her, making her even more angry with her mother.

"Listen, Squirt," he said as he dropped down into a squat in front of her and put his hands on her small shoulders. "I'll come and visit all the time and you can come here too, I promise. You've got to go back home with Mummy. Don't you think Trevor and Alan are missing your old home?"

"Twevor's dead," Rosie said miserably. "We buwied him– member?"

"Ah... yes–"

"Anyway... I got loads more fwiends for Keith now. And I founds them a new home – they likes it in your pants dwawer."

Jamie suppressed a grimace at the thought of twenty or so woodlice infesting his boxer shorts, and pressed on.

"They'll be just as happy back in your old room once you settle them in."

"I *hate* you and I *hate* Mummy!" Rosie shouted, crying in earnest now as she pulled away from Jamie's hands. "Beauty's the only one who loves me and I know we can't take her to live with us because of Mr Tully being a gwumpy fastard!" She tore out of the room before either of them could stop her and threw herself onto Beauty, who was now lying in her huge dog bed.

"Thank you," Libby whispered as Jamie straightened up from the floor.

"I won't contradict you in front of her. But that doesn't change how I feel. I want you to stay."

"I can't."

They stood staring at each other. A couple more tears slipped down Libby's cheeks but she didn't say any more. After a long moment Jamie sighed and looked down at his feet.

"She's right," Libby said. "Mr Tully *is* a gwumpy fastard – I had better pack up and get back there before it gets too late, or he'll complain about "late-night comings and goings". It's happened before when Kira laughed in the corridor after nine at night. To be fair to Mr Tully, Kira's laugh is probably louder than most environmental health hazard noise pollution." She gave him a weak smile. He didn't have it in him to reciprocate.

"Okay, you go and separate the woodlice from my pants and I'll go and get the suitcases I hid."

"Right," Libby said, and pressed her lips together, clenching her jaw. Jamie's feet took him over to her of their own accord and he laid his hands on her shoulders just as he had her daughter. She looked up at him with those wide ice-blue eyes, and he sucked in a sharp breath at just how stunning she was. That was the strange thing about Libby – you'd think you'd adjusted to her appearance but every so often the sheer intensity of it would hit you like a sledgehammer out of nowhere.

"Stay," he whispered, not above begging. She reached up to his face and slid her hand from his hairline down to his neck, then pressed a small kiss on his cheek. Before he could move she had backed away, out of his range. She gave him one last, long look, shook her head, and then started opening drawers, removing all trace of their presence from his home.

Jamie watched her for a moment, then turned to leave. Whatever she said, it wasn't over. So he'd let them go for now, if that's what she needed.

But he wasn't giving up. Not by a long way.

Chapter 30

There'll be a riot

"Mummy. Muuuummmy! Mummy?"

"I... uh... what...?" Libby tried to focus on her daughter's voice but her brain had temporarily stalled. All she seemed to be able to take in were the words swimming in front of her eyes.

"I've called you *three* times, Mummy," Rosie told her with supreme four-year-old indignation at being ignored. "I do not want to have to repeat myself."

"Okay, Little Louse," Libby muttered, clutching the paper she was reading in two hands, her head not lifting from her frantic re-reading of its contents.

"Mummy!" Rosie's latest shout caused Libby to jump in her seat and she managed to tear her eyes away from the letter.

"Right, yes – what is it, honey?"

"I *need* a dog."

Libby rolled her eyes. "You don't need a dog. You need to eat your lunch and you need to put your knickers on... but you don't need a dog. We're not allowed pets here, darling."

"Ugh!" Rosie huffed out a disgusted breath. "I *do* need one. My tummy hurts without a dog." Libby put the paper down and moved out of her chair to drop down in front of Rosie and cup her small face. She was smiling. She couldn't stop smiling. Five years of struggle. Five years of worry and difficulty and she was finally, finally getting her lucky break. The words swam up into her brain again:

Dear Miss Penny,

We have reviewed your application for a grant covering the clinical portion of your study. Given the demands of the course and your academic record at the school we are pleased to be able to offer you a more robust package of financial aid...

They were going to help her. The people in charge at the Deanery who'd signed this letter were finally going to help her. No more beg, borrow or steal. No more sleepless nights. She pulled Rosie in for a fierce hug and swung her from side to side. "I love you, gorgeous, funny girl."

"Mummy!" Rosie said, pushing back and squeezing Libby's face between her small hands. "You're still not listening."

"I am," Libby said, pulling Rosie back in for another hug. "I'm sorry your tummy aches without a dog. As soon as we get back from Granny and Bumpa's we'll go and see Beauty, okay?"

At the mention of Beauty, Rosie's body went from being stiff with anger to melting into Libby, and Libby felt a pang of guilt that she hadn't let Rosie go back to Jamie's house since they moved out two weeks ago.

She'd been avoiding him. To be honest she had thought it was probably for the best. She hadn't been able see a way to make it work. But now... now, with this money, she wouldn't have to dance anymore. Well, she'd still do some choreography, still coach the girls, but that would be enough. Finally she could concentrate on her studies and Rosie. And maybe, with this obstacle out of the way between her and Jamie, maybe if they could sort out the Educational Director stuff, there was a chance for them too.

Once Rosie had pulled away to eat her sandwich Libby began to hunt for her phone. For some bizarre reason it was in the bread bin. She smiled as she remembered Jamie's anal little shelf in his entryway for his keys, wallet and phone. The two of them must have driven him nuts when they lived there.

For a moment she paused before she hit the green button to dial his number. His frequent phone calls had stopped three days ago. A shiver of worry went down her spine. He couldn't have forgotten about her that quickly, could he? She shook her head – this was Jamie, her Jamie. Of course he wouldn't have forgotten about her already. She tapped the screen and waited whilst it rang. Her shoulders sagged when the answerphone kicked in. She didn't want to leave a message – she wanted to scream and shout with him over the phone; hear his reaction to her news for herself. She straightened her shoulders and pressed again. On the ninth ring he answered.

"Libby?" There was some sort of music in the background and the low murmur of voices.

"Hey," she started, feeling her elation dip slightly, but soldiered on. "Listen, I had to tell you. I'm so excited. I got this grant from the ..."

"Hey, loverboy." Libby heard the voice of another woman over the music on the line and she froze mid-sentence. "We've still got some unfinished business over here. You ready?"

Loverboy? *Loverboy*? It was mid-afternoon on a Saturday. What was Jamie doing somewhere with loud music and women that called him *loverboy* at this time of day?

"Lib," Jamie sounded distant, distracted. No wonder, if he had some sultry woman with him. The weird thing was Libby thought she could almost recognise the voice. Was it somebody from the hospital? Her leaden feet took her over to the sofa and she sat down heavily. It was like somebody had taken a knitting needle to her balloon of happiness and she was watching it slowly deflate. "I'm sorry but this really isn't a good time. I'm..." the pause that ensued was long and incredibly awkward, "I'm just in the middle of something. Can I call back later?"

"I have a show later," she said dully, staring down at her painted toenails. Just as she had managed to perfect the technique, her stripper days were almost over. She'd work this one weekend – she owed that much to Steve – but then, other than coaching the girls, she was gone. Her rent, fees, nursery, food – all of it would be covered by the grant.

"Oh... right, yeah, okay." He didn't sound annoyed by the fact she was going on stage again. She hadn't danced properly since she'd been ill. Steve had just asked her to train the other girls, and other than a couple of short dances at the beginning of the night she was told to stay away from the actual performing for a few weeks. She'd convinced him to let her come back this weekend.

At first he'd remained resistant but a couple of days ago he phoned out of the blue and asked her if she still wanted to work a full shift. It was a relief. Rosie needed new shoes and her winter outfits would be too small by the time the weather got colder, so Libby could do with the tips. So yes, she'd been relieved; but she'd also been worried about what Jamie would think. Bloody hell, she'd been worried that she'd *upset* the bugger. Not much chance of that. It didn't sound like he gave the first shit about what she did.

Why was she phoning him anyway? Nothing had really changed. True, she now had a better way of supporting herself, but that didn't alter the fact that her relationship with Jamie had put his career in jeopardy and would continue to do so.

Her mouth pressed into a thin line and her chin tilted up. Why should she suddenly feel good enough for Jamie just because she didn't have to strip for a living? She wasn't ashamed of how she'd earned her money. Maybe she wasn't earning the prizes and trophies she had for her dance and gymnastics anymore, but she was still bloody good at what she did.

"Right," she responded, her voice flat and her knuckles aching where she was gripping the phone.

"Look, Lib, I've really got to go. I'll see you soon, okay?"

"Okay," she whispered, but he'd already rung off.

Rosie was so wrapped up in her plans to see Beauty that she thankfully didn't notice the change in her mother. On the bus Libby gave her the iPhone and Rosie played on a numbers app whilst her mother sat opposite and simply stared out of the window. She re-ran conversations she'd had with Jamie, the affection they'd shared, all the amazing sex – trying to work out how she got it all so wrong. Got *him* so wrong. Her chest felt tight and there was a heavy weight in her stomach. Usually she found it a real pain to starve herself before a performance, but today it was easy. The very idea of food made her feel physically ill.

Her thoughts then moved to the last few years and how lonely she'd been. If she didn't have the comparison between that and her time with Jamie she wouldn't feel so devastated. Everything now seemed a struggle. It was like she was working her way through a thick fug of misery. Her eyes felt unnaturally dry, as if she was forgetting to blink enough, and there was a vague ringing in her ears, which made sounds seem very far away.

When she arrived at her parents' house they were strangely

upbeat. Her mum couldn't stop smiling, which, if Libby had been functioning on any sort of normal level, she would have thought was weird: Rita Penny had been almost as upset as Libby was over the break-up with Jamie.

After settling Rosie, Libby threw all her stuff into a bag and, like a zombie, made her way out. Her mum was fussing that Libby would be late, something she had never normally worried about before, but Libby was too far gone to notice that either. She would usually arrive at the club in the afternoon to rehearse with the girls, but Steve had insisted they didn't need her to come in early today. So now, what with the fog she seemed to be pushing through, she was late.

She stared at her phone for the entire tube ride, oblivious to the people jostling her on either side and the cat-calls of the drunken Saturday night crowd around her. But however much she stared at the screen it remained blank. No texts, no phone calls, nothing. She rubbed her chest absently. Her heart actually felt like it hurt.

As she pushed through the double doors into the large foyer of the club, Barry surged forward to intercept her, steering her away from the entrance to the main room.

"What the...?" she asked as she was herded down the corridor towards the dressing room.

"No time to scope the atmos tonight, Lib," Barry said, his tone firm and his large hand on her back guiding her forward. "The girls are all waiting for you, and you know you shouldn't keep Claire waiting." Libby was about to complain but she allowed the fog to settle over her again and walked forward towards the excited feminine chatter. If she was going to perform she knew she needed to snap out of this – one wrong step, jump or spring and she could do herself some serious damage.

"You're here!"

Libby blinked as she was descended upon by at least five over-excited strippers. Yes, these women were affectionate, but a massive group hug on her arrival, nearly knocking her out with the force of their combined perfume, was not the norm. Just when Libby thought she might suffocate, Claire fought her way through the semi-clad bodies and grabbed Libby's hands to pull her to one of the make-up chairs. Tara picked up Libby's bag and two sets of hands pushed her down to sitting.

"Bloody hell," Claire said as she tipped Libby's head back. "You look like total crap. What have you been doing to yourself?" Libby pressed her lips together and tried to fight back the stinging behind her eyes but it was no use, a tear escaped. "Bugger," Claire muttered, scanning Libby's face with concern, then turning to the women around her. "Right, move out, bitches," she snapped. "Give Libby some goddamn room – go and get your outfits sorted, we've only got half an hour."

Libby's mouth dropped open as she listened to Claire. Now she realised why she'd recognised that voice on the phone earlier, although her brain had refused to compute so big a betrayal. Claire ignored her shocked expression and knelt down in front of her, gathering both her hands in her own.

"Libby, gorgeous, do you trust me?" she asked softly.

"It was you," Libby whispered, and Claire's brows drew together.

"What do you mean, hun?"

"It... it was you. I heard you."

"You're not making any sense," Claire told her, giving her hands a firm shake.

"I heard you with him. You... you called him... *loverboy*."

Claire groaned and rolled her eyes, and the lack of shame in her expression made Libby suddenly furious. She yanked her hands away and made to stand up, but Tara's freakishly strong hands on her shoulders kept her in place.

"Ugh! Please don't tell me you've been getting yourself all worked up over nothing."

"Nothing! How dare y–"

"Listen, you silly sod–"

"I will not listen, you–" Libby fought to stand but was yanked back again by a now furious looking Claire.

"I'm a lesbian!" Claire shouted, and the entire changing room fell silent.

"But... but ..." Libby trailed off and sank down into the chair.

"I've been in love with you for four bloody years," Claire muttered, her hold on Libby loosening as her cheeks heated slowly. Libby hadn't seen Claire blush the whole time she'd known her.

"Wh... what?"

"Look, I challenge anyone, gay or straight, not to fall in love with you after spending any time with you. You're just too beautiful and quirky and... well, you're just too freaking lovable. Seeing as I was a goner the first time I ever did your make-up, and given the fact it was obvious how straight you were, I thought it would be easier if I pretended to love meat and two veg rather than lady-gardens." The silence stretched as everyone stared at the two of them.

"Get back to work you lazy bitches," Claire snapped after a few seconds. "I'm not the weirdo around here. If anything it's you lot that's strange: fancying hairy, testosterone-fuelled, smelly, stubborn things with unattractive dangly bits." She made a face and a few stifled giggles were quickly suppressed. "Anyway," she sniffed, "I've got a girlfriend now and we're looking into Norwegian sperm together, so don't think I'll come panting after any of you tarts any time soon."

"What's wrong with English sperm?" asked Tara, hands on her hips. "I made a perfectly good baby with English sperm."

Claire made an eek face at Libby behind Tara's back, and despite her confusion Libby had to cough to stifle her own giggle – Tara's baby *was* cute, although that was a straight-out miracle since her partner Dave was decidedly *not*.

"So now you know," Claire said, drawing Libby's attention back to the problem in hand, "and there's no way I would be calling your bloke "loverboy" in any capacity other than to take the piss out of him."

"But... but ..." Libby trailed off and rubbed her temple, feeling a serious case of information overload, "why the varp were you with him then? It doesn't make any sense."

Claire's face softened before she dropped her head into her hands and sighed. "See, that's why I fell in love with your stupid nerdy arse," she said into Libby's lap. "You don't even realise you're doing it anymore."

"Doing what?"

"Varp is not a swear word in this universe, Libby."

"I know that, it's from Alderaan."

"Jesus," Claire breathed, before she lifted her head and looked back at Libby. "Okay, babe, please trust me. I was with Dr Sexy for a very good reason, not to bonk his brains out. I. do. Not. Like. Penises. Okay?"

"Um... okay," Libby said slowly.

"Now, tonight is a bit different," Claire told her, pulling back so she could open up her make-up case. "And you're just going to have to trust me about that too. Close your eyes."

Libby's mind was whirling as Claire went to work on her face. But she knew better than to move, having had years of experience being poked or tweezed when she ruined Claire's concentration whilst in the Torture Chair. After twenty minutes Libby was turned towards the mirror.

"Open your eyes, honey," Claire said softly. Libby's eyelids fluttered open; they connected with the image in the mirror and she froze.

It was safe to say that Libby was not adept at applying make up herself. So apart from when Claire put it on her for work (a look that was firmly in the "Drama!" category), she had rarely seen what she might look like any other way. After a long moment she leaned forward to the mirror, her hand coming up to her face but not daring to actually touch the skin. Her lips were a pale, shimmering nude colour. Her skin seemed to glow and her cheekbones were subtly defined. Instead of heavy dark make-up around her eyes she had lighter eye-shadow, more blended eyeliner, and mascara to thicken her lashes. The overall effect was absolutely stunning. Libby had no idea that she could look like this. She gripped Claire's hand.

"Why...?"

"Like I said, the routine is a little different tonight," Claire told her, standing behind Libby and putting both hands on her shoulders. Some of the other women came to stand around her chair, and Libby's eyebrows shot up into her hairline as she took in their appearance. They were all wearing dresses in different shades of grey. The material was soft and layered, with a torn effect around the short full skirt. It was not dissimilar to something Libby would have worn for a modern dance routine back in the day. None of them were wearing heels and they all had long leggings under the dresses. *Leggings!*

"Is it some sort of fetish night or something?" Libby asked, and the women just smiled.

"Hmmm, something like that," Claire muttered, reaching behind her to pull another outfit off the rack and dumping it on Libby's lap. It was similar to the other dresses but a much lighter shade – almost white. Memories of gym and dance competitions came flooding back to Libby as she fingered the material. "We're switching it up a little as well," Claire continued, "going for more of the new routines you taught us; and this time it'll be you starting off on the stage. Just you. Like when we make you dance in practice."

"But that's not a club routine. That's not what Steve expects. How am I even supposed to get this thing off on stage for Sith's sake?" The light material was stretchy and there were no hidden zips or tags to pull. Grappling to pull it off was not going to look sexy in any way.

"You're not taking anything off."

"What?"

"Nothing comes off," Tara said firmly. "We all stay in these get-ups for the whole routine. Waps are to be firmly tucked away tonight."

"There'll be a riot," Libby muttered, but smiles of the women around her just got bigger. Claire squeezed her shoulders.

"Have we ever let you down? In five years have we ever fucked you over?" Libby shook her head. "Then trust us, please."

She looked at all the faces of the women behind her in the mirror. They were so sure; they looked so happy.

"Okay," she said slowly, and was engulfed in another perfume-suffocating multi-stripper hug.

Chapter 31

Supergirl

It was completely pitch black. Libby couldn't see the audience at all; only hear the low murmuring of their voices. Claire and Tara were holding her hands on either side of her, ushering her forward.

"Where are the poles?" Libby whispered to Claire when they reached the centre of the stage.

"We're not doing pole work tonight," Claire told her, giving her hand a light squeeze.

"Claire, the poles were bolted to the ceiling and floor – Steve wouldn't have removed them for just one night. What the Varp is going on?"

Claire and Tara moved to face Libby and she could just about make out their faces in the dark. They seemed nervous but excited, and they were both smiling.

"You said you would trust me," Claire reminded her, and Libby nodded slowly. "Okay, when the spotlight comes on I want you to concentrate on the dance, nothing else. Can you do that? We'll come in like we practiced, but its just you at the start. Don't look at the audience. Don't get distracted." Libby frowned: she was an expert at ignoring the audience; Claire and Tara knew that.

"What aren't you telling me?" she asked.

Instead of replying the idiots just grinned at each other, gave her *another* hug, and then retreated. Libby was about to turn to go after them when the spotlight suddenly blinded her. A huge cheer went up from the crowd as soon as she was lit up on stage; the audience sounded larger than normal, and bizarrely there seemed to be a fair few female whoops and shouts in amongst all the noise. Libby smiled uncertainly and the first chords of "Tears" by Clean Bandit filled the space.

Having been drilled since she could remember, Libby closed everything off: the change of outfit, the removal of the poles, the audience, everything. She let the music take her over and she dropped down into a crouch for the opening bars.

The feel of the leotard and dress, rather than the skimpier but more restrictive outfits she normally wore to perform, seemed to make everything more fluid. She could arch further, spring higher: she felt invincible. The gasps from the audience as she flipped and the cheers when she finished her double pirouette filled the space. It was an atmosphere she'd never experienced before.

As the faster beat came in she felt the girls filling the stage behind, with Claire and Tara flanking her until the lights finally came up. They all started the routine Libby had taught them. Somehow everyone was step-perfect: they had been practicing. Just as Claire and Tara moved to the two raised aisles through the club and Libby to the front of the stage, she saw something that almost made her lose her footing. Jamie was standing there. And in his arms was her daughter.

"Focus! Trust me!" Claire shouted, and despite her shock Libby fell into the flip off the edge. The cheering, combined with the music, was now deafening, and as Libby dropped down into the crowd, balancing on the benches and flipping from table to table, she started to really take in the audience.

Kira was jumping up and down on one of the chairs, pumping the air with her fist and cheering madly. Libby's goddamn parents were next to Jamie and Rosie, smiling and clapping. She could see other students from her year, a couple of her neighbours, some of the doctors she worked with in the hospital, Dan and Amy were there with their kids, and Jamie's parents were jumping up and down on the spot, just like Kira. Libby's eyes widened with shock but she managed to flip back up onto the stage and complete the routine with the rest of the dancers.

As the last chord sounded, all the girls fell into each other laughing and crying. Libby's heart felt like it was beating out of her chest. The cheers from the crowd were even louder. Everyone was up on their feet, and lots of them had climbed onto their chairs like Kira. Out of the corner of her eye Libby saw one person who wasn't cheering: a disgruntled Toby moved through the crowd, his face set tight in anger as he pushed out of the back door.

"Okay everyone." Libby jumped as Jamie's voice filled the space. She turned to see him striding towards her across the stage, speaking into a microphone and still holding an extremely excited Rosie, who squirmed out of his arms and ran to her, colliding with her legs full force. Libby picked her up and hugged her like a lifeline.

"You were amazin', Mummy," Rosie said into her ear, giving her a tight squeeze. Libby squeezed her back, then refocused on Jamie, at a complete loss for words.

"Right, settle down," he said into the microphone, but the audience continued to cheer. Claire snatched the mic with an impatient look on her face.

"Let the man speak, you buggers," she shouted into it, then handed it back to Jamie as the crowd slowly started to quiet.

"When can I say bugger?" Rosie asked in Libby's ear.

"When you're fifty-eight," Libby replied automatically, still watching Jamie in bemusement.

"You all know this amazing woman on the stage," Jamie said, his eyes sweeping the audience and then focusing on Libby. "Some of you work with her; some of you have studied with her for years. But very few of you were aware of how talented she is. I knew she would never have agreed to do this tonight. That's why I had to surprise her, and I am so grateful to Steve for allowing me to do it, and to all the girls who helped me plan.

"Libby is the most determined person I know. She is also the kindest, funniest... and of course the biggest nerd." Another cheer went up from the crowd and Jamie paused until it died down. "She's raised a wonderful daughter who is as beautiful, clever and quirky as her. And both of these fantastic females have blown me away." Libby stopped breathing as Jamie moved to her and sank down on one knee, pulling a small box out of his pocket. "Libby, I love you. I will spend the rest of my life proving that to you and Rosie, if you'll just give me another chance." He produced a small box and opened it up. Inside, sitting on a plush little cushion was a Boba Fett, in pristine condition. Instead of answering, Libby sank to her knees and she and Rosie collapsed into him. As always, and as was his way, he caught them, he held them both, he supported them.

He made them feel safe.

He made them feel loved.

"Look, you haven't actually given me an answer," Jamie said in her ear as he pulled them all up to standing and wrapped his arm around Libby to walk her down the steps and off the stage. Libby just kissed his cheek and gave him an adorably dazed smile. Yes, she had Boba Fett clutched in her hand, and yes, she looked relatively pleased at this development; but Jamie wanted a firm reply.

"How did you–?" Libby started, but was cut off with a few aggressive pats on her back.

"That was the dog's bollocks, girl," Steve shouted over the clamour of the crowd. For a man whose club had been changed beyond recognition for what Libby supposed was just one performance, he was surprisingly upbeat. "I was a horse's arse not to put all those routines in the show. From now on you have complete discretion with the choreography."

"Listen, Steve," Jamie cut in, and felt Libby stiffen, no doubt bracing for another tirade of his disapproval, "and you, Libby. I want you both to know that I totally respect what you do here and I'm completely supportive of–"

Libby's fingers came up over his lips to stop him mid-flow. He frowned but she just gave him another smile, this one slightly more focused. "I love you, Jamie," she said, "but I can speak for myself."

"But–" This time a smaller set of fingers squished his face from both sides to cut him off.

"Mummy's tawkin'," Rosie told him, her speech and the slightly lacklustre face-squish reflecting how tired she must be (it was now ten o"clock at night). Jamie made fish faces at her, then tucked her head into his shoulder, but decided he'd better let Libby have her say.

"I got a grant from the Deanery," she told him and Steve, and Jamie's head whipped round in surprise. With her free hand Libby reached over to touch Steve's forearm as she stared up at him. "You'll never know how grateful I am for everything, but I *need* to study. I won't have time to work the nights. I can still help with the choreography, but I'm sorry, I–"

"Thank Christ," Steve cut in, snatching her out of Jamie's grip and engulfing her in a forceful hug. "You live that dream, Supergirl," he said into her hair. "'Bout time you stopped hanging around this place and did what you were supposed to do. I've got a bonus cheque for you here and I don't want any arguments. You know you've at least doubled my profit over the last four years. If I wasn't such a stubborn old sod you could have probably quadrupled it." He shoved the cheque into her hands and her gaze dropped down to the figure written across it.

"Steve," Libby breathed, her eyes wide and confused, "I..." She blinked, and blinked again, before her vision misted over with tears.

"That's enough of that now, Supergirl," Steve said, his voice rough before he cleared his throat. "It's what I owe you, that's all."

"Thank you," Libby whispered, a single tear escaping, which she wiped away before standing on tiptoes to kiss Steve's cheek. The big bastard actually blushed and did some rapid blinking of his own before he reached up to muzz Rosie's hair, telling her to "Take care of your mum" and giving Jamie a significant look before melting back into the crowd.

"Darlings!" Jamie rolled his eyes as his mother ploughed dramatically through the bodies to get to them, dragging Libby's mum in her wake. "Fan-bloody-tastic!" she shouted, throwing her arms into the air on the last syllable and giving them all jazz hands. She pulled Rita forward to stand next to her and then manoeuvred them all into a group hug. "You *have* to teach me and Rita all those moves. I will not be satisfied until I can flip my way across the lawn at my next Parish Council fundraiser."

Rita and Libby were laughing, but Jamie sighed: they might think his mother was joking, but bitter experience of all the myriad ways she had of embarrassing him had taught him different. The dads arrived at this point, both of them hugging Libby and Jamie in turn.

"Haven't seen that since you were fifteen, honey," Libby's dad said to her, then turned to the group. "My girl won the Nationals two years running. Could have been in the Olympics if ..." He trailed off and Jamie caught Rita giving him a sharp elbow in the ribs. Libby's smile faltered but her dad shook his head and put both hands on her shoulders. "No, sweetheart. You don't get it. We're so *proud* of you. So goddamn proud of everything you've done." One of his hands moved from her shoulder to reach out and stroke a now sleeping Rosie's hair. "*Everything*, honey," he told her, and she gave a little hiccup before she launched herself into his arms and hugged him fiercely.

That was when Jamie noticed the slow clap that had started in the crowd. He glanced around at Libby's friends and family and saw that they were all turned towards her. "Encore!" somebody in the crowd shouted. Rita approached Jamie to take Rosie away, and the clamour of the crowd became louder and louder. Jamie gritted his teeth. This was not in the plan. He wanted to take Libby back to the room he had booked at the Savoy and he wanted to get a firm answer out of her.

"Get up there, you lazy lump!" Kira shouted as she bounced up to them with a tray of tequila shots, which she pressed on Libby, Jamie and all their family. "Give the punters what they want!"

"Ki-Ki ..." Libby paused as Jamie felt her body jolt. Claire had jumped down from the stage and was yanking her arm from her other side.

"Come *on*," Claire shouted above the increasingly loud shouts of the crowd. "We've done the soul-wrenching, fancy-pants stuff. Let's have some bloody fun." Jamie tightened his grip on Libby as he felt her giggle and start to slip away.

"I'll be back," she told him on a smile, kissing his cheek and ducking under his arm. He crossed his arms over his chest and clenched his jaw as he watched the girls on the stage descend on Libby and form a little huddle. Kira gave him an enthusiastic shoulder bump and he scowled down at her in annoyance.

"Loosen up, Big Syringe. She's got your weird *Star Wars* figure tucked down her bra hasn't she?"

Jamie rolled his eyes and went back to watching Libby. The sound man was now on stage with the girls and Libby was shaking her head at him. She cupped his ear with her hand and stood on tiptoes to say something into it, after which he grinned, then jogged off stage. Minutes later the slow clap was drowned out by the beat. Despite his annoyance, when the piano kicked in and Jamie realised what song was starting, he shook his head, a reluctant smile tugged at his lips, and his ears started to feel decidedly hot.

The women on stage spread out in formation, all of them grinning madly. Once they were all in position Libby led the dance from the front. They moved in unison and with almost inhuman speed. The crowd went wild. After the first verse Libby and the two blondes started flipping down the aisles and back again, then all the women turned to the audience and started dragging people up onto the stage. Jamie had worked his way to the front. Once there, the chorus line *I need a hero* blasted out through the speakers, and he braced when Libby came sailing through the air towards him.

"Omph!" he said as she knocked him back on his heels, her legs circling his waist and her smiling face looking up at his. "You're heavier than you look, Supergirl."

"Shut up and kiss me."

Epilogue

Worthy

Libby ran her hands through her short hair, and smiled. Even four years after she'd cut it all off into a layered bob, it still made her happy. No more grappling with elastic bands every five minutes. No more tension headaches from the sheer weight of her messy bun. It was perfect.

"Hello," she said as she pulled the curtain of the cubicle back. "I'm Libby." They were all encouraged not to use their first names. Everyone reasoned that for some patients it felt over-familiar. But Libby just couldn't ask children to call her Dr Grantham all the time. "Are you Milo?" A mop of dark hair with two wide eyes peering at her below were visible above the blankets, but nothing else. And when she'd finished talking even that disappeared into the bed.

Mum sighed. "Come on Milo, love," she said, attempting to pull the blankets down with no success. "The lady's here to help you." Milo burrowed even further down the bed until there was only a small ball in the middle. He whimpered once, and then there was silence. Mum looked up at Libby. There were dark shadows under her eyes and her lips were trembling.

Her grip on the side of Milo's bed was so tight that her knuckles were white.

"It started yesterday. He won't move at all and when he does he cries out in pain. I don't understand it. He hasn't fallen over, hasn't hurt himself in any way, but he won't walk. Libby sat down on the edge of Milo's bed and fished in her pockets.

"Well, if Milo won't let me see what's wrong I guess I'll have to give this Luke Skywalker Lego mini-figure away to the little boy in the next room." She waited a minute, and then started to stand up. A small hand crept out from under the blanket and a little face followed. The movement caused another whimper of pain and the small face flinched, but he held out his hand for the figure nonetheless. Libby smiled and handed the Lego over. She had a never-ending supply of mini-figures she kept behind the nurses' desk for difficult cases. Taking her opportunity, she whipped out her stethoscope to show him.

"I'm going to listen to your chest and feel your tummy now, Milo." Her voice was soft but firm. "Mummy will be right here holding your hand, okay?" Milo narrowed his eyes but gave her a slow nod. When she got to his tummy his knees were still curled up and she had to coax him to get him to lie flat. It only took a very brief exam to determine what was wrong.

"Okay, Milo, we'll get some medicine to make you feel better, then you're going to have a sleep so that the other doctors can take this pain away."

"How they gonna do that?" Milo asked.

"They need to do an operation. One of your bits down there has got itself twisted and it needs to be put right."

Milo looked horrified. "But it's gonna hurt if they untwist somethin'."

"Okay, I pinky promise that it'll be way less hurty once they untwist it – and you'll be asleep the whole time." Libby held out her little finger. Milo frowned and then whimpered again in pain before he linked his little finger with Libby's.

"Right, I'm going to talk to another *two* doctors about you because you're such an important little boy today, and they'll be here to see you in a jiffy."

Milo's eyes went wide again before he shot back under the covers. Libby explained the procedure to Mum whilst a nurse brought Milo something for the pain.

"ARE YOU ON CEPOD TODAY?" LIBBY ASKED INTO HER phone and she heard Jamie sigh.

"You know I'm not on CEPOD, Libby. I've just finished with the students and I'm about to do all my admin from the last two months." Jamie had long been reinstated as Programme Director after the disastrous run of Dr Maitland's SIM teaching, which resulted in most of the student body complaining, and the Deanery threatening to withdraw the students altogether. As Libby and her cohort had received the best marks ever recorded in their OSCEs under Jamie's supervision, it had all seemed a little pointless. There was also the small fact that Jamie and she had married some time ago.

"Its just there's this little boy..." She trailed off and bit her lip. Paediatrics had always been her dream and she was loving the start of her rotation, but she tended to be a little overprotective of her patients. She knew the anaesthetist doing the emergency list today, and quite frankly he wouldn't do. He was perfectly safe but as far as reassuring seven-year-old boys went – no. "Are you with Pav?"

Another sigh. "Yes."

"Please come down, there's a torsion here and I don't trust

anyone else. Tell him I'll speak to you-know-who again if he doesn't."

She could almost hear him rolling his eyes but she knew he wouldn't let her down. "Come on you lazy arse," he said to what she hoped was Pav, and she smiled. "Have you had lunch? Libby?"

Libby started as she realised Jamie was talking to her, and then rolled her eyes, her hand going to her ever-expanding belly to rub in small circles.

"Between you, Millie and Kira I'm the most well-fed pregnant woman alive. I'll be the size of a small planet by the time this little chap puts in an appearance."

"And I've told the sister to make you raise your feet whenever you're sitting today," Jamie went on as if he hadn't heard her. "Did she take your blood pressure?"

"My blood pressure is fine, you freak," she muttered.

"Well, your ankles were really puffy last night and–"

"They're just fat," she cut him off hotly, drawing a few curious stares from the nurses behind the desk. She looked up at the ceiling and contrived to lower her voice. "They're just fat because *I'm* fat, because I'm carrying your big fat baby. Now stop fussing."

"I'm taking Rosie to swimming today. I swapped my on-call and–"

"Jamie," Libby said in a warning tone. "We've been through this. The swimming pool enclosure is a perfectly reasonable temperature."

"It's thirty degrees in there!" he said. "You looked like a lobster after it last week."

"Some pregnant people spend their whole lives at thirty degrees. I hardly think that forty-five minutes on a bench at the Wimbledon Lido is going to–"

"Do you want me to come and see this torsion or not?"

"Fine."

"Fine."

There was a beat of silence, then: "I love you."

Libby smiled despite her annoyance. "I know you do." She twisted the two rings on her left hand and her mind flashed back three years.

"MOTHER OF G .. GAH!" RITA PENNY SHOUTED FROM outside. It was the closest Libby had ever heard her mother come to taking the Lord's name in vain.

"What?" Libby said, and tried to turn but received a sharp swat to the side of her head for moving. "Claire, I've got to see what's happened."

"Stay still or I *will* burn you," Claire threatened, and Libby froze. Claire didn't do empty threats, and how Libby looked on her wedding day was now a matter of extreme personal pride to her. If Libby was honest (which she would definitely not be with Claire wielding the curling tongs) she didn't care what she looked like when she married Jamie. She didn't really care about any of this faff. But it was what The Mothers wanted, so she'd let them have their fun. Unfortunately Claire was so honoured to be bridesmaid that she'd gone slightly crazy about the prep work, even resorting to portable heated hair tongs for last minute touch-ups.

"Argh!" Libby heard Bunty scream. This time she did manage to twist around and slip away before Claire could clamp her ear between the two-hundred-degree surfaces. Libby turned to grab her dad and pull him along with her to the church garden. Her hand flew to her mouth and she stifled a bark of laughter. Rosie was standing in the middle of a pool of muddy water just outside the church alcove. Her bridesmaid's dress, which had been a lovely cream colour, was now very, very brown; and she had leaves and twigs in her hair and a streak of dirt across her face. Next to her was an equally bedraggled Seb in a totally ruined pageboy outfit.

"They were gone for thirty seconds!" shouted Bunty, her face red with anger. "Rita and I were just discussing canapés for *thirty seconds* and these minions of Hell managed to roll in the only patch of mud for miles around."

"I think you might want to ease back on the old blasphemy, Bunts," Kira said, leaning against the ancient oak doorframe to enjoy the show. "I doubt these two are actually Hell's minions. Haven't you seen *The Omen*? I guess we'll all find out now – if the holy water starts to boil over out of the font I'd say that's a good sign."

"I did warn you," Libby said. "I did say to–"

"We cannot bring our grandchildren to church in their pants, Elizabeth."

Libby had warned The Mothers that keeping this particular five-year-old and six-year-old pristine in cream silk outfits might be a challenge, but changing them into their wedding attire in the church vestry had been deemed too extreme.

"Rosie," she said (her shoulders were shaking but she managed to suppress actual laughter). "What's in your hands, Little Louse?" Both sets of Rosie's small fingers were bunched into tight fists. Not a good sign. She opened them up very reluctantly and at least ten woodlice started crawling up her arms. "*Seb*," Libby said to the little boy in warning, and cringed when he opened up to reveal two fat, slightly squashed slugs.

"I founds 'em," Seb said, very proud of his haul.

"They look like homeless children," Rita moaned as she started wiping away the worst of the dirt with a kitchen towel. Libby's dad allowed himself a small snort of laughter and Libby smiled but elbowed him in the ribs.

THERE WAS LOW, MUTED LAUGHTER AS THE BRIDAL PARTY started down the aisle. Seb and Rosie were still mostly covered in mud, and the four bridesmaids behind them – Amy, Claire, Tara and Kira – were struggling not to laugh themselves. But silence fell when Libby stepped into view. She might not care how she looked on her wedding day, and she might have a couple of burn marks on her neck, but she had to admit Claire had done a good job. Her dress was simple lace with cap sleeves, her short hair was pinned up with flowers that matched her bouquet, and her make-up was subtle but effective.

The church seemed to be groaning with people and Libby felt a wave of nerves. But as she started down the aisle she passed Steve, who gave her a wide grin and a wink and she breathed a sigh of relief; all the people here were people who cared about her. She smiled back at him, and if she hadn't known the tough bastard better she would have sworn there was a tear in his eye.

Rosie had abandoned Seb (who was taking his ring-bearer's duties rather more seriously than she was her bridesmaid's ones) to run up the aisle and collide with Jamie's legs at pace. The quiet of the church was broken again with laughter, and he picked her up to settle her on his hip. When Libby arrived next to him he shifted Rosie to the other side so he could take Libby's hand from her dad's. Libby and Jamie stared at each other and the church fell silent again.

"Are you my daddy yet?" Rosie shouted, breaking the silence with another round of laughter.

"Yes, honey," Jamie said without hesitation, and Libby felt her eyes fill with tears.

"Right, well, let's go and have some cake then."

"Can you give me a minute to marry your mum?" he asked,

and she huffed but gave an imperious nod. Any form of cake delay was a major inconvenience to Rosie. Pav took the opportunity to wrestle the rings off Seb's cushion, which was wobbling precariously, and Kira came up to lead both the children away to the front row.

An amused vicar started the ceremony, but Libby didn't hear a word. With Jamie's large warm hand encasing hers and his smile filling her field of vision, all she could do was beam up at him.

No more beg, borrow or steal. No more guilt and shame. She *was* worthy of this amazing man.

She always had been.

Acknowledgments

I'll start by saying a massive thank you to my readers. I never dreamt that people would take the time to read the stories I have thought up in my freaky brain, and I am honoured beyond words. I am also eternally grateful to the reviewers and bloggers that have taken a chance on me – your feedback has made all the difference to the books and is the reason I've been able to make writing not just a passion, but a career. Special mention for Susie's Book Badgers - you are wonderful humans and your support means the world.

Huge thanks to my agent, Lorella Belli, for your support and encouragement. Thanks also to my editor Martin Ouvry, and to Steve Molloy for the fantastic cover design.

Thank you to my wonderful beta readers: Jess, Ruth, Curly, Alexa, Carly and Susie for their invaluable feedback. Jane from Texas deserves a special mention as she struggled through the book with a broken arm and still sent me screenshots of suggested changes with the help of her husband (thank you Vic).

As always thanks to my wonderful husband for his unwavering support and my kids for providing endless comedy material; in particular Sammy, my five-year-old, for his undying love of all creatures great and small which inspired much of Rosie's antics.

About the Author

Susie Tate is a contemporary romance author and doctor living in beautiful Dorset with her lovely husband, equally lovely (most of the time) three boys and properly lovely dog.

Please use any of the links below to connect with Susie. She really appreciates any feedback on her writing and would love to hear from anyone who has taken the time to read her books.

Official website:
http://www.susietate.com/

Join Facebook reader group:
Susie's Book Badgers

-

Find Susie on TikTok:
Susie Tate Author

Facebook Page:
https://www.facebook.com/susietateauthor

Email Susie at:
hello@susietate.com

Printed in Great Britain
by Amazon

50061094R00179